FINDING HOME

St. John Sibling Series, Book 2

by Barbara Raffin

This is a work of fiction. People and locations,
even those with real names, have been fictionalized
for the purposes of this story.

When life handed Dixie Rae (St. John) Carrington lemons, she made lemonade. Widowed in her mid-twenties, her husband's life insurance depleted by a custody battle with her father-in-law over her son, and the mortgage on her dream restaurant more than she can handle, she starts over with a defunct farm alongside a rural Michigan highway. She turns the first floor of her grandmother's farmhouse into a restaurant, the upstairs spare room into a rental, and the empty barnyard into a haven for cast-off animals.

When life handed Sam Ryan lemons, he ran. But, after running away from his problems and obligations all his adult life, Sam's uncle offers him a means back into the good graces of his family. Unfortunately, what the family patriarch wants Sam to do is vilify his son's widow, Dixie.

But Sam quickly realizes there is no dirt to dig up and the family he really wants is Dixie's. Now he just has to hope she doesn't find out what's really brought him into her life before he can win her heart.

Special thanks to my dear friend Chris for her never-failing optimism and to the cousins whose glacial family photo served as an inspiration.

OTHER BOOKS & STORIES

BY BARBARA RAFFIN

Taming Tess: St. John Sibling Series, Book 1

The Mating Game

The Scarecrow & Ms. Moon (novella)

Jaded (novella)

The Sting of Love (short story)

The Visitor (paranormal)

Time Out of Mind (paranormal)

Wolfsong (romantic suspense)

The Indentured Heart (historical)

FINDING HOME

St. John Sibling Series, Book 2

by Barbara Raffin

CHAPTER ONE

"That woman's not fit to raise my grandson!" The old man slammed his palm down on the mahogany desk in front of him.

Sam Ryan shifted in the ancient leather chair on the one-who'd-been-summoned side of the desk. So much for pointing out the old man's son had chosen to *wed that woman.*

"As for Michael's good judgment," the old man growled, bracing both hands against the broad desktop and leaning toward Sam. "She seduced him. Trapped him into marriage."

Strike two. If the old man was implying she'd gotten pregnant to force a proposal from Mickey, then the pregnancy would have been a record at thirteen months post wedding.

Not that Sam was going to make the mistake of pointing out yet another flaw in the old man's reasoning. He had nearly a lifetime of being reminded how futile it was to argue with Stuart Carrington. Twenty-five years, to be exact, since he'd first sat in this chair under the scrutiny of an uncle who had it within his power to decide his future. He still felt every bit the six-year-old boy he'd been then.

And that brought Sam to the question that had nagged him ever since his uncle had summoned him from the banished lands abroad. Why welcome the family black sheep back into the fold now? It couldn't be to replace Mickey. Hell, Mickey had died over two years ago. If the old man wanted a replacement son, he'd have called him home a hell of a lot sooner.

Not that Sam wanted to replace Mickey…not that he could. Michael—Mickey to Sam—had been the big brother he'd always wanted—needed, giving him the sense of family his globetrotting mother hadn't and buffering him from his uncle's wrath when Sam screwed up…which had been most of the time. He'd idolized Mickey—loved him. The one thing his uncle-slash-surrogate father and he had in common. They both loved Mickey.

No, Stuart Carrington would never replace his son with his sister's mongrel whelp. But a grandson…

Sam sighed in resignation, having known deep down all along the reason he'd been summoned. It was the specifics he didn't know. "Why am I here?"

His uncle's flinty eyes narrowed at him. "I need you."

Sam's heart lurched in his chest before his brain could intercept the reflex. To be *needed* by the only father figure he'd ever known fed into the hunger of the lost boy still inside him. Yet, at the same time, he hated the notion because he knew whatever his uncle asked of him, he would do.

#

So here he was, some two hundred plus miles north of Chicago sitting in an empty parking lot under a darkened restaurant sign, the Ducati bike engine rumbling with a throaty purr between his legs. Another perk of doing the old man's bidding—getting the keys to whatever vehicle he wanted from his uncle's priceless collection, along with the promise that when he finished the job and headed back to Paris, the bike went with him. But, did he love the bike enough to ruin a woman's life? That was the one question that had sent him riding aimlessly along country roads rather than sticking to the highway and its direct route to his objective.

Sam gazed up at his destination, the white-washed farmhouse gilded by a setting sun. Its multi-gabled upper floors cast soft shadows across the scalloped shingles of the inviting wraparound porch. Beneath the overhang, warm yellow light filtered from the curtained windows of the Victorian era farmhouse's first floor. Even the sidewalk was flower-lined. Norman Rockwell couldn't have painted a more idyllic scene. Hardly the setting he'd expected of a gold-digger.

But appearances could be deceiving. He knew.

For all the mischief and decadence of his thirty plus years, for all the running away from his uncle he'd done, what he truly coveted was family acceptance. Yup, all he had to do was dig up some dirt on a woman who'd never done him any wrong and he'd be back in Uncle Stuart's good graces.

He flicked off the bike's engine, dismounted and stepped out from under the free-standing sign above him that read *The Farmhouse*. Appearances indeed could be deceiving, he thought, as he gazed into the warm glow coming from the windows of a home turned restaurant.

With his Ducati silver and red helmet tucked under his arm, Sam climbed the broad front steps. A figure moved beyond the first floor curtains, a distinctly female figure. Mickey's widow cleaning up after a day of diners? He hesitated ever so briefly at the top of the porch stairs, doubt still niggling at him. Would Mickey approve of what he was about to do?

He would if it saved his son from a mother who used the boy to gain her own end. Stuart was certain she was holding his grandson as collateral against the inheritance he denied her. And ransom had been the kindest of the words Stuart had used to describe his daughter-in-law's refusal to give the boy up to his care—his very money-advantaged care.

Sam stood there facing the leaded glass panel of the front door—facing his dilemma. Was he really doing this for Mickey's family or for himself? Mickey, after all, had chosen her—married her— fathered a child with her; and Mickey had never been fooled by womanly enchantments.

Then again, perhaps he could do right for both family and self. What harm would there be in visiting Mickey's wife and kid if there was no dirt to dig up? After all, Uncle Stu's army of detectives hadn't ferreted out anything he could use in court. What were the odds he, the family screw-up, would find anything?

And if he did?

Mickey would want his kid protected. The kid was all that mattered.

Still, Sam opened his silver windbreaker with its red Ducati emblem and let in the balmy breath of the summer evening. As if anything could warm him— make him feel less reptilian about introducing himself to his cousin-in-law as a friend.

"Simon Legree had more heart," he muttered and raised his hand to knock on the door.

Yet something stilled his hand from completing the motion. Mickey, who'd raised a child with this woman for two years? Mickey, who'd emailed him pictures of a happy family and written endlessly of his love for them? Was the memory Mickey's way of trying to give him one more chance to do the right thing—the honorable thing? And was the right thing to *leave*? Stuart's needs be damned?

Sam backed away from the door. That's when he heard the clatter of toenails coming fast toward him from the side porch—when the vibration of heavy footfalls reverberated up his legs from the old floorboards. He turned toward the stairs just as the biggest dog he'd ever seen skidded around the porch corner, ears flying, jowls flapping, strings of drool trailing from a fang filled mouth.

He flung his helmet at the black and white blur of a dog coming at him, turned, and threw his body against the front door. But the door didn't budge. The next thing he knew, he was plastered against the leaded glass panel of the door and a pair of massive paws had him pinned by the shoulders.

#

Dixie Rae Carrington stepped into the entry hall just as the guy she'd spotted prowling her porch hit the door. With cheek and lips smeared across the glass, he didn't look so menacing. In fact, he looked downright comical.

A glance the length of the door's oval glass insert and she amended her opinion yet again. He had on a pair of jeans faded out in all the right places. Yessiree. Faded and polished thin in the very best of places...those jeans. Set the mind of a widow to pondering on activities she hadn't partaken of in a couple years. That's what those tight, faded jeans did to her.

Too bad the fellow wearing them had been prowling around her front porch. No good ever came from a skulking man.

Or maybe it had been the motorcycle helmet he'd been carrying that had her thinking ill of this comical-looking man wearing decidedly sexy jeans. Though the helmet had been an innocuous silver color. That's what had caught her attention first; the light reflecting off the helmet as the man had skulked past her dining room windows. What kind of man wore a silver motorcycle helmet? Not a Hell's Angel. That was for sure.

Still, any guy lurking about had to be trouble. So much for that thick mop of chocolate-brown hair making her fingers itch for a feel.

Then again, his big brown eye was huge with a plea for help. And was that Ben on the end of Bear's leash shouting for the dog to get down? Blast that kid, but he was getting good at giving her the slip. She'd better get out there and rescue the stranger from dog and four and a half-year-old.

#

An image of blond hair and buxom shapeliness imprinted upon Sam Ryan's brain as his head hit the glass. But the fact that his uncle's Dobermans were trained to bite chunks out of trespassers on command, and whatever had pinned him to this door was easily three times the size of any Doberman, prevented him from fully enjoying the view. Besides, the shapely blonde had just fled what appeared to be an entry hall and whoever controlled this doggie King Kong sounded suspiciously like a kid.

Sam chanced a glance over his shoulder. A biscuit-scented muzzle huffed in his face and a huge, pink tongue sliced through the saliva strings and over glistening fangs. He shouldn't have dropped his helmet. Better high-impact plastic jammed between those canine teeth than any part of him.

"Nice doggy," Sam croaked.

"Get down, Toto," cried a child-like voice as the hound from hell pawed Sam's shoulders. He'd be two inches shorter by the time anyone hauled the beast off him and, at five foot ten, he couldn't afford to lose any height.

Sam squinted past the gleaming fangs. Yup. It was a kid swinging back and forth on the handler end of a dog leash like a midget Quasi Moto. What responsible adult put a pint-sized kid in charge of the jolly giants of dogs?

An unfit mother?

That's what Uncle Stuart had sent him to ferret out. That's why he was now on the porch of an old farmhouse turned restaurant along a highway in North-eastern Wisconsin about to get his jugular torn out by a dog big enough to saddle and ride.

"Auntie Em," the kid shouted. "Help me, Auntie Em."

Auntie Em? Toto? Either he'd taken a wrong turn out of Chicago and wound up in Kansas, or Cousin Mickey's widow had relatives in residence that his uncle's detectives had missed.

Arruf, went Hellhound in his ear.

"Shhh, Toto," the kid pleaded. "Icky witch'll hear."

A witch, too? Make that a wrong turn to Oz.

"Bear, quiet," commanded a decidedly feminine voice from behind them.

"Quiet?" Sam choked out, straining to see over

his shoulder and through the droopy jowls of Toto, or Bear, or whatever the dog's name was, at this 'Auntie Em'. He was about to be turned into kibble and all the woman could say was *quiet*?

"How about getting this beast off me?" he asked.

"Bear means no harm," the languid female voice responded, nearer this time. "He's just a puppy."

"Some puppy," Sam grumbled, trying to dodge the huge tongue lapping up the side of his head. "You should post a warning sign. *Beware of greeting by big, rambunctious puppy.*"

"Bear, down," the woman commanded in a voice smooth as a thirty-year old single malt liquor, closer this time.

The weight of the dog's paws lifted from Sam's shoulders. But the hot breath against the back of his neck warned him the dog hadn't gone far. Cautiously, Sam turned, faced the Godzilla of Great Danes and...

Angel of all angels.

She stood behind the dog, just out of reach...the golden-haired vision he'd glimpsed in the entry hall. An ankle-length skirt draped her womanly hips and a white, tailored blouse was buttoned to her throat. But the frilly bib-apron cinched to her narrow waist defined every inch of her female ripeness. Those curves made every woman his Uncle Stuart had tried to marry him off to seem anemic by comparison.

Auntie Em?

The woman placed a small, porcelain-pale hand on the kid's shoulder. "Go in the house, Ben."

Sam's attention snapped to the boy. Ben? As in Benjamin Carrington, only grandson of Stuart Carrington?

As in, Cousin Mickey's son?

"But Toto an' me gotta get to the Em'rald City 'fore Icky Witch catches us," the kid protested.

Maybe Uncle Stu hadn't overstated his case this time. Under the mother's care, the poor kid had clearly developed an identity crisis.

The mother's care. Sam thumped the back of his head against the leaded glass door insert. If Benjamin thought he was skipping along the *yellow brick road* and *Toto* was really Bear, of course Auntie Em must be the nefarious Dixie Rae Carrington whom his uncle had sent him to expose as an unfit mother and extortionist.

"Into the house," she said in a tone that brooked no argument. "You know you're not supposed to play outside after dark."

Okay. So, she didn't *let* the kid stay out this late.

"Ah, gee," the kid protested.

"Go. But leave Bear."

Leave Bear? Hellhound's abandoned leash slapped across Sam's toes, reminding him he still had a dog the size of a mini-van holding him at bay. The Dane's ears swiveled in the direction of a door slamming at the back of the house. Now it was just him, Hellhound, and—

"So," the woman who was no doubt the kid's mother drawled in the flirtatious timbre of the late, lusty Mae West, "What are you doing snooping around my porch?"

"Looking to see if the restaurant is open?" Sam ventured. A voice like that could distract a man from the worst of circumstances...or most stalwart of plans.

"Sign's not lit." She nodded toward the parking lot where his bike stood alone beneath the towering restaurant sign. "That usually means closed."

"The dining room lights are still on," he returned hopefully.

"Just a few," she leveled and cocked her head to one side, setting in motion the soft curls that had come loose from her upswept do. The movement stirred the air, carrying the aroma of fresh-baked bread and spiced apples to him, a distraction he couldn't afford.

He forced a smile over the Dane's pricked ears. "How about calling off your dog and we talk things over?"

She planted her hands on her hips. "Whether I call off my dog depends on whether or not you're a process server."

Process server? What the hell? No wonder she was in no hurry to call off the dog.

He shook his head. "I'm no—"

"We string up process servers in this neck of the woods," she leveled back at him, not a hint of flirtation in her tone now.

"I'm not a process server. I'm Mickey's er Michael's cousin…Sam, Sam Ryan," he rushed out.

She reached past the dog, caught Sam's chin between her fingers, and tipped his face into the light shafting over his shoulder.

"I know we've never met," he hastily added.

"I've seen pictures," she said, kneeing the dog out from between them.

"Great," he murmured. His life and limb depended on stiffly posed family portraits which depicted a tightly collared lad with slicked back hair. The only thing the boy in those pictures had in common with the man he now was extreme discomfort.

"I'm surprised all photos of me weren't purged from the family records?" He tried to laugh, but all he managed was a lame squeak.

"Spoken like the Sam our Michael knew and loved," she said, smiling once more and releasing his chin.

The Sam Michael knew and loved.

The air went out of Sam as if he'd been sucker punched. But who had delivered the final blow—an uncle who slanted the truth to fit his purpose, or a gold-digger with the voice of a seductress?

Or did Mickey somehow reach out from the grave to get his attention? Mickey who'd been more brother than cousin to him, and had accepted him just the way he was.

A sense of loss cut through Sam. Maybe if he hadn't run off to Europe to escape yet another of Stuart Carrington's attempts at turning him into a corporate clone, life wouldn't have taken the turn it had. Maybe if he'd followed suit of the cousin who'd been a big brother to him, Mickey would have stayed with Carrington Corporation. Maybe Mickey wouldn't have followed his ill-thought out example, wouldn't have rebelled and married a woman his father disapproved of…and died.

That's what had happened, right? Mickey had taken a page out of his younger cousin's book of rebellion. Mickey, the responsible one. Mickey, the honorable one.

Mickey, the golden boy for whom things always went right…until the day he died.

Sam studied Mickey's widow. Stuart had told him Mickey's son needed rescuing from Dixie Rae's clutches. But his cousin had chosen to marry this woman who wasn't tall and willowy or anything like the women Sam remembered Mickey dated. This woman was petite and voluptuous, like some sexy cherub with all the cushioned invitation of a Reuben's woman. Not Mickey's style.

Then again…

Dixie Rae was doll-like, almost fragile in a porcelain doll sort of way. It made Sam want to protect her, not unmask her. Is that what had appealed to Mickey?

Then she laughed.

She threw back her head, the light tangling in the blond curls that defied restraint, and laughed a full, lusty laugh. It reminded him how easily she'd used her sexy voice to lure him in, then interrogate and intimidate him, how ready he'd been to buy anything she said for a chance to lose himself in her soft curves. So much for the fragile doll.

Protect her, hell. This woman could have manipulated Mickey into turning his back on his family. Maybe he should stick around and give her enough rope to hang herself.

#

Dixie knew she shouldn't be amused. She was one disaster away from bankruptcy—away from losing her livelihood and her grandmother's home. She didn't want to think about what that might cost her son. But she was so relieved the guy prowling her darkened porch hadn't been another of her father-in-law's legal lackeys that she couldn't contain herself.

"Sorry, Sam," she chirped, shooing the dog out from between them. "But a woman can't be too careful these days."

She offered him her hand. "I'm Dixie, and the little tyke who thinks he's a wizard, is your second cousin, Benjamin."

"So I gathered," he said in a tight voice, his hand meeting hers in an uncertain handshake.

The Carringtons weren't a touchy-feely bunch, Dixie reminded herself. Even Michael had been a tad formal in the beginning. But, given Michael's description of Sam, she hadn't expected Sam to bear that particular family trait...Sam of the worn-in-all-the-right-places jeans. The latter was definitely not the norm in Carrington dress codes.

She settled back on her heels, planted her hands on her hips, and studied him. "Imagine, mistaking a fellow family exile for a process server."

"Get many of them on your doorstep, process servers, that is?" He wiped dog drool from his neck and frowned at his palm.

Dixie bit the insides of her cheeks to keep from laughing. "Not lately. But a while back, every time I turned around, some guy was handing me a legal document."

"Most of them from Stuart Carrington, no doubt," he grumbled.

"*All* of them from Stuart Carrington," she said, paying way too much attention to the lean hip against which he wiped his damp palm.

"Bully the opposition with legal brawn. That's Uncle Stu's style."

"Spoken like a man who's experienced Stuart's wrath first hand," she retorted, unsure of what she was trying to evoke from Sam Ryan.

"In spades," he returned, shoving his hands into the front pockets of his jeans and dropping his chin so he peered at her through thick eyelashes fringing heavy eyelids.

There. That sad, hungry look. That's the telltale sign she'd been looking for in Michael's cousin...the wounded Sam Michael had told her about, the litmus test of the real Sam. That lost boy look made her want to reach up and smooth down the tuft of hair moussed with Bear's saliva.

Of their own volition, her fingers slid through the thick, dark hair that was a tad shaggy. Michael's hair had always been close-cut. Nor did Michael have a full bottom lip like Sam. And Michael's eyes were blue and clear as a cloudless sky while Sam's were...

Surprise glinted from the eyes the color of strong coffee. What was she doing noticing Sam's eyes and hair...and lips?

Lips that now tugged an uncertain, crooked smile. *Not at all the typical straight-laced Carrington.*

"Do I pass muster?" he asked.

She pulled her hand away, his hair slipping between her fingers, tickling. It'd been a long time since she'd run her fingers through a grown man's hair, too long.

She hadn't realized how much she'd missed that kind of contact until now. Though that wasn't what surprised her. Twenty-eight year old widows had plenty of life yet to live. But, did the first man to kick-start her hormones have to be her husband's cousin? A cousin-in-law was definitely off limits, especially one that was more brother than cousin to Michael.

Especially one who'd boycotted hers and Michael's wedding. But then all the Carrington clan had been a no show. That had hurt Michael; though he'd forgiven Sam. He'd been an ocean and half a continent away when they'd impromptly wed. And strangely, she suspected she understood why Sam had missed Michael's funeral. Still, why would he show up now?

#

"Tell me Stuart sent you here with an olive branch," she said, her tone closer to the one she'd used when she'd sent her son off into the house.

Sam gaped at Dixie. She'd just slipped her fingers through his hair and looked up at him as though he were the answer to her prayers.

"Olive branch?" he questioned, confused by the mixed signals this woman put out.

"Yeah. A peace offering." She bent and plucked up his helmet. "A gesture demonstrating Stuart has given up trying to take my son away from me." She handed him the helmet that, in the moonlight now slipping between them, turned a dove gray. "Did Stuart send you here to mediate peace between us?"

This was just the kind of question a conniving gold-digging woman asked. Wasn't it?

"Aren't you the direct one," he said, vying for time to…to *what*? Come up with the right answer?

"Comes from a lifelong habit of having nothing to hide." Cornflower-blue eyes narrowed at him. "How about you, Sam? Why the evasiveness?"

What could he tell her that she'd believe without revealing his true purpose for coming to her restaurant—her home—that he'd come to dig up dirt on her as a means back into the good graces of his family?

He braced the helmet to his hip and rubbed the

back of his neck. A reasonably true explanation came to him and he peeked at her. "Blame it on road weariness."

"Sure. But, did Stuart send you here or not?"

Just his luck, Mickey had married a woman with the focus of a homicide detective. Indeed, looks were deceiving.

"And before you answer," she said without a hint of flirtation, "You should know I rank liars right up there with process servers."

Having run out of time for further debate, Sam sighed. "I think Stuart has exhausted every legal means at the disposal of his considerable wealth." *True enough.*

"That's something." She drew her arms across her stomach. "But no olive branch, huh?"

"He didn't send me here with an olive branch." *Absolutely true.*

"Thanks for the warning."

Is that what he'd just done, warn her? If Stuart found out, the old man would filet him.

Make that, *when* Stuart found out. There were no *ifs* where the senior Carrington was concerned.

"Then what's the deal, Sam? Surely you didn't come here looking for a hideout."

He glanced at the Ducati a mere dozen yards away. Escape or...

He shrugged. "Just passing through, I guess."

"And thought you'd stop by for a visit?"

The dubious note to her question snapped his attention back to Dixie. He expected to see condemnation in her eyes, something that damned him for dropping by now that it was too late to ever see Mickey again...or for Mickey to see him. Instead, he found a sadness in her eyes that edged on pity. Damn, but he couldn't get a fix on Dixie Rae, and that made her almost as lethal to his wellbeing as his uncle.

"Guess I came too late," he said, regretting the words before they were completely out of his mouth, knowing he was too late for a lot of things.

"Never too late to visit," she said, snagging him by the arm and tugging him toward the corner of the porch. "Ben is going to love getting to know his second cousin."

"I'm not staying," he said, dragging at her pull, hell-bent on saving his own hide. "I heard you ran a restaurant. Thought I'd stop for a bite to eat. Meet you and Ben."

"Great." The seductive lilt was back in her voice. The restaurant kitchen may be closed but mine isn't."

Sam eyed the closeness with which she hugged his arm as she towed him along the side porch, felt the intimacy as his arm pressed into the cushioned side of her breast. She sure had a familiar way about her, maybe too familiar. The modus operandi of a gold-digger?

But the Mickey he'd known would have been too smart to get snared by a woman who used sexual wiles to trap a man. He was certain of it.

Dixie Rae raised a Cheshire cat grin at him. "If you're not too fussy, we can find you a place to sleep."

"I'm not staying the night."

"But it's late, already past Ben's bedtime. If you don't stay, how will he get to know you? Besides, you're tired. Road weary, you said."

She had him with that.

"Unless it's our sparse accommodations that are scaring you off."

A "yes" would gain him freedom. But a "yes" would also be a lie, and something warned him Dixie Rae could spot a lie at a hundred paces.

"I don't travel first class near as much as you might think," he said, not sure why he was admitting anything about himself to a woman who might be holding her child, Mickey's son and Stuart's grandson, as collateral against a trust fund.

"Sorry I can't offer you the guestroom," she said, blinking up at him. Or had she batted her lashes at him?

"We had to rent it out," she continued as she hauled him around the back of the house. "Can't afford the luxury of an empty room these days."

Stuart had said she'd spent her way through everything Michael had left her, that she'd even lost the Chicago restaurant Michael had bought for her. Maybe she could read a lie so well because she was a master at telling them?

They stepped into the light slanting across the porch from the back door, illuminating a speculative look in Dixie Rae's eyes. Was she sizing him up for what worth he might be to her?

Before he could be sure what he saw in her expression, boyish hoots blasted them and the expression in Dixie Rae's eyes softened.

"Sugar high," she said above the din, any hint of calculation gone from her features...if there'd been any there in the first place. "He went to a birthday party this afternoon. My Cousin Annie's girls turned twelve. You'll meet them tomorrow. Annie waitresses for me and her girls help watch Ben."

Babysitters barely twelve years old? Was that old enough to be responsible for a four-year-old? He'd never been around kids younger than him so he didn't know.

Beyond the rusty screen, Ben wheeled about a small sitting room, a towel tied around his neck flaring back from him. Was letting the kid over-indulge bad parenting? Is that what he was supposed to reveal...if he stuck around?

Dixie ushered him across the threshold into the pandemonium she declared their private quarters. A couch, television, two over-stuffed chairs and a dated assortment of side tables crowded the boxy room. The kid bounced around the space like bubbles in a pot of boiling water.

"It's best to let him burn off the energy before trying to put him to bed," Dixie explained, leaning into Sam in what he considered a too familiar way.

He didn't know whether to question that flirtatious nature or her parenting skills. Not that he felt qualified to judge the latter. Though there did seem to be good rationale to letting the kid burn off his high. Maybe had his own high-energy childhood not been stifled, he might not have screwed up so much.

Or maybe he'd have turned out a lot worse.

"Scoot on over here, Ben," she called, the lilt of her voice tickling Sam's nerve endings.

Do not walk. Run.

"Come meet Cousin Sam," she said.

The kid glanced off one stuffed chair, ricocheted around the coffee table, and scrambled up onto the arm of the couch where he tipped a smudged face up at Sam. A pair of blue-gray eyes studied him from beneath tawny lashes, Mickey's eyes.

For the second time since arriving at The Farmhouse, the breath went out of Sam as though he'd been punched in the gut.

"I'm the wizard," Ben declared, drawing a makeshift cape over his narrow shoulders.

Mickey's kid.

Dixie bumped her cheek against Sam's shoulder. The scent of cinnamon enveloped him. "He's been fixated on the Wizard of Oz ever since seeing it."

And how long ago was that? Sam wanted to ask, needing to know how long she'd allowed her child to fixate on some mythical land and its fanciful characters—needing to know if that was normal or lax parenting...or worse. What if the mother really was using the kid to gain her own ends, to gain control of the trust fund that would one day be little Ben's?

But Mickey had chosen her. Sensible, perceptive Mickey.

The kid smeared a grimy finger across the silver dome of the helmet tucked under Sam's arm. "Are you the Tin Man?"

The Tin Man who went to Oz for a heart.

Sam's chest tightened. For the life of him, he couldn't feel his heartbeat.

Heartless to spy on a mother. Heartless to prove her unfit. Heartless to cost a child the only parent he had left. Sam knew what it felt like to grow up without parents. He knew what it was like to be left with no one but a stern uncle to share the anger and a nanny to wipe away the tears.

What would Mickey do—Mickey who'd had enough heart for them both?

Watch out for the kid. That's what Mickey would do—what Mickey had done for him. Perfect Mickey who had loved him in spite of all his failings.

But he didn't have Mickey's integrity, Mickey's smarts, or Mickey's charm. What passed for Sam Ryan charm was better labeled sham. He'd connived his way out of more than a few tight spots and into a few choice positions...including his share of beds.

Was that what Stuart had in mind when he'd offered Sam a way back into the good graces of the family? Bed the curvaceous Dixie Rae so he could play the morality card? But it would take a string of documented bed partners before any court would take a child from his mother, and surely Stuart could get that list without him.

Dixie was laughing at her son calling him Tin Man. Not the head-thrown back kind of laugh she'd given out on the porch that had dispelled the illusion of china doll fragility. No, this one was far more subdued, but still came from deep enough that the side of her breast bobbed against the side of his arm.

Sam shifted uncomfortably. Had Stuart enlisted his aid because he thought it would take a con to catch a con? Is that how Stuart thought of him, a conman?

Disappointment pulled at Sam's shoulders. He'd hoped for more. He'd hoped Stuart might finally have seen whatever it was Mickey had always managed to see in him. Maybe then he could see it, too.

Sam stared into the Mickey blue eyes looking back him from Ben. Not a hint of an answer reflected from those eyes. Just Mickey's kid, scrubbing a grubby finger against his helmet. Did the kid *really* need his help?

Maybe if someone had helped him when he'd been dumped on the doorstep of a stern uncle he'd be able to read the signs.

Aaah, but someone *had* helped him. Mickey.

Mickey, whose kid might well need his help now. And if that meant bedding the kid's mother to get close enough to her to dig up dirt on her...to make sure he was alright, so be it.

Sam sighed. For a guy who'd spent a lifetime avoiding responsibility, he'd gotten himself hip deep in it this time.

CHAPTER TWO

"How about that bite to eat?" Dixie asked.

"Bite to eat." The lips almost too shapely to belong to a man flexed an uneasy smile. "Yeah. Sounds good."

In spite of the hint of apprehension, there was a definite suggestive note to Sam's voice that took her back to her truck-stop waitress years; years when she went to school by day and slung hash by night, weekends and every off-school holiday. That's how she'd paid her way through college...and where she'd met Michael. Back in her truck stop days, she'd made use of the skills she'd learned under the merciless tutelage of four teasing brothers to keep the gropers at bay and banter with the harmless flirts. She figured Sam fell somewhere into the harmless flirt category.

She looked him in his puppy-dog-brown eyes. Damn, but why did he have to have such sad eyes? That was trouble. Blatant sexuality she could easily resist. But vulnerability did her in. Just ask anyone who'd ever dumped an unwanted animal on her doorstep. She'd been called everything from a soft touch to a sucker.

She preferred to think of herself as a mother hen, which would be the safest approach to Michael's cousin, provided she could keep the lid on the libido the all-too-appealing Sam seemed to have nudged to life while she figured out what brought him to The

Farmhouse.

Ben hopped down off the couch and lapped the room while shrieking like a banshee. She urged Sam forward through the room littered with party-favors. "It'll be quieter in the kitchen."

She steered him ahead of herself into the private kitchen partitioned from the living room by a wide arch and toward the table and chairs tucked under the stairs. "Have a seat, why don't you?"

"Been on my backside most of the day," he said.

Don't even look at his backside.

"I'll stand, if it's all the same to you," he finished and faced her, stopping so close to her she couldn't ignore the cool freshness of the outdoors wafting off his clothes, his hair, his skin.

"Suit yourself," she said, stepping around him and busying herself gathering a plate and glass from the cupboard. She needed to keep her head on straight and her hormones in check if she was going to figure him out. No way did she believe he just happened by and stopped for a meet and greet even though he'd been hesitant to accept her invitation to stay the night.

She handed him the place setting. "Mind putting these on the table?"

He took the plate and glass in his free hand, giving her a heavy-lidded look that reminded her of how the Big Bad Wolf might look Little Red Riding Hood over. Michael had never described his cousin as a wolf.

"Today's beef roast was particularly good," she said, holding his gaze, certain a good stare down would make Sam back-off and stop sending her hormones into a tizzy. "I'll make you a sandwich. You want that hot or cold."

"Cold will be fine," he said, his thumb stroking the smooth, silver dome of the helmet still braced between his elbow and ribs in a way that made her skin tingle. She'd almost forgotten what it was like to have a man touch her like that.

So much for cooling Sam's draw.

"I'm melting, melting, melting." Ben's voice corkscrewed from the living room.

Melting just about summed up her body's response, too.

Ben shrieked and Dixie snapped back to reality, a reality that drew a line between her and any possibility she'd ever be lucky enough to be on the receiving end of Cousin Sam's stroking thumb. Sam, above all else, was Michael's cousin and cousins were off limits. Besides, she mothered lost souls and there was still a lost little boy behind those eyes.

"You were going to put those on the table," she said, nodding at the plate and glass caught between his fingers…his very long fingers.

His smile twitched and he turned toward the table tucked under the stairs. She shook her head against her own failure to resist. Maybe what had changed from porch to kitchen had been her perspective, not his. Maybe she, with her revived libido, was the one seeing what she wanted to see.

She opened the refrigerator door and bent into the cool air, gathering containers. "How about an ice tea with that?"

"Sounds great."

The nearness of his voice jerked her upright and she turned to find that he now stood in the space between table and appliance…where she stood with arms full. For a moment, she forgot about the condiment jars and packages of beef and cheese she hugged against her chest in spite of their chill. It was his eyes that made her forget, those heavy-lidded, bedroomy eyes. Michael had said women were drawn to "Sam's underdog quality." But a puppy was the last thing she thought of under the seductive invitation of Sam's steady gaze. So much for maintaining motherly thoughts.

So much for thinking his flirtation was all in *her* mind.

"Aren't you quick on your feet," she said, "and quiet about it, too?"

He plucked a precariously balanced pickle jar off the stack in her arms, and winked. "Comes from years of sneaking past Uncle Stu. The less I encountered him, the better."

What kind of flirtation was he plying on her? The kind meant to camouflage pain or the kind meant to score a conquest?

"Michael told me Stuart was pretty hard on you," she tested.

His smile froze. "Michael told you that, huh?"

"Yeah." *And a whole lot more.*

He turned away from her and set the fat jar on the countertop beside the fridge.

"Want the works?" she asked, dumping her load onto the counter next to the pickle jar, closely watching Sam for further reaction.

Only a hint of the puppy dog remained in his eyes as he responded. "I place myself completely in your capable hands."

Did he mean to sound so suggestive?

He hitched one lean hip against the cabinet where she worked and drummed his expressive fingers against the silver dome of the helmet propped against the other. She couldn't seem to stop herself from glancing at those fingers.

"There are hooks by the back door," she said, hoping even a few seconds of being out-of-sight would give her a chance to get her head back on straight. "Why don't you hang up your helmet and jacket?"

But the wide grin he flashed her before heading off toward the back door sent another flush of hormones through her.

"Get a grip, Dixie," she muttered under her breath as dumped her armload onto the counter by the sink, turned on the faucet, and scrubbed her hands. "He's a relative."

Sam reappeared in the kitchen sans helmet and jacket just as she dried her hands. The black t-shirt he wore detailed a trim build with just enough muscular definition to intrigue a woman of modest tastes, and she'd never been one to favor the overly-muscled.

Related by marriage, not blood, whispered a wry voice behind her left ear.

Dixie tossed the towel aside and sliced a couple slabs off her homemade wheat bread. "You want hot mustard or regular?"

He hooked his thumbs into his jeans pockets, leaned a shoulder against the fridge, and grinned. "I'll take spicy."

"Why doesn't that surprise me?" she said, certain now she wasn't the only person in the room aware of the electrically charged air between them. Or, was he using that charge to divert her attention from places he didn't want her going?

She dropped a stack of thinly sliced beef atop the

hot mustard on the bread. "How long have you been back in the states?" she asked.

"A couple weeks."

She slapped cheese on top of the beef and rolled a fat tomato onto the cutting board. "Didn't take you long to annoy Stuart."

"I can annoy Uncle Stuart without even being on the same continent."

There was a hint of pain to his voice. Her fingers paused in mid-slice, juice seeping from the tomato where the tip of the knife had perforated its skin.

There's more to Sam than he lets people see. Michael had told her that, too.

The mother-protector in her wanted to gather Sam into her arms and smooth back the unruly hank of chocolate-brown hair from his wounded brow. The woman in her with the awakened hormones wanted something entirely different.

Just slice up this tomato, peel off a few leaves of lettuce, pluck out a pickle or two from that big jar Sam had set on the countertop and pile it all on his sandwich. Feed him. That's all she intended to do...and find out why he'd come to northeast Wisconsin.

"What'd you do to invoke the Carrington wrath this time?" she asked, dipping more hot mustard from the jar, trying to keep the conversation traveling a less provocative path.

"Just being the family screw-up is enough," he quipped, leaning against the counter—leaning too close.

The knife slipped from Dixie's fingers, its impact against the countertop sending golden flecks of mustard flying from its blade.

"Follow the yellow brick road," Ben's little boy voice recited from the next room.

And a yellow brick road was exactly the path she tripped as long as she reacted to every flirtation Cousin Sam sent her way. Look at the trouble she'd created in the Carrington clan falling for Michael. If only she didn't have to touch Sam. But she'd spattered his shirt with mustard. It would be impolite not to wipe it off.

Yeah, right. Impolite. Who was she kidding?

"Sorry," she offered, as she dampened the corner of a hand towel. "I'll just dab those spots away before they dry."

He'd followed her to the sink, trapping her in the tight space of the corner sink. She slipped her hand into the neck opening of his tee, her fingers cushioning the underside of the spatters, her knuckles brushing his warm skin. Couldn't let her guest get wet now, could she?

She dabbed the damp towel at the yellow spots on the black shirt. She concentrated on the task, ticking off each speck as it disappeared—a masterful job of diverting herself. She could almost ignore the heat of his skin against the backs of her fingers. Then, just as she blotted the last speck of mustard, he swiped his thumb across her cheek.

Lucky, the woman on the receiving end of his stroking thumb.

Involuntarily, her heart lurched and she blinked at him. Sam held up a thumb sporting a dollop of mustard. He winked. "Some dishes don't need spicing up."

The sweep of Sam's tongue as he licked the mustard from his finger made Dixie itch in places she'd forgotten. No doubt about it. Sam Ryan was flirting with her and she had better put a stop to his game before she made a fool of herself and fast.

She released his shirt, folded her arms across her chest, and leveled on him her best *this chick's got your number* smile. "I bet you charm the socks off your mama."

The gleam in Sam's eyes evaporated, his lips flattened, and he lowered his mustardy finger from his lips. "The last time anyone charmed anything off my mother, she wound up with me."

#

She'd read him like a first grade primer while luring him in with sultry, sideward glances and quippy comebacks. So much for testing *her* character. Much more of this, and he'd be spilling his deepest, darkest secrets to her.

And at the top of that hit parade would be the reason he'd come to The Farmhouse. How did Stuart expect him to dig up dirt on a woman to whom even Mickey had succumbed, Mickey who had been infinitely more experienced with women than he, Mickey with his leading man looks and lady-killer charisma?

Sam jammed his hands into his pockets and wheeled away from Dixie. The maneuver failed to take him out of spiced apple and hot mustard scent range of her, though. The kitchen was just too damn small.

"Sorry," she said with a quietness that penetrated his defenses with the ease of a hot knife through soft butter. "I didn't mean to stir up bad memories."

Did she or didn't she?

Heck, she'd by-passed current faults like where

had he been the day she and Mickey got married, the day she buried Mickey, and the years in between, instead hitting him deep in his soul. Not that he had a burning desire to explain the cowardice that prompted most of his life choices. He'd just expected the questions at the top of Dixie Rae's hit list to be about his absence from Mickey's life these past five years. He'd expected her to demand those answers the way his uncle had...the way Mickey would have.

Wrong. Mickey wouldn't have demanded. He'd have asked, his hurt—his disappointment masked by concern. Mickey who smiled back at him from a snapshot fastened to the front of Dixie Rae's fridge by fruit-shaped magnets. What had Mickey been so blasted happy about in that photo? Didn't he know he'd been seduced into marriage by a gold-digger?

And Dixie Rae *had* to be a gold-digger. She was too smart not to know what Mickey was worth. Even with the rift between Mickey and his father, she probably figured they'd work out their differences eventually and she'd be swimming in Carrington wealth. She'd even had the foresight to provide the requisite heir which came in handy in the absence of a husband. But she didn't know Stuart Carrington if she thought she'd get anywhere near her son's trust fund as long the old man drew breath.

Could that be the reason she flirted with him, because she figured Stuart couldn't be long for this world—because she figured Sam would be the next Carrington she'd have to fight for control of any trust fund? If that was her thinking, she was in for a big disappointment. Stuart would never put a ne'er do well nephew in charge of a dime of his money.

"That was the day we brought Ben home," she

said, bringing him back to the moment, back to her world of cinnamon-scented, golden hair tickling his cheek as she touched the corner of the photo.

Don't get suckered in.

"That's Ben Michael's holding," she elaborated.

The reason Mickey grinned in the photo. A son would make any man smile. At least a man *should* smile at his son. He doubted his father had ever smiled at him and he couldn't remember Stuart ever favoring him with one. Was that the life he would be saving Ben for?

"Ben was barely two when Michael had his accident," Dixie said. "Half his life ago. It's getting harder to keep Michael's memory alive for Ben." She looked up at him, barely a hand's width separating them. "I bet you have loads of stories about Michael that Ben would love to hear."

But to share stories, he would have to stay and risk being found out by Dixie. Or unmask her and condemn the boy buzzing around in the next room, thinking he was the Wizard of Oz, to an old man's regimented idea of life.

Ben entered the kitchen, scuffing the rubber soles of his tiny tennies across the linoleum, his narrow shoulders drooping. He sidled up to his mother and laid his head against her hip.

"Bear won't play with me," he said.

Dixie smoothed the hair back from Ben's forehead. "He's probably tired, honey."

Ben stomped a foot. "But I *want* him to be Toto."

Dixie squatted and encircled the child in her arms. Motherliness or indulgence? The actions of a woman who cared for her child's wellbeing, or a woman who play-acted to gain her own ends?

"It's past Bear's bedtime," she said, her tone gentle in its reasoning.

Ben squirmed in his mother's embrace. "But I want to play."

"I've already let you stay up way past your bedtime."

"No!"

She winked at Sam. "Somebody's sugar high just came crashing down."

Then she took the boy by the shoulders, held him away from herself, and looked him in the eye. "No argument. It's time the Wizard hit the sack."

Ben rubbed his eyes with his fists. Such little fists. Too small to protect himself.

The kid *needed* protecting. But from the mother who ruled his world?

His own mother had blithely handed him over to the care of her stern brother when her new husband didn't want a six-year-old in the bargain. It shouldn't have surprised him, given his own father had abandoned him.

"Sorry to cut our visit short," Dixie said, straightening, "but the wizard needs to go to bed."

She tipped her head to one side and murmured in that sultry timbre that called to him like a mermaid's song, "Me, too."

Was that an invitation?

"Our days start pretty early," she said. "And tomorrow morning I'm opening for Sunday brunch for the first time. I'm hoping to cash in on the after church crowd."

Cash in.

There it was. Her motive. The reason she fought Stuart for the kid. Maybe the underlying reason she had flirted with him tonight. The way her eyes had turned all dreamy when he'd swiped the mustard off her cheek could have been as much an act as his action had been.

"But the restaurant's closed on Mondays so we could have a real nice visit then. You're more than welcome to stay as long as you'd like, Sam."

"Thanks." *But staying has nothing to do with what I'd like.*

She hefted Ben in her arms, braced him on her hip, and nodded toward the stairway. "How about I show you your room? That way if I get tied up with the Wizard here, you'll know where to stow your gear. Bear will come with us so your sandwich will be safe."

Just like that, she assumed he was staying, this woman who posed in front of him like a Rubenesque Madonna with child.

There was looks could be deceiving thing again. He knew. He was the family black sheep come to spy on a woman who'd never done him any wrong.

"Lead the way," Sam said, not sure he wouldn't sneak out after the household went to sleep.

She climbed the steps ahead of him, the hem of her skirt swinging back and forth across her ankles. Correction, make that the backs of a pair of red high-tops. What kind of woman wore sneakers, red ones no less, under a primly long skirt?

The same kind that cinched a frilly apron to her very narrow waist, hugged a man's arm to the side of her plump bosom, and spoke with a voice that made a man's nerve endings cry out for more.

"You can move your bike into the garage behind the house," she said as her red-shoe-clad foot cleared the top step.

He glanced up at the sound of her purr and nodded, knowing he could as easily ride off as park in her garage.

"Gotta say g'night to Nana." Ben reached for a door from behind which the gentle strains of Brahms drifted.

"After your bath, Mr. Wizard," Dixie said and continued down the hall. Over her shoulder she explained to Sam, "That's my grandmother's room. You'll meet her tomorrow."

The elderly relative off whom Stuart said Dixie Rae now mooched. Maybe he'd meet her. Maybe he wouldn't.

A skittering noise sounded behind the next door they passed, as though someone withdrew in a hurry.

"Our renter," Dixie explained.

"Icky Witch," Ben said, ducking his head against his mother's shoulder.

Dixie swung Ben to his feet and gave his behind a playful swat that propelled him ahead of them toward the far end of the hall. "Go get your pjs."

As they followed, her head tipped close to Sam's, she explained in a lowered voice. "Miss Weston isn't into chaos which, unfortunately, is the hallmark of four-year-old boys."

"Aaah," Sam sighed as though he was focused entirely on what Dixie was saying rather than how her arm brushed his in the narrow hallway.

"Odd for someone who claims to be a teacher," she commented and stopped in the doorway where Ben had disappeared.

Peeking inside, Sam saw the sloped ceiling side of the bedroom where Ben dragged pajamas from a sunshine-yellow dresser. The room had been painted sky-blue with a bright rainbow arcing from wall to wall. A cartoon bear dipped honey from the pot where the rainbow ended while bees circled his head and a plethora of toys spilled across the floor at his feet. It was a room decorated by love, not design. But whose love created the room, Dixie's or that of a grandmother who listened to Brahms?

"I changed sheets this morning so the bed's fresh," she said through a dazzling smile. "It's yours as long as you need it, or can tolerate it."

He tore his attention away from that mind-numbing smile and eyed the low-set bed tucked beneath the room's single window. The bed looked barely long enough to accommodate a full-length male. At least it wasn't a set of bunks.

Dixie nodded over her shoulder at the closed door of the neighboring room. "If you need anything, you'll find me right next door."

Right next door. Was that *another* invitation?

What to do? Leave and save himself, or stay and save the kid? He knew what was the right choice. What Mickey would do.

By the time Sam ate his sandwich and moved his bike into the garage, the last tendrils of steam were wafting from the bathroom across from Dixie's bedroom. Her door stood ajar.

The most brazen invitation of all? If so, should he accept?

Should he learn right now what kind of woman Dixie Rae was?

He resettled his travel-pack over his shoulder and tiptoed closer to the door. He could hear Dixie's voice. Sweet. Rhythmic. Playful. That voice invited him.

But the words were all wrong. Though they were familiar words, words he'd heard over and over again, a very long time ago.

He stopped outside the partially open door and spied on the woman with the voice of a temptress. She was curled up on the edge of a double bed, one shoulder against the headboard and a large, thin book cradled in her lap. Ben was snuggled under the covers beside her listening to her read the bedtime story.

He'd misread her intention, misinterpreted what she'd meant when she'd informed him that her room was right next to his. She hadn't invited a rendezvous, not with her son tucked in beside her. Stuart had to be wrong about her.

Tomorrow morning, right after a hardy farmhouse breakfast, he was outa here.

CHAPTER THREE

Dixie charged the length of the upstairs hall after a giggling Ben. She couldn't yell for him to stop running without waking the entire household, something she was trying to avoid at this early hour. If only she'd thought to retrieve a few of his toys before giving Ben's room to their houseguest. If only she'd remembered last night that an active four-year-old needed more than leftover party favors and Sunday morning TV to occupy him until Nana woke or the twins arrived with their mother when her shift started. But toys had been the last thing on her mind when she'd shown Sam Ryan, with his boyish grin and puppy-dog eyes, to her son's bedroom.

Just as she snagged her son by the back of his crew-neck collar, he turned the doorknob to his room. Being an old house, nothing was quite square any more. Windows no longer sealed out drafts, walls had grown lumpy with layers of wallpaper, and floors were slanted. Slowly, the bedroom door swung open.

Light fanned inward across the scuffed floorboards and climbed a tangled, Winnie the Pooh sheet. That sheet covered the sleeping form beneath only to his naked shoulder blades. The sight of all that flesh could set a girl to wondering what the man under that sheet wore...or didn't wear.

Ben squirmed in her grip, demanding, "Want my Hot Wheels."

She squatted, turned him to face her, and whispered, "If you go in there, you'll wake Sam."

Ben's faced brightened. "Then you get them, Mommy."

Her in a bedroom with Michael's very appealing, half-naked cousin. Nothing like flying into the face of temptation.

"I can't go in there, either," she told her son.

"But I want—"

Dixie pressed a finger against Ben's lips. "Sorry, Honey Bear, but we don't always get what we want."

She knew. She wanted Michael back. She wanted for him never to have gotten into his car on that fateful night when icy roads had conspired to end his life. She wanted Ben to grow up knowing his father.

She wanted Sam Ryan *not* to be a relative.

Whoa. She would not entertain romantic notions about her husband's cousin. Heck, she didn't have time for romance with anyone, especially not today when she was about to serve Sunday brunch Farmhouse style for the first time.

Ben stomped his foot. "Want my Hot Wheels!"

Across the room in the narrow bed, Sam stirred and the tangled sheet slipped down to his back. If she didn't head off this tantrum, that sheet would be around Sam's ankles and she wouldn't have to imagine what else he did or did not wear.

Besides, she had to go into the room to close the door. How much further was it to the car collection that had passed from Michael to his son?

She peeked inside. All the way across the room to the dresser next to the bed where Sam Ryan slept. There, two dozen miniature cars over-spilled their carrying case.

"Figures," she muttered, making a mental note to work with her son on what 'picking up your toys' meant.

"Mommy, please?"

Heavy-lashed eyes pleaded up at her. She knew Ben was trying to manipulate her. She also had a cranky chef downstairs in her kitchen who expected her to be helping him with prep-work, a restaurant minutes away from opening and no one to babysit Ben until her cousin arrived with her girls. Nana couldn't have chosen a worse time to suffer one of her *spells*. The *Proper Parenting Police* were going to have to forgive her this morning.

She gave Ben's shoulders a gentle squeeze. "I'll get your cars."

His face lit up.

"But you have to promise me something in trade. You have to stay in the living room and play quietly until Lola and Lulu get here."

He nodded enthusiastically. She hoped he'd remember his promise fifteen minutes from now when Cousin Annie was due.

Midway through the room, the floor squeaked under her foot. Sam rolled toward the sound—rolled onto his back, the movement ripping the top sheet from its last, tenuous mooring at the foot of the bed. One leg slipped out from under the sheet. It was a rather nicely turned, darkly furred leg.

For an instant, Dixie wondered what that leg might feel like entwined with hers. But only for an instant. She didn't have time for fantasizing, not this morning and certainly not about Sam Ryan.

Besides, it wasn't like she'd never seen a naked, male leg before. Growing up with four brothers, she'd seen plenty. Of course, the sight of her brothers' legs had never made her heart go pitter-patter.

Then there'd been Michael's legs, tan and sinewy—a runner's legs. Judging by Sam's exposed limb, he wasn't the athlete his cousin had been. Yet Sam attracted her.

Probably all that wounded boy stuff Michael had told her about. And she was a sucker for the walking wounded. Come to think of it, Sam did remind her of a ten-year-old boy what with his shaggy mane ruffled against the pillow beneath his head, lush lashes fanned out across cheeks, and full lips puckered ever so slightly in blissful slumber.

A boy with the dark shadow of a beard and wide-flung, woolly limbs. Yeah, right. This was all about his wounded boyishness...*not*.

She finished her trek to the dresser where she swept the tiny toy cars into the rectangular compartments of the carrying case. The metal cast bodies clicked together and tiny tires whirred. Beside her, Sam stretched. The sheet worked its way down around his waist.

She flipped the soft lid over the loosely packed toys, tucked the little case under her arm, and turned. Ben still stood in the doorway, but something or someone down the hall had caused him to tilt his little, round chin away from her. In the next instant, Ben wheeled away, shouting, "Nana!"

Beside Dixie, Sam jerked upright in the narrow bed, his uncovered foot simultaneously hitting the floor. Reflexively, she glanced at that naked limb below where the Winnie the Pooh sheet dipped low over Sam's hip. As low as it was, she no longer had to wonder if Sam wore anything.

#

"You wake up all your guests this way?" Sam asked through a yawn.

A slow smile spread across Dixie's lips. "Only the cute ones."

He settled onto his hip, braced an elbow against the edge of the mattress, propped his head in his hand, and gazed up at her from beneath sleepy lids. "So, you think I'm cute, huh?"

One corner of her mouth tugged upwards; and she leveled in a voice that, this morning, reminded him more of a young Lauren Bacall than a salty Mae West. "You figure it out."

He half expected her to give him a lesson in whistling next. Oh, he'd happily put his lips together and blow for her. Never mind that she wore another ankle-length skirt and another buttoned-to-the-throat blouse, both cinched to her narrow waist by another ruffled apron. In his dreams his fingers had spanned that waist...and slowly popped the pearl buttons on her blouse from their buttonholes at her throat...and lower.

"I think I'm cute enough," he said, smiling dreamily.

"Hate to burst your bubble of self-delusion," she returned, "but I came in here to get something for Ben to play with."

"Something to play with, huh?" He was tempted to fold his hands behind his head and roll onto his back—to let fate, accident, or desire rule the precarious perch of the sheet over a certain part of his body. A rapidly responding part of his body.

"Toys—" Her grin twitched. "—for Ben."

Ben. Mickey's boy. The child he'd vowed to

protect in a weak moment. The child this woman mothered...Mickey's wife.

Sam drew a quelling breath, willed the blood to stop pooling in the lower regions of his body, and glanced at the empty doorway. "Where is the Wizard this morning?"

"Abandoned me like a rat off a sinking ship."

Funny, she didn't look a forsaken woman. She looked downright amused to have been caught at the side of his bed. And here he was, in the all-together, baiting her. Maybe if she hadn't wakened him in the middle of an erotic dream that featured the very woman at his bedside. Maybe if she weren't so damned desirable.

Maybe if he weren't so weak.

No, he had no business flirting with Mickey's widow, especially since she'd passed his test of her moral resolve last night. Maybe he best pass on the farmhouse-style breakfast and leave before he compromised them both.

                                #

"It's burnt," shrieked the woman who'd invaded Dixie's restaurant kitchen. "That's what's wrong with it!"

Dixie examined the omelet on the plate her boarder shoved under her nose while, behind her, her chef grumbled over the grill. "First she complains it's too runny, then I don't have enough cheese in it for her liking, now she says it's burnt."

"It is hard cooked," Dixie allowed.

The chef slapped his spatula against the griddle. She hoped he was flipping pancakes and not eggs.

"But not burned," she added in part to appease her irate chef, but mostly because it was true.

Miss Weston's thin lips disappeared altogether.

"If it is too well cooked for your taste," Dixie offered, "we'll be happy to cook another to your liking."

"I ain't cookin' nothing more for that woman!" howled the chef. "She's as impossible to please as my ex-wife!"

It wasn't by accident that she'd placed herself between her chef and her renter when the woman stormed into the restaurant kitchen. Every day, these two fought. It was like mediating between two six-year-olds.

Though her chef was right in this instance. There was no pleasing Miss Weston. Still, Dixie had to try. She had a dining room full of breakfast customers within earshot of the woman's screeching complaints.

"I'll cook it personally," Dixie offered, hoping to appease both boarder and chef.

"No," Miss Weston commanded in a screech that was sure to clear the bats from every belfry within a thirty-mile radius, not to mention the customers from her two small restaurant dining rooms. "I want *him* to cook it—" She jabbed a bony finger over Dixie's shoulder at the chef. "—and I want him to cook it right."

"That does it," roared the chef. "I'm outta here!"

Dixie spun at the man. "You don't mean that."

But he was already halfway to the door, apron untied. Dixie caught up to him just as he reached the service entrance.

"Please. You can't leave. I have a restaurant full of customers who love your cooking."

"As long as that woman—" It was his turn to jab a finger. "—eats under this roof, I don't cook here."

Dixie placed her hand on her chef's forearm, reined in her panic, and lowered her voice. "Carl, I hired you out of a drug rehab program when no one else would give you a chance."

Never mind that no one else had applied for the job.

"And for that, I've put up with her—" He jabbed his finger again in Miss Weston's direction. "—for two weeks. No more. I'm gone." He swiped off his chef's cap, peeled away his apron, and dumped them both into Dixie's hands.

The next thing she knew, the door had slammed shut between her and her chef and the scent of scorched pancakes curled across her nostrils. Her boarder had just cost her her chef when she needed him most. Forget the needed rental income the woman provided. Miss Weston had to go.

Dixie wheeled about, mayhem in her heart, and stopped dead. Sam stood in the doorway between restaurant and private kitchens.

Okay, he wasn't quite that far into the restaurant kitchen, he held the door open barely a foot. But his presence was enough to remind her of something else Michael had told her about his cousin, something that might keep her from killing Miss Weston and winding up in jail, which would no doubt bring Stuart Carrington circling like a buzzard.

She grabbed Sam by the front of his jacket, and hauled him into the restaurant kitchen—hauled him close. "Michael said you're a European trained chef and that's exactly the kind of help I need right now."

#

"Ah-ah," Sam stammered partly because the fingers gripping his jacket also had a fistful of t-shirt and a pinch of skin, but mostly because he didn't know how much to confess to Dixie.

She jerked him closer still, her chin almost touching his. "Michael said you trained at the Cordon Bleu. Is that true?"

Her eyes were more like blue flames than sun-soaked cornflowers. There was nary a hint of the temptress left who'd teased him from bedside this morning—the temptress with whom he'd flirted shamelessly. He'd already decided he needed to get away from *that* woman ASAP or suffer the failings of his weak will. *This* woman was even more of a threat—this Dixie with the no-nonsense focus of a homicide detective. Shades of last night on the porch flashed through his mind. He needed to be careful how he answered her questions.

With a slight nod, he murmured, "Technically, yes. But…"

She shoved the chef's apron and hat into his fumbling hands, muttering, "Whatever. Just play along with me."

Turning, she towed him between prep table and cooking surfaces toward the kitchen's far end. Not the least sure of what he'd agreed to *play along with*, he followed. Besides, she had the grip of a wide receiver on his wrist.

When Dixie stopped short, he nearly ran into her. He blinked over her shoulder at a stiff-postured woman garbed from throat to toe in black. The border no doubt.

Mud-brown eyes peeked at him from between cut-to-the-eyebrows, dark bangs and the mound of omelet on the plate she held in front of her face as though she were hiding from him. Did she know him?

Should he know her? Weirder yet, was that a hint of fear he saw in the wide eyes peering at him?

Heck, nobody feared him; and the harpy he'd heard moments ago shrieking complaints didn't sound like the sort to shrink from anybody. Though, Ben had called her a witch. Maybe the expression he read as fearful was her version of the evil eye.

"Miss Weston," Dixie said. "This is Sam Ryan, my husband's cousin and our houseguest. Sam is a European trained chef."

When had he last called himself a chef? When had he last even considered himself a chef? He ran a fingertip along the starched edge of the white chef's cap in his hand. Something akin to nostalgia bubbled up in him.

He glanced at the rack of pots and utensils hanging over the prep table running the center of the room, surveyed the stainless sinks beyond, wire racks of supplies, and stainless steel cooler and freezer units back by the service door. He eyed the multi-burner gas range, flattop, and deep fryers occupying the nearest wall. A familiar environment. Comfortable.

"How about if I ask Sam to cook your omelet?" Dixie asked.

His attention jerked back to Dixie. *What had she just asked Miss Weston?*

He blinked from Dixie to her renter just as Miss Weston gave the scantest of nods. What had the woman just agreed to?

Releasing him, Dixie steered Miss Weston out the kitchen door. "You go back to your table and get comfy. I guarantee you an omelet that'll knock the socks off your obviously sophisticated taste buds."

Had he, somewhere in his befuddled state, agreed

to cook an omelet? This was why he had to give Dixie a quick good-bye, hop on his bike and ride away. She distracted him with her smoky voice and soft curves, with the promise of what her high-collared, long-sleeved, ankle-length attire hid from him…aside from a resolve of steel. Steel magnolia type of woman scared the bejeebers out of him. But she needed him now, what with her chef walking out and Sunday brunch to serve. He'd overheard that much from the doorway separating the kitchens.

She needed him.

It struck him then, for the first time in his life, someone *really* did need him. And she needed him in a way he could help. His fingers tightened on the chef's apron she'd stuffed into his hands. Helping her would mean sticking around longer.

The swinging door swept to and fro behind the departing Miss Weston. Dixie strode toward him, Weston's rejected omelet in one hand and red tennis shoe toes peeking out from her swirling hem.

No. No. No.

He couldn't stay because even one more day near those voluptuous curves and ridiculous red high-tops were enough to do him in, let alone the way she now looked at him—smiled at him. Those inviting lush lips too easily made him forget the steel maiden behind them. Good intentions be damned, a hot kitchen and tight quarters was no place to be with his cousin's widow.

"Look, Red—"

Her eyebrows rose questioningly as she stopped short of the corner of the prep table—short of him. "Red?"

"Yeah, because your shoes."

She glanced down at the toes of her tennies poking out from under her ankle-length skirt, nodded and cocked her head at him. "They *are* red."

She planted her free hand on one hip, expectancy sparkling in her eyes. "You were about to say?"

He stared into the bright eyes peering back at him like he was her hero. No one had ever looked at him that way. Damn, he'd hate to chase that look away, but he was nobody's hero. Besides, Mickey's widow deserved the truth and the truth was...

"I didn't finish my training at the Cordon Bleu."

The hero-worship gleam didn't dim one iota from Dixie's eyes. "You telling me you left the program before you got even as far as omelet making?"

At least she hadn't assumed he'd been kicked out. Then again, that her first thought had been that *he'd* left training could mean she knew about his tendency to bail when the going got tough.

Heat climbed his cheeks and not because of the bacon spitting on the griddle behind him. Eager to end the exchange—to get away from Dixie and her wonderful kitchen—the words rushed from him.

"I just figured you should know the truth about my limited training before turning me loose in your kitchen. I'm hardly qualified to be called a chef."

She set Weston's plate on the dirty dish counter with a definitive clunk, the hero-worship melting from her eyes like butter on a hot grill. "I wasn't planning to hand my kitchen over to you, Sam. Nor do I expect you to cook any omelets."

He'd given her the truth. He should feel good about that. But the truth had chased that glint of hero worship from Dixie's eyes. It made him feel like a heel. Why, he didn't know. He was used to seeing disappointment in the eyes cast his way. But then, none of those other eyes had ever looked at him with anything akin to hero worship.

She edged past him to the flattop, took up a spatula and scraped aside the burnt pancakes and over-cooked bacon, the sweetness in her voice a tad forced. "I hadn't meant to impose on you, Sam."

He pivoted after her. "It's not an imposition. It's—"

"It's okay, Sam." She gave him an understanding smile, turned away from the grill and scrubbed her hands in the sink. "You don't have to be polite and manufacture some excuse. Asking you to cook would be an imposition. That's why I didn't exactly ask that of you. I only asked you to play along."

"I don't understand," Sam said as she returned to the griddle.

"Miss Weston can be a bit of a snob," Dixie said without looking at him. "All I need is for her to think a European trained chef has prepared her omelet and she won't dare complain again."

"Aaah," Sam exhaled. "You never intended for me to cook any omelet." *You just hoped I would.*

She moved to the walk-in cooler, opened its door, and, before stepping inside, said, "I can make Miss Weston's omelet and she won't know the difference."

Did she doubt his ability? Is that what this was about? He didn't like it, as evidenced by the knot forming in his stomach.

"And while you're making omelets on the stove, who'll be running the flattop?" he called, testing her true intent, hoping it wasn't about her doubting him.

As she emerged from the cooler with bacon,

eggs, and milk, her gaze went to the big flat cooktop and worry lines pinched vertical troughs above her nose. Still, she said, "I can handle that, too."

Beginning to think her reason for dismissing him was more about imposing on him than doubting him, he ventured, "There's a lot more to running a flattop than the uninitiated might think."

She all but threw the contents in her arms down on the prep-counter before facing him, one hand on hip. "I waitressed in more than a few greasy spoons, and when a cook didn't show up for his shift, I took over the flattop, the grill, and the fryers. I can do this."

He leaned a hip against the prep-counter. "Smart enough to run a business, sweet enough to attract honey bees, and experienced enough to run a restaurant kitchen. Aren't you a woman of many talents?"

She blinked and turned to the ingredients she'd brought from the cooler. Was that a *tell*? A man didn't successfully maneuver around life's pitfalls without learning to read people; and he'd swear that blink— that turning away from him hid a lie. He decided to push a little harder.

"Cooking eggs, bacon, sausage, pancakes, and hash browns on a flattop while whipping up omelets is quite a talent."

"Carl did it," she said, frowning at the ticket for the ruined breakfast she'd scraped off the flattop.

"Not many can do both and keep their cool and you did it as a waitress just filling in."

She scowled at him. "Okay, the places I worked didn't exactly make omelets. It was mostly hamburgers, French fries, and grilled sandwiches."

He laughed. "Hell, Red, you were fibbing."

"I do not lie." She peeled a slice of bacon from its tray and slapped it on the griddle with far more force than was necessary.

"But you said—"

"That I'd *ask* you to cook her omelet." She looked him in the eye. "Sam, will you cook Miss Weston's omelet?"

Before he could answer, she turned her attention back to the flattop. "There. Now I've asked you."

"Integrity to the letter," he said.

"Lies cause trouble," she said, slapping another slice of bacon onto the hot grill. "There's never a good reason for lying."

Hisssss, went the bacon.

"I used evasive action to prevent myself from strangling Miss Weston," Dixie muttered, a third bacon slice hitting the griddle with a sizzle.

Taking the package of bacon from Dixie's hand, he said, "I, for one, am glad you didn't strangle Miss Weston. I couldn't bear to see you in jailhouse stripes."

She gave the pitcher of pancake batter a stir. "You saying horizontal stripes won't work on my figure?"

He caught himself taking a quick inventory of Dixie's luscious curves before shaking his head. "Heck, Red, stripes, horizontal or otherwise, would work their little dyed fibers threadbare for an hour wrapped around you."

She peered over her shoulder at him, the fire in her voice replaced with a dubious lilt. "Are you flirting with me, or just trying to smooth my ruffled feathers?"

"A little of both, I guess."

"A truthful enough answer," she said, uncertainty a mere shadow in her tone. "I like that." She poured out three perfect circles of pancake batter, their edges immediately bubbling against the hot surface of the flattop.

"So, Samuel Jefferson Ryan—"

"Mickey gave you the full tour of my name, did he?"

She faced him. "Among other things."

I just bet he did.

"Thanks for playing along, Sam."

Playing along. He didn't believe for one minute that's all she'd expected from him, not given the hero worship in her eyes. Nor did it sit right in his gut that her opinion of him so easily shifted—that she so easily let him off the proverbial hook...even if his history made him a bad bet.

He should stick to his original plan and leave before she learned how bad a gamble he was. But, something deep within him wanted to prove to her he could be what she needed him to be.

He took the hand she held out to him, held her bacon-greased fingers. But he didn't shake her hand as her gesture had implied he do. The gesture seemed too impersonal—too final.

"You saying you don't want me to cook for you?" he asked.

A plethora of emotions flashed across her face. Surprise, hope, and something like relief. She slipped her fingers from his and turned back to the cook surface where she turned the bacon with the corner of a spatula. "I told you, Sam, you're a guest here. I wouldn't dream of imposing on a guest."

"How about family?"

She paused in mid-flip of a pancake. "Careful about volunteering your services, Sam. I'm likely to take you up on the offer and I can't handle two chefs walking out on me in the same day."

He could still escape, just tell her what a sham he was.

"I make an omelet that's to die for," he said.

She tossed down the spatula and threw her arms around Sam's neck, crushing the chef's apron and cap between them. "Thank you, Sam. Thank you. I promise I'll call Carl as soon as I have a free moment and beg him to come back."

He wanted to say there was no hurry to call Chef Carl, not if she kept hugging him like this. What he should be doing was smacking himself up alongside his head for *volunteering* his services. The best he could say for the situation was that at least he'd be stuck in this torture chamber of heat and close quarters with Dixie Rae for only one day. Certainly good old Carl couldn't resist her any better than he had, right?

Like a stone skipping across the surface of a tranquil pond, the fact that the man had already rejected her pleas that he not quit sent a ripple of doubt across Sam's logic. Or was it the gliding of her hands down his arms that set his nerves ajumble?

"Of course you mean *die* in the figurative sense," she said, leaning back from him and looking him in the eye. "Preferable as that would be where Miss Weston is concerned, it's never good form for any restaurant customer to die from the food."

Take the out. Tell her there's nothing figurative about his word choice.

"I mean it figuratively. Promise."

She snatched the apron from his hands. "Okay. Here's what we'll do." She looped the apron over his head, for a moment her arms draped once more around his neck. Too close. Too tempting. Too late to run.

"You make Miss Weston's omelet. I'll do the rest." With quick, efficient hands, she urged him around, tugged off his jacket, and began tying the apron strings.

"What do you mean, you'll do the rest?" he asked, trying to ignore the brush and bump of her fingers against the small of his back.

"Having you make Miss Weston's omelet is imposition enough," she replied. "If there are any other omelet orders, we'll worry about them then."

"What do you mean, *we'll worry about them then*?"

"I mean, we'll worry about making more omelets if anyone orders any."

"You don't believe I can make an omelet to die for, do you?"

She tugged the chef's cap from his fingers, rose onto her tiptoes, and placed it on his head. "I believe you can do anything you set your mind to, Sam Ryan."

Anything you set your mind to. So it was his ability to follow through she doubted, not his talent. An accurate assessment.

He escaped past her to the sink and turned on the hot water. He couldn't blame her for doubting his commitment. He'd never followed through on anything.

He scrubbed his hands harder than was

necessary. He didn't like that Dixie doubted him. It wasn't like he wasn't used to being doubted. His family did it all the time. But they doubted his abilities while Dixie...

With scalding water flowing over his hands, it struck him. Mickey had told him the same thing Dixie had. *You can do whatever you set your mind to.*

But he'd never had anything to set his mind to...unless avoiding Uncle Stuart counted. So, he'd let Mickey down.

But, he wouldn't let down Mickey's widow, at least not today. At least not as long as Sunday brunch lasted.

Sam dried his hands, selected a spatula from the rack above the stainless steel island, and tested its weight in his hand. How right it felt being back in a kitchen.

"I can handle every aspect of a restaurant kitchen," he said.

She grinned at him when he joined her at the flattop. "For now, just keep to the stove and Miss Weston's omelet. At least then we'll know who to blame in case of death."

"There you go again, Red, underestimating my talents."

Before she could counter, the door to the dining room swung open and a blonde wearing an apron similar to Dixie's burst into the kitchen, reading from an order pad, "I need two farmhouse specials, one scrambled with ham, the second hard cooked with bacon." Then, looking up, she added, "Hey, who's the new chef?"

"This is Sam Ryan," Dixie supplied.

"Your chef du jour," he said.

"He's Michael's cousin," Dixie added, stating the facts as they stood between him and the very enticing Dixie.

"How do, Sam Ryan," the waitress said, her chin cocked in an angle reminiscent of the tilt Dixie had given her own chin as she'd bantered with him at his bedside, but nowhere near as provocative. "Dare I ask what happened to our former and far less handsome chef?"

"Sam, this is my cousin Annie, my very *married* cousin Annie."

"Just because a girl has already bought the goods doesn't mean she can't still window shop," Annie returned with a wink. "So, what happened to Carl?"

"He and Miss Weston had a difference of opinion," Dixie explained.

"And Sam's taking his place?"

"Sam's making the omelets…for today."

"Cool!"

Next to where Dixie flipped pancakes, Sam one-handedly cracked two eggs onto the griddle.

"Wow," Annie said. "I never saw Carl do that."

Dixie gave him a sidelong look. "Okay, so you know a few tricks." To her cousin, she said, "Don't you have coffee to pour, or something?"

"Yeah. Sure."

Annie disappeared in a flurry of swinging doors.

Sam cracked open three more eggs into a deep bowl, drawing Dixie's attention.

"I can handle the kitchen," he said.

"There's more to cooking for a restaurant than tricks and being a whiz with omelets," she said.

He nodded at the flattop in front of her. "Over easy on those eggs, right?"

She flipped them. "It takes coordinating, lots of it."

He tested the temperature of his pan, poured the beaten eggs into it, and read the ticket Annie had just delivered. "What's a farmhouse special?"

"Two eggs your choice with hash browns, toast, and a side of bacon, ham, or sausage. Why?"

He buttered the flattop and scooped out two portions of shredded potatoes.

"You're trying to make a point here, aren't you?" she said.

"Me? No." He added three strips of bacon and a slab of ham to the mix, and nodded at the griddle space in front of Dixie. "Your eggs are about to pass the over easy stage again."

She smirked at him and scooped the eggs onto a plate. "If I didn't have you distracting me—"

Annie burst into the kitchen. "I just seated the Fieger family."

"All nine of them?" Dixie gasped.

"From Gramma Fieger right down to baby Ruth."

"I don't suppose they're the pancake and sausages types?" Sam asked.

He loaded the cooked pancakes and bacon onto the plate in Dixie's hand. She looked at the plate, then at him.

"I can handle the kitchen," he said. "Trust me."

"Trust you, huh?"

"Yeah."

She nodded. "This is going to work."

"Of course it is."

"We will make it work," she said.

He gave her a thumbs up and she nodded again, then backed out the swinging door. He'd win her over…at least in the kitchen. It was the one place where he could be honest.

CHAPTER FOUR

"This will work. It has to." Dixie murmured the words like a mantra as she stepped into the front dining room whose walls she'd bordered with hand-stencils and windows she'd covered with lace curtains. Customers filled better than half the tables with Sunday brunch getting underway. Everything was as she'd envisioned it...except for handing over her kitchen to Sam. She reminded herself she'd done that as much because she needed someone cooking for her as much as because Sam needed someone believing in him.

What *had* she been thinking? She stood frozen in place just outside the kitchen doors. She needed Sunday brunch to be a hit for her, for Ben, for Gran. This shouldn't be about Sam at all. That's what she got for being the local saint of all lost, broken, and unwanted creatures. What was this penchant she had for fixing the walking wounded?

She drew a quelling breath and took a step away from the kitchen doors. Now was not the time to ponder her shortcomings, or Sam's...unless he decided to exercise his number one failing. When the going gets tough, Sam runs. Michael had well acquainted her with that pattern of Sam's. But he wouldn't walk out on her in the middle of brunch, would he?

Of course not. He'd volunteered his services—fought to get her to accept his offer to cook for her.

Besides, you can't fight fate. Sam's being here at the very moment when she most needed him was proof of that.

Yup. Everything would be fine. Every cloud has its silver lining. The glass is half full. The sun always rises.

With a smile, she set the egg and pancake filled plate along with a brown paper bag in front of a bird-like man with thick, black-rimmed glasses. "I'm sorry your order took so long, Mr. Patterson. We had a little mishap in the kitchen and had to start over. As an apology, I wrapped up a couple of my apple-cinnamon muffins for you to take home."

His wizened face crinkled into a smile. "You are a sweet girl."

For a small man, he sure had a big smile and a healthy appetite—a contradiction not unlike Sam Ryan who could be vulnerable one minute and flirtatious the next.

Make that sexy.

Quite a talent, to go from tousled boy to tempting man in the blink of a waking eye...and the slip of a sheet. Michael had said there was more to Sam than met the eye. Thank goodness, because that black t-shirt and jeans he wore under his apron didn't fit the persona of a chef one iota...at least not the kind of chef who cooked gourmet omelets.

"If you need anything," she said to Mr. Patterson, "you just give me a call."

He gave her a wink, his eyes huge behind the thick lenses of his glasses.

Everything would be okay. She had a chef in her kitchen who had at least some European training. Catastrophe averted. Nothing else was going to go wrong.

The front door rattled open and Dixie turned toward the foyer, eager to greet her next customers. But the three women filing into her entry were the Hostettler sisters, the most gossipy women in town.

For months, Dixie had tried to entice them to dine in her restaurant—wanted them to sample her good, home cooked food. Their word of mouth advertising was worth half a year's budget of newspaper and radio ads.

And they had to pick today of all days to come to The Farmhouse—today when she had an untried chef in her kitchen.

"So much for silver linings," she muttered under her breath.

Dixie pasted on a smile and greeted the trio. "Hortense, Penelope, Esmeralda, don't you all look lovely in your Sunday finery."

Penelope and Esmeralda smiled and nodded, their widened eyes exploring every corner of the dining room. Hortense, the eldest, sniffed. "We'll have a table away from any drafts."

No drafts in an old farmhouse. Swell. Why didn't the woman just ask for the moon?

She seated the trio by the window that over-looked the flower garden. Hopefully, the view would distract them from the imperfections of an old parlor-turned-restaurant dining room. Hopefully, they'd order something simple, like muffins or croissants. Just nothing…cooked.

Not that she doubted Sam.

I make an omelet to die for. What if he'd lied to her?

Even if Sam *could* make an omelet to die for, it

had to pass the impossible to please Miss Weston's taste test. To be on the safe side, she should steer the Hostettler sisters away from ordering any omelets.

Just as she handed them their menus, Sam emerged from the kitchen with Miss Weston's omelet—Miss Weston who occupied the next table. Dixie cringed. Why hadn't she seated the Hostettler sisters along the far wall?

Because the only table open there was between the Fieger family and the entrance. One never seated important clients next to the door or a noisy family. Silently, she prayed Miss Weston wouldn't reject Sam's omelet.

Sam served the dish with a flourish. Dixie tried to block the Hostettler sisters' view of Miss Weston's table, but there were too many of them and not enough of her.

She felt Sam at her back, lingering. Why didn't he go back to the kitchen, him with his black tee and longish hair? What was he waiting for?

She glanced over her shoulder just as Miss Weston sank her fork into the omelet. Sam, his hands folded behind his back, his legs splayed, was waiting for Miss Weston's verdict. Dixie faced the Hostettler sisters and held her breath.

Then, a sound like none she'd ever heard—at least not in a public place—emanated from the vicinity of Miss Weston's table. Dixie turned and gaped as the woman chewed and moaned, her eyes rolled back in her head. Sam grinned that wonderfully boyish grin of his, gave Miss Weston a bow, pivoted on his heel, winked at the Hostettler sisters, and strode off toward the kitchen.

"I'll take whatever she's having," Esmeralda

Hostettler said with a nod in Miss Weston's direction.

"I'll have the same," Penelope said and nodded after Sam, "as long as he serves it."

Dixie smiled weakly at Sam's backside disappearing through the swinging doors. He did cut a dashing figure in that crisp, white apron and jauntily set chef's cap. But the close-cut jeans and black tee sent out an entirely different signal—one that made her think of leather-clad bad boys. Hortense Hostettler, eldest sister and family matriarch, was sure to find fault with that last.

Dixie held her breath and waited for Hortense to harangue her younger siblings for their obvious lapses in propriety and her for employing an improper young man. Hortense handed her menu back to Dixie unopened. Here it comes, Dixie thought. But to her surprise, Hortense said only, "I'll have the same as my sisters."

Sam Ryan may not be reputed as the most reliable man in the world, but he was clearly a man of his word. He'd promised her an omelet to die for, and considering the sounds Miss Weston had still been making when she left the dining room, he'd delivered.

"You are one hell of a silver lining to my latest dark cloud catastrophe," Dixie said as she charged into the kitchen.

Pancakes, eggs, hash browns, and every side meat listed in her menu lined the flattop. Sam flipped and scraped and nudged, all the while whistling. She stood there, gaping at him.

He looked at her, stopped whistling and gave her a grin that made her go weak clear to her toes. "Told you I could handle the kitchen, Red."

She strode closer, surveying the quality and

quantity of what he cooked. "And I repeat. You are one hell of a silver lining."

"Thank you," he said, his grin turning almost sheepish. But it was the quietness of his tone that made her feel like she'd just done him a favor instead of the other way around.

#

"Don't volunteer anything you're not prepared to deliver, Sam. I can't handle two chefs walking out on me in the same day."

Sam trod the well-worn path that led away from the back of the house to the garage, his duffel under his arm and helmet dangling from his fingers. He didn't know why he was feeling guilty. Brunch was over and the kitchen clean. Even her Cousin Annie had gone home. The job he'd promised to do and more was done. He wasn't abandoning Dixie.

I can't handle two chefs walking out on me in the same day.

Okay, so he was technically doing the one thing she clearly stated she couldn't abide. He was sneaking off without so much as an "it's been nice meeting you." The cowardice of his act pressed down his shoulders.

But, if he lingered long enough to say good-bye to Dixie, he'd never leave. He'd already tried when he'd gone into the kitchen early this morning to tell her he was leaving. Look what being polite had gotten him. A job cooking all morning and into the afternoon.

Not that he minded it. It was the most fun he'd had in a long time. But still…

He focused on the corner of the garage where he'd parked the Ducati. If he stayed, he would disappoint her. Sooner or later, at the very least, he'd lose interest in this latest adventure and run off to the next. Lack of responsibility his uncle called it. Worse yet would be if she figured out Stuart had sent him to spy on her. Better that he sneak off with his memory of the way her eyes had shined when she'd returned to the kitchen and essentially decreed him her knight in a chef's cap.

He was almost to the garage. The old swing type doors would open soundlessly on well-oiled hinges and nothing would be between him and the open road.

...Provided no one sounded the alarm.

He eyed Bear who loped ahead of him and willed the dog to remain silent. One yip out of him and Dixie was sure to be routed from whatever task had taken her to the barn beyond the private drive that circled from the front parking lot between the side of the house and outbuildings and around an apple tree occupied patch of grass.

As for the rest of the household...

He glanced back at the house. Miss Weston was parked in a wicker chair on the side porch huddled over a book. She'd said nothing as he'd passed. Actually, she hadn't said anything to him since making those ungodly sounds over the omelet he'd cooked for her. He hoped she wouldn't speak up now. She had the potential volume to be heard in the next county.

A curtain fluttered in the window of the room at the top of the back stairs. The grandmother's room. Someone had said she'd "gone up" for a nap. He assumed Ben had gone with her. Four-year-olds took naps, didn't they?

Bear disappeared around the corner of the

garage. Sam blew out a breath. All he had to do was roll his bike out of the garage and to the front of the house where it would be too late for anyone to stop him, even if they heard him start her up.

With one eye trained on the barn, the largest and furthest from the house of the outbuildings, he stepped around the garage corner after Bear.

"Hiya, Tin Man."

Sam skidded to a halt in front of Ben. The kid looked up at him, head tilted back as far as it would go. Ben's thin little boy arms hugged a huge black and white cat to his chest—a cat with long ears. Make that a rabbit.

"Hey, I thought you were with your grandmother."

"Nana's napping."

"And you're not," Sam murmured, scanning the buildings clustered around the circular driveway for any sign of Dixie. If the grandmother wasn't watching the kid, then Dixie was.

"Where ya goin'?" The kid was eyeing the helmet dangling from his fingers.

"Where am I going?" Sam repeated, vying for time as he pondered whether lying to the kid was the same as lying to Dixie. He opted for a half-truth. "I'm going for a ride."

A one-way ride to parts unknown. Once Stuart figured out he'd screwed up yet again, the more continent he had between him and his uncle, the better. Now all he had to do was get the kid out from between him and the garage doors.

"Can I go fo' ride with you?" Ben asked.

"Maybe next time."

Yeah, like he hadn't heard that one a thousand

times from his mother during her semi-annual visits post marriage to the creep who didn't want another man's castoff kid. Not the image of himself he wanted to leave with Mickey's son.

"Look, kid. Motorcycles eat up little boys. Besides, I don't have an extra helmet."

The kid screwed up his mouth like he was gearing up to debate what Sam said while Bear plunked his behind down beside Sam and leaned into him. Things were getting worse by the minute. Maybe a little diversion was called for here.

Sam tweaked the rabbit's ear. "What ya got here, kid?"

"Checkers. Nana said he could be my pet. Sh-she said we would never eat him."

"It's good not to eat your pets." Bear licked Sam's neck and he added under his breath, "Better yet, if the pets don't eat you."

The rabbit wriggled in Ben's grip, his back legs scrabbling for the ground.

"Be still, Checkers," Ben scolded, sounding more like an elderly Nana-type than a kid. Was that the role model Sam should leave the kid with?

Far better that than a stern uncle, an absentee mother, and an overly efficient nanny.

The rabbit stopped struggling and hung in Ben's arms, its nose twitching and round eyes shiny as black marbles. That pretty much summed up Sam's take on his current position.

"How about you and Checkers take Toto off to Oz?"

The kid squinted up at him as if he'd suffered his own tornado-induced delirium.

"Bear," Sam said, nodding at the dog.

"Don't want to. Playing with Checkers now."

The rabbit erupted into a flurry of wiggles. Ben scrabbled to hang onto the over-sized rodent. Before Sam could help, the rabbit got his hind feet on the ground and vaulted out of Ben's arms. Instantly, Bear bounded after the rabbit. Pet dog eating pet rabbit definitely ranked among those experiences no child should ever witness.

Sam dropped his helmet and duffel and lunged after Bear, yelling, "Get the rabbit, kid."

But Ben wasn't as quick nor as coordinated as the rabbit. Just as he grabbed, Checkers hopped. Sam got a grip on Bear's collar and wound up stumbling after the Great Dane who seemed to think proper hunting methods involved mimicking the movement of its prey.

Across the gravel and onto the grassy oasis mid driveway the unlikely quartet hopped, lunged, and stumbled, a virtual Keystone cops-like parade of prey, predator, and would-be rescuers. Checkers paused to nibble clover. Bear sniffed the rabbit's tail. As much as Sam preferred to stay out from between Bear and anything the dog might consider lunch, Sam acted on the opportunity. He dove between dog and rabbit, grabbing for Checkers...who scooted out of reach. Belly-first, Sam hit the ground hard and skidded face-first into a pair of rubber boots...red ones.

"I could learn to like a man falling at my feet," Dixie said in that sultry voice of hers.

Sam forgot about rabbits and dogs and little boys. He forgot about the motorcycle helmet tottering in the gravel back by the garage—forgot about escaping. Denim jeans melded to Dixie's legs like they'd been custom woven for her shapely limbs.

She squatted and the denim tightened across her knees and up her thighs. "Sam?"

He loved how that throaty voice said his name. He loved it almost as much as the way one blouse button strained across—

"You okay?" She brushed a hank of hair out of his eyes, her fingertips tickling his forehead. He'd happily lie at her feet for as long as she touched him like that.

He grinned. "Never better."

"You sure you're okay? You hit the ground pretty hard."

"Ground. Hard. Yeah," he said through a sigh, reality slow to hit him. But when it did...

"Jeez, the kid's rabbit!" Sam was half way to his feet when he spotted the rabbit grazing on clover under the apple tree mid-oasis, the dog nose to tail with him.

"No," Sam wailed, reeling toward the furry pair.

But once again, rabbit and dog were faster than man. Checkers spun, reared up, and batted Bear on the nose. With a yelp, the Great Dane crumpled back onto his hindquarters.

Grimacing, Sam checked his forward momentum. "I should have known you'd own the Arnold Schwartzeneger of rabbits."

"Checkers grew up with dogs," Dixie said, moving to his side, her eyes twinkling with silent laughter.

"He didn't grow up with the kind of dogs I grew up with," Sam countered, brushing dirt from his jacket sleeve.

Following the movement of his hand, Dixie's eyes dimmed and she plucked a blade of grass from his jacket above where his heart would have been...had he had a heart. Clearly he didn't or he wouldn't be sneaking off and causing disappointment to shade across Dixie's cornflower blue eyes as realization dawned on her. He winced.

"Kind of warm out to be wearing your motorcycle jacket," she murmured and looked him in the eye.

And getting hotter by the minute.

Her eyes cut to the garage door where his helmet and duffel lay. Damn, why hadn't he just set the kid aside, shooed the dog off, and hopped onto his bike? Now he'd have to run the gauntlet of excuses why he couldn't stay, none of which would be the truth...unless he confessed that he'd come here under Stuart's orders...not to mention he was far too attracted to her to be decent.

"I hope you were going to say good-bye before you left," she said, her purr a tad tight.

"Sure. Of course." He stared at the red toes of Dixie's footwear—boots this time, which was about as close to looking her in the eye as he could manage. Maybe if she didn't see into his eyes, she wouldn't see the lie in him.

But the seconds stretched and he knew he hadn't fooled Dixie one iota. He shoved his hands into his pockets and confessed.

"I *was* sneaking off."

"Poor Sam."

He blinked at her—gaped at her. Hardly the response he'd expected.

"You don't need to sneak off from us, Sam." She brushed at the dust on his sleeve. "You can come and go here as you please." She turned his hand over, her fingers light on his wrist, her thumb soft against the grass stain on the heel of his hand.

If she kept touching him like that, his pleasure would all be in the staying. Was that her plan, entice him with provocative caresses?

One corner of her lips tugged further upward as though she knew her secret was out. "Just making sure I'm not sending you off with any of my gravel imbedded in your hand. Blame the mother in me."

"The *mother*, huh?"

Her crooked smile stretched further still. "That's what mothers do."

"Not mine," he answered without thinking.

The flirtatious curl of Dixie's lips slipped and the message in her eyes couldn't have been clearer if she'd said it aloud. *Poor Sam.*

He should be disturbed by her pity. He should be so shamed by it that he couldn't face her—that he'd all the more need to leave. But he couldn't turn away, couldn't stop exploring the sympathy in Dixie's eyes. Suddenly he wasn't so sure he wanted to leave the world of a woman who knew what it was like to be cast out by the Carringtons.

"You said the restaurant was closed Mondays," he said. "So I knew you wouldn't need a chef tomorrow."

"I'll have all day to talk Carl into coming back."

He had no doubt she could talk any man into anything.

"Besides, I've already imposed on you enough," she added.

"We already had this discussion. I'm family, remember? Besides, it was fun."

"Good." Her lips curled into their seductive smile

and her hand in his warm—comfortably so, invitingly so.

Ask me to stay.

"We'll miss you."

Don't send me away.

"Come visit us any time you want."

Would it count as a visit if he drove down the road a few miles, then turned around and came back?

"I'd love for Ben to get to know you better."

Ben. The kid...who was rolling around the grass with Checkers and Bear at the moment. That's who she invited him to visit. Not her. Sam forced a smile. "I'm not much of a role model for kids."

She tugged at the front of his jacket. "Boys need a little rebel in their lives, especially little boys who live in a household full of women."

Rebel? *Him?* That label was for men who didn't care what others thought of them. That wasn't him. He cared, especially about what Dixie thought. Dixie who was giving him an out—an excuse to change his mind and stay. Why didn't he jump at it?

Because his staying would have nothing to do with the kid. The kid was safe and happy. He knew that now. He could see it in the way Dixie cared for her son.

Dixie's fingers spread across his forearm. "Thanks again for helping out in the restaurant. I don't know what I'd have done without you this morning."

"You'd have managed."

"Not without more than a few singed edges."

"Couldn't let that happen."

"Not to Michael's wife, huh?"

"Not to any woman as fair and beautiful as you."

"Careful there, Sam. You'll turn my head." She

looped her arm through his, walking him toward the helmet and duffel that lie in the dust like his wasted past. "Sorry we had so little time to visit."

"Me, too," he murmured, aware he wasn't just being polite in his answer, willing her to remind him if he stayed they'd have all day tomorrow to share stories about Mickey.

They stopped and Dixie snatched up the helmet and handed it to him. "Have a safe trip."

Ben squeezed in between them, peered up at his mother, and said, "Want to go fo' a moto'cycle ride with Sam."

She looked Sam in the eye, her smile stretching a little. "I wouldn't mind taking a ride with Sam myself."

The idea of Dixie's arms wrapped around his waist and her curves pressed into his back made him itch in places he hadn't scratched in a while. He shifted from one foot to the other.

Her smile faded. "The open road in front of you and the wind in your face, right Sam?"

And responsibility left behind in the dust. That's what she was probably thinking, not that she'd have been wrong. Still, he couldn't fully admit his biggest failing to Dixie, however obvious it was, and he shrugged.

She flashed him a sympathetic smile and said to her son. "Maybe next time Sam visits he'll give us a ride on his motorcycle."

Sam wanted to shout for her not to give the child empty hope. There would be no *next time*. Not if he left now.

Dixie's arm slid out of Sam's and settled around her son's shoulders. She pulled Ben in front of her, held him there against her legs as she smiled and tilted her head from one side to the other.

"We'll miss you," she said.

"You already said that."

"Some things are worth repeating."

He nudged the duffel with his toe, trying to figure why he couldn't just tell her he'd changed his mind—that he wanted to stay.

She ruffled Ben's hair. "Say good-bye to Sam."

Ben stretched his arms up at him...as Sam had so often reached out to his uncle. Sam hoisted the kid in his arms the way Stuart had never done him. Ben folded his arms around Sam's neck and squeezed. The child was so small, his arms thin and his back narrow. Yet, the power in that hug took Sam's breath away. Had Stuart finally figured out this was what he'd denied himself all these years? Is this why Stuart wanted the child?

Is this why Sam needed to stay? To protect Ben from Stuart?

"Bye, Tin Man," the kid said against the side of Sam's neck.

"Good-bye, Ben," Sam whispered into Ben's hair.

"Uh-oh," Ben said, straining back from Sam and looking up at the sky. "Rain drop hit me on the head."

Dixie lifted Ben from Sam's arms and set him on the ground. "You better put Checkers in his hutch."

The kid darted off. A second raindrop splatted against Sam's forehead. Dixie laughed and eyed the sky. "Those clouds don't look too good. You got rain gear?"

Dumbly, he nodded.

Tell me to stay!

She took his hands in hers, her fingers warm

against his own. He wanted her to never let go.

Please.

"You visit us any time you want, Sam." She rose onto her toes, leaned in, and pressed her lips to his cheek.

Her kiss was like a summer breeze across his skin. Balmy. Gentle. All too fleeting. He wanted to turn his face and test her lips against his. He wanted to explore Dixie mouth to mouth and body to body. He wanted to know her inside and out. That's why he couldn't stay—why he had to leave. She was *Mickey's* wife.

She stepped back, her lips lifting from his cheek, her fingers sliding from his hands. He felt the cool tracks of her departure—felt its sting on his cheek, his hand, his forehead where she'd earlier swiped the hair back from his brow.

Or was it the raindrops that fell in fat droplets that stung his skin and made him think there was more to her touch than there really was?

Dixie lifted her face and smiled into the rain, seemingly heedless of how it wet her cheeks, her hair, and her clothes. Sam knew there was nothing ordinary in the way Dixie touched anyone.

Mickey, if this is your handiwork, I hope you know what you're doing.

Looking Dixie in the eye, he said, "Maybe I should stay until it stops raining."

#

Dixie opened her mouth and laughed, letting the rain pelt her lips and splash against her tongue. She didn't care that it ruined her hair and drenched her clothes. Sam was staying. At least for a little while.

It'd been hard to leave the choice to him, and not

because she could use his chef's talents. Good enough to knock the socks off Miss Weston or not, she didn't need another chef who had it in him to walk out on her. The reason it had been hard to leave the choice whether to stay or go to Sam was because she wanted him to stay...and not just for Ben's sake, either. She wanted Sam to stay because *he* needed to stay, even if he wasn't willing to admit it.

And because *she* wasn't ready to let him go. Though, what exactly that meant she wasn't ready to explore too deeply. That she hadn't figured out yet why he'd come to The Farmhouse in the first place was reason enough.

Dixie scooped up her squealing son as he dashed across the driveway, snagged Sam by the arm, and ran for the house. Bear slipped through the door ahead of them, trapping them in the narrow back hall as he shook himself off, showering them anew. Sam's laughter mingled with hers and her son's.

It was a hearty, from the belly laugh—the kind of laugh that chased the shadows from a man's soul and blew the cobwebs from his heart. A laugh free of self-doubt. She got the distinct impression he hadn't laughed that way much in his life.

Oh yeah. They were good for Sam Ryan. Now all she had to do was convince him of that before it quit raining.

CHAPTER FIVE

Sam descended the stairs off the end of the kitchen, dry and warm in fresh jeans and black cotton turtleneck. Changing had given him just enough time to convince himself he could be useful to Dixie, and not for the money he represented. At the very least, he could tell Ben stories about his father just as she'd suggested the night he arrived. Having looked her menu over, he might even be able suggest some ways to streamline what she served—lighten the load on a one-chef kitchen. Maybe even add a recipe or two that would make The Farmhouse stand out even more. He had enough to offer Mickey's family to merit staying another day.

Dixie's and Ben's giggles drifted up from the living room and he felt even cozier. This definitely beat a wet ride on the back of a motorcycle.

He stepped into the opening between the narrow kitchen and boxy living room and stopped. Mother and son sat together on the loveseat-sized couch under the window on the far side of the room. Dixie had changed out of her t-shirt and into a pale blue, cowl-neck sweater that was all fuzzy invitation, especially the way it threatened to slip off one shoulder.

She and Ben had their heads together over a photo album cradled in their laps, Dixie's arm around Ben. Sam tried to remember a time when his mother had hugged him to her side with as much familiarity. But the Carringtons didn't do displays of affection, public or private.

They did, however, *connect* when they had issues with each other. He already had a half dozen *missed calls* from Stuart on his cell phone. He'd turned it off last night when he thought Dixie had invited him into her bed. No doubt the old man expected a progress report.

But, he'd already decided whatever it cost him, he no longer wanted to be part of Stuart breaking up this happy home. Lingering with Mickey's family might still be a mistake. Dixie and her son needed him like they needed a case of food poisoning.

If he backed up real quiet like, he could retreat to the second floor before they even noticed him. From there, he could escape down the front stairs and out the front door, slip on his rain gear in the garage and roll out of their lives forever.

He hadn't taken a single step backward when Dixie looked up, immobilizing him with her bright smile. "Hey there Sam, we've been waiting for you."

"We got the pictchoo al-album," Ben said, kicking his legs and making the book that covered his narrow lap buck.

"How about that," Sam said through a forced grin, trying to figure out how he was going to rectify yet another of his mistakes—how he was going to escape yet leave this family intact.

"I've been telling Ben that you knew his father when he was a little boy." Dixie tilted her head toward her son, the angle causing her to peer up at Sam through her thick lashes. Flirtatious?

He wished.

"Maybe you two could swap stories," she said in her throaty voice.

"Swap stories?" Sam scratched the back of his neck, a feeble attempt at breaking the spell of her look—her voice.

"Ben would love to know about his father when he was a little boy."

Trapped like a rat on a sinking ship, Sam jammed his hands into his pockets. Maybe if he looked relaxed where he stood, she'd have no reason to summon him closer. "Something about his father when he was a kid, huh?"

"Yeah." That voice turned even a single word into a sultry invitation.

He drew a deep breath. "Okay. Stuart—"

"Your grandfather," Dixie explained for Ben.

"—used to take us on tutorial visits to the corporate offices."

"Your Dad and Sam visited your grandfather's office," Dixie interpreted.

"Mickey always played the good soldier."

"Your daddy liked the office." She looked up at Sam. "How about you, Sam, did you like playing office?"

"I liked playing with the photocopier, copying body parts."

"Body parts?" She raised an eyebrow as though she could guess what shenanigans he'd pulled.

He couldn't resist a sheepish smile for Dixie. For Ben he opted for a G-rated example.

"Once, I copied this really goofy shot of my face. It got a laugh out of your father."

The boy grinned as though Sam had imparted some mystical story about his father.

"And Stuart?" Dixie asked.

Sam grimaced. "Unfortunately, none of my

copier projects amused Stuart."

"Not corporate enough for his standards?" she quizzed.

He eyed Ben, who seemed absorbed in a photo in the album in his lap. "Suffice it to say, the crowning glory of my *Photocopier Incidents* involved a body part that many an employee would like to show his boss but seldom dares to do."

"And was that body part yours, Sam?"

Damn, but he loved the way she said his name. "Guilty as charged."

The corners of Dixie's lips curled upward. He could spend a lifetime watching her mouth quirk into a smile and never tire of the view.

Dixie patted the couch cushion next to the one she and Ben sat on. "Come sit with us. Our turn to share a story about Michael with you."

He glanced at Dixie's fingers spread across the cushion where she expected him to sit. Too close for comfort. He glanced at the two over-stuffed chairs angled at the couch...in front of which a blissfully snoring Bear stretched.

Dixie cupped her hand over her son's shoulder as though she understood his hesitation. If he stayed, that womanly second sight would see him for the snake in the grass he'd been willing to become for his own selfish needs.

"Which picture do you think we should show Sam first?" she asked her son.

"The mommy with the baby in her belly," Ben said, bouncing beside his mother.

Sam raised an eyebrow.

"It's not as gross as it sounds," Dixie said, peering up at him. "It's just a picture of me a week before Ben was born."

"See." Ben flattened the photo album across his little lap and pointed at a snapshot.

He was going to regret this. Stiffly, Sam strode across the living room and lowered himself onto the edge of the couch beside Ben. He took care not to bump the slender hand cupping the child's shoulder as he looked at the photo of Dixie and Michael in the album.

"That's the Mommy," Ben said, pressing a finger against the woman in the picture. "That's the Daddy." Ben next pointed out a grinning Mickey who framed Dixie's voluminous belly with his hands. Damned if Dixie didn't look as beautiful with that paunch as she did in a tightly cinched apron.

"And that's the baby in the Mommy's tummy." Ben poked a finger at Dixie's belly framed between Mickey's hands.

Family, the way it was meant to be.

"That's you inside me," Dixie exclaimed as though she were revealing a secret.

Ben threw his arms up and his head back and hooted with delight. "That's me inside the Mommy!"

Sam smiled at the kid's enthusiasm. He smiled at Dixie who encouraged that enthusiasm. He smiled at his own good fortune for being there to witness a happy family in action.

"It's a game we play every time we look at that picture," she explained over Ben's head, her face as radiant as an angel's.

He smiled softly at Dixie Rae, who created memories for the child of a father who'd died too young. Dixie Rae, who encouraged boisterousness and freely handed out hugs.

Dixie, whom Mickey had loved.

Sam blinked away from the cornflower-blue eyes he feared would see him for the fraud he was if he stayed too close too long. The photo of a happy moment frozen in time sharpened before his eyes. He wished he'd known them then—Mickey and his bride. He wished he'd been there to touch Dixie's belly, feel the baby move inside her. She'd have invited him to share the experience. He knew she would've.

Then again, he was glad he wasn't there, because the pain of being that close to that much happiness and knowing it could never be his would have been more than he could bear.

"Tell us more about Michael as a kid," she said, breaking into his commiserating.

"His favorite food was hot dogs," he replied readily, grateful for the change in topic.

"Mine, too," hooted Ben, tipping his head back and peering up at Sam.

Sam gazed into the shining face of the boy with Mickey's eyes—the boy who'd dubbed him the Tin Man.

If I only had a heart.

"They're my favorite, too," Sam said. "But, while I like my hot dogs with the works, your dad wanted only ketchup on his."

"Just like you," Dixie said, tickling her son in his ribs.

Ben giggled and wiggled. Sam wanted to tickle Ben the way his mother did—the way his father would have were he here. But, he wasn't comfortable with kids—wasn't sure if Mickey's boy would welcome his teasing.

Sam nodded at the book in the kid's lap. "What

else ya got there, buddy?"

Ben flipped album pages and squealed. "There's Uncle Renn on his horse!"

"It's a favorite picture of his," Dixie said, beaming.

Was that gleam in her eye for him or the man in the photo wearing a cowboy hat? And why did it matter? Why did it make him want to dislike the man in the picture?

"Who's *Uncle* Renn?" he asked.

"My baby brother," Dixie answered.

Sam's mood lightened appreciably. Ah yes. Upon closer evaluation, even in the shadow of the Stetson, the man's eyes shone a blue that hinted they were as bright as Dixie's.

"He rides horses at a theme restaurant," she said.

"Horses? Theme restaurant?" Sam looked up at Dixie, his gaze sliding over the bare expanse of skin exposed by the wide neckline of the over-sized sweater she wore.

"The restaurant features a jousting tournament while you dine…with your fingers…as befitting medieval times, naturally." She wagged her fingers in the air for emphasis.

"Naturally," he murmured, watching her fingers flex, imagining sucking chicken grease from those perfect appendages. Better yet, her pouty lips sliding from knuckle to fingertip—

"Did my daddy like horses?" Ben asked.

Sam blinked, slow to return to the subject he should be focused on. "He sure did. Your dad played polo as often as he could."

"That's a sport you play while riding horses," Dixie explained to her son. "When you were *real* little, you and he would watch matches on TV. Your dad even took us to a match once."

"Did I like it?" Ben asked.

She stroked the hair from his brow. "You liked the horses."

"And you?" Sam asked, studying Dixie.

She looked at Sam, hesitating ever so briefly before answering. "I found the whole thing interesting."

"Interesting, huh?"

"Ben," she said, lifting the album from her son's lap. "Get the postcard from Uncle Renn off the refrigerator and bring it here."

The kid slid off the couch and dashed for the family kitchen.

"I found the whole thing a little formal for my taste," she said.

Sam chuckled. "All that *etiquette* used to give me headaches."

Her mouth slanted a sad angle. "I think polo was the one thing Michael missed about his old life."

Sam sobered, the words escaping his mouth before he could edit them. "I can't imagine him missing anything as long as he had you and Ben."

A speculative look crossed Dixie's face a breath before Ben came bounding back onto the couch between them. His movement stirred the air between them, making it eddy and rise like a cold front butting up against two hot land masses.

Ben knelt between them, holding up a glossy postcard of two knights in medieval regalia astride horses. They were caught in mid charge toward one another, each man's lance leveled lethally at the shield the other man held over his heart. Such small shields.

At least they had hearts to protect unlike him. Sam winced.

"This is the kind of stunt riding he does," Dixie explained, breaking into his thoughts.

"Looks like a lot more fun than polo." Sam said, forcing a grin. "Ben's lucky to have his Uncle Renn's influence in his life."

"Renn texts us nearly every day with exciting tidbits," she continued, "and sends postcards for Ben every month."

Ben dropped the postcard onto the album page and Sam noticed the Texas postmark on its back just before the kid turned the page. Okay, so the stunt-riding uncle wasn't readily available to his nephew for daily demonstrations of masculinity. Maybe Dixie's kid could use a man around the house after all.

And Dixie?

He searched her face for a hint of any flirtatiousness that said she needed a little manly influence in her life.

"This is Uncle Dane," Ben said, pulling Sam from his thoughts.

The guy in the photo Ben now stubbed a finger against looked like a slightly older, more polished version of *Knight* Renn. "Is it just because he looks so much like his brother that he seems familiar to me or have I seen him somewhere else?"

Dixie unfolded a glossy poster from the album pages. It depicted cars flipping through the air and fireballs exploding outward toward the viewer. It was a smaller version of the kind of movie poster plastered all over theaters and used in televised promotions. And the dashing actor dead center of the mayhem was...

"Dane St. John," Dixie said. "One of my older brothers."

One of my older brothers?

"Just how many brothers do you have?" he asked.

"Three older."

"One of which is an action movie star," Sam murmured, adding Dane St. John's machismo to that of the younger brother who stunt-rode horses. Sam felt his purpose as a male influence for Ben growing smaller by the brother. Then again, he hadn't planned to stick around long enough to make that kind of a difference anyway. He was just going to share some Mickey stories, offer a few restaurant tips, and be back on the road twenty-four hours or so from now.

"And that's Uncle Jake," Ben said, pointing out a photo on the opposite page of a dark haired man with serious eyes and a subdued smile.

"Doesn't look much like the rest of the St. Johns," Sam said.

"He's our half-brother," Dixie said. "From Mom's first marriage."

"Divorced?"

"Widowed. Jake's dad died while on a mission as a Navy Seal."

"Sorry."

"Th-that's why Uncle Jake became a Seal," Ben said. "Because his daddy was one."

Though he'd just been introduced to another testosterone laden brother, something other than his own diminishing importance to Ben...and Dixie...niggled at Sam.

He looked at Ben. "Are you going to follow in your daddy's footsteps when you grow up? Are you going to be what he was?"

"I'm going to a wizard," Ben hooted, all boyish enthusiasm and innocence.

Hardly realistic. Not at all what his father was. A choice of child who didn't yet realize how hard it was to follow in the footsteps of a father who'd left none.

But Mickey had left footprints in the hearts of his family. And Ben had people around him who could and would share with him the memories of what his father did in life—of what kind of man his father had been.

He met Dixie's gaze and saw in her eyes that she understood why he'd asked Ben what he had. Her empathy tore through his skin and knotted in his gut.

The ringing of a phone cut between them.

"It's Uncle Roman time," Ben squealed, scrambling off the couch and sprinting to the wall-mounted phone on the kitchen side of the archway. The ringing ended abruptly with an excited, "Hiya Uncle Roman."

He and Dixie continued to stare into each other's eyes, his pleading with hers not to probe. And she didn't. Good, kind Dixie guided the conversation back to her brothers.

"Roman is the contractor who renovated the side parlor into a restaurant class kitchen," Dixie said. "He calls every Sunday night."

"He *calls?*" Did that mean the contractor, like the Hollywood actor, Texas stunt-rider, and God-knows-where Seal didn't live nearby?

"Calls at precisely the same time," Dixie elaborated. "Promptness is Roman's middle name. Of course he also emails us on a regular basis. Heaven help us if I don't respond by day's end."

Definitely did not live near. "What happens

then?" Sam asked, relieved to keep the conversation going in the direction of her family.

"An unscheduled phone call."

"And if you aren't here to answer the call?"

"He calls my cell."

"And if you don't answer that?"

"I *always* answer Roman on my cell. If not, he's likely to show up on my doorstep."

"He lives close by, then."

"A couple hours."

Not quite close enough for daily infusions of testosterone, but close enough to get to them in an emergency. Sam let out a relieved breath, not that how far away her brothers were should matter.

"Unless he's not in the Upper Peninsula of Michigan but in Chicago, his wife's home*town*, Dixie added. "Then it's a much longer ride."

How well he knew.

Dixie flipped album pages until she came to one of a dark-haired woman and light-haired man gazing into each other's eyes. "This is Roman and Tess. He watches over us a little less intensely since they married."

"She settled him down a bit, huh?"

"More like distracts him, a lot." Dixie chuckled. "Roman's the staid one in the family. Has plotted out his life course for as long as I can remember. Then Tess contracted him to renovate a house she wanted to flip. I knew the night he called me, grousing about her pigheadedness, he was hooked. And when her house caught on fire—"

"He set her house on fire?"

"Actually, the fire turned out to be her fault."

Sam shook his head. "That doesn't sound like a

formula for love."

"Haven't you ever heard opposites attract?"

"Yeah, but these two sound pretty extreme in their differences."

"Michael and I were opposites," she said.

Not as opposite as you and me. Dixie was honesty personified while he was a...liar.

He headed off a shudder with, "You two weren't *that* different."

"And you know this how?" she asked, amused curiosity shaping her face.

"His phone calls. He always sounded happy when he spoke to me. I could even see it in his emails. You brought a passion to his life that I'd never seen in him before."

Her expression softened. "Thank you for telling me that, Sam. I often wondered what a man as handsome, educated, and cultured as Michael saw in a mouthy waitress like me."

"You're not mouthy. You're open and honest. You're giving and full of optimism. You're...inspiring."

"Careful there, Sam. Words like those could turn a girl's head."

And he wasn't the kind of man who should be turning this woman's head. He shifted, breaking eye contact and shrugged. "I got those impressions from how Michael talked about you."

"He always made me feel special," she said, her voice soft, wistful.

"He had that talent," Sam said, remembering how good he felt when he was with Mickey.

Out in the kitchen, Ben spoke excitedly into the phone. "Then the house fell on the Icky Witch."

Dixie's smile widened. "Roman has the patience of a saint, at least with kids. He's going to make a great father someday."

A great father.

Like Mickey had been.

Like Stuart had never been and he, Sam, would never be.

"I better get out there and rescue my brother," Dixie said. "Ben'll recite the entire plot of a movie we've all seen dozens of times if we let him."

Dixie crossed the room, leaned against the wall separating kitchen and living room, then waited patiently while Ben wrapped up his conversation with his Uncle Roman. Stuart would never have allowed him or Mickey to ramble on about any movie plot. He'd never have wasted the time listening.

"And all Do'thy had to do to get home was click the groovy slippers together," Ben said.

Groovy slippers. Sam thought of Dixie's cherry-hued boots and red high-tops. He eyed the crimson velvet slippers she now wore. He liked that she was secure enough in herself to wear red foot gear, hammed it up for a photo of her profile in her most voluminous pregnant state, and filled out a sweater, a t-shirt, and a frilly apron with equal pizzazz. He liked that she looked for the best in people—in him. He liked how kind and intuitive she was. A fine example for a growing kid. And he suspected he knew exactly where she'd learned all those good traits.

He saw it in the photo album spread in his lap—in one prominent picture center page. Seven people bundled up in bright orange cold-weather gear in the midst of a bleak plain of snow looked out at him from the snapshot. It was hard to see their expressions what with the orange hoods cinched around their faces. But a wild array of blond hair had escaped one hood and was frozen in a wind-whipped frenzy.

Four young men were down on one knee, a youthful Dixie on her side on their raised knees vamping it up for the camera. Behind them, heads tipped together and arm in arm, stood an older couple. He had to look close to see in the father the eyes Dixie had inherited and in the mother the flirtatious lips. He saw in all the faces of the family bundled together on that snow-blown plain merriment and zest for life.

He saw a family not afraid to touch each other.

The perfect family.

A perfect legacy for a little boy who'd lost his father at too early an age.

Ben scrambled up onto the couch beside Sam. Sam slung an arm loosely around the boy, oddly pleased that the kid came back to sit with him while his mother said her good-byes to the contractor brother who called them every Sunday night.

"That's Uncle Roman," Ben said, leaning into Sam as he pointed out one of the faces framed by the hood of an orange parka. "And that's Uncle Dane and that's..."

Sam listened as Mickey's boy identified his uncles, mother, and grandparents. Dixie's parents. The two people who had raised four sons who cared enough about their sister to keep weekly tabs on her—parents who had raised a daughter secure enough in herself that she dared to be unapologetically unconventional. No wonder Mickey had fallen in love with her.

Dixie in her close-fitting jeans and over-sized

sweater that drooped off one shoulder stepped in front of Sam. She smiled down at him.

"Checking out my family tree?"

"Looks like you had fun together," he said.

"We did. How many families do you know would pick an Icelandic glacier for a family portrait?" Her chin dipped at the photo in the album.

Reluctantly, Sam shifted his attention from the cherubic chin beneath the angelic mouth and coquettish eyes to the family in the photo so unlike his.

"What were you and your family doing in Iceland?" he asked.

"Daddy wanted us kids to see the world. So, whenever a military transport had the spare space for us, he and Mom would pack us up and go."

She leaned forward and tapped the picture in his lap of the orange-clad explorers. She smelled of strawberries, distracting him from the icy suggestion of the photo—from any question about her reference to *military* transports.

"That particular trip we took when they were working at the Consulate in Germany," she said.

Her pale shoulder made him think of whipped cream—made him want to lean forward and sample that slope of skin with his tongue. He was a lick away from exposing himself for the degenerate he was rather than the guy with stories of interest to a little boy—the man who wanted to save that boy from the austere world of his grandfather.

"Consulate?" he asked, distracting himself...curious. "Germany?"

"They worked in foreign service."

"Foreign service? Impressive," he said.

"Don't get overly impressed. They were support staff."

"Where are your parents now?" he asked. *Now that you need them.*

"They retired to Japan...for the time being."

"You need them closer," he said. *Where they can protect you against a father-in-law bent on taking your son away from you and a black sheep of the family cousin-in-law who wants even more.*

"I'm more than fine here. We may be scattered around the world, but we're close where it counts," Dixie said, tapping her chest. "In our hearts."

And here he was, a man without a heart. She and Ben needed better. They deserved better.

"Besides, we'll all be together for the Fourth of July. A mini family reunion."

"Family reunion," he murmured, knowing he'd be gone well before the entire St. John clan descended on him.

Behind him, the windowpanes rattled with a gust of wind. Dixie ducked her head to see out the window and the fuzzy sweater slid further down her arm. He looked longingly at what the sweater exposed. He *wanted* her and all she represented. But *his* wants weren't a good enough reason to stay longer. He knew that. He accepted that.

"Looks like an all-day rain," she said. "We might even get a storm out of this. Good thing you changed your mind about heading out tonight. Safer here."

Staring at the perfect, naked shoulder within easy reach, he knew there was nothing safe about his being here. Not for him, and certainly not for Dixie.

Tree limbs scraped against the porch roof. He jumped and his foot bumped the side of hers. "Sorry."

She smiled at him and her eyes twinkled. "No harm done."

For the life of him, he couldn't remember a place or person he didn't leave untouched by the dark cloud that followed him. Mickey's was the last family he wanted touched by his penchant for failure.

Thunder rolled across the house—across him and Dixie, who stood too close for his comfort. Yet, at the same time, not close enough. An imperfect soul like him had no right to wish the touch of perfection like her, but he did. He wished it like he'd never wished for anything in his life.

Lightning lit the small room, burning away the warm, yellow glow of the table lamp—burning its message into what passed as his soul. He was like the lightning; a momentary, blinding blaze. When the charm faded, she'd see him for the misfit he was. That's how it always went.

Run, the thunder rumbled. *Run*, it echoed through the rooms.

"Run," shrieked a banshee-like wail from the stairway.

Dixie wheeled toward the wail, Bear popped to his feet barking, and Ben chirped, "Uho, Nana wake up too quick again."

"Sweet Noah," howled the tiny, white-haired woman flying at them from the stairs on the far side of the room. "To the ark, children. Two by two."

The little woman charged into the front room and ducked behind the television set, grabbed a fistful of electrical cords, and jerked on them, plunging the room into blackness. From the darkness lifted Dixie's sweet voice.

"You haven't met my Nana yet, have you?"

#

Dixie listened through the darkness for the sound of fleeing footsteps and the slam of a door. Sam could have tucked tail and run and she wouldn't have faulted him. Not now. Not with Nana in one of her confused states. But the only sound coming from the couch behind her was the creak of the sofa springs— Sam poising for flight, no doubt. So much for convincing him that he needed them.

Whatever the end result, her undoubtedly horror-stricken houseguest would have to fend for himself for the time being. She hadn't the time to explain the pitfalls of an aging mind to Sam, not right now when Nana demanded her immediate attention.

Dixie felt her way to the table lamp between the over-stuffed chairs. In a click, warm light illuminated the room again. Joining Nana behind the television stand, Dixie slipped an arm around her grandmother's shoulders. "Come on, Nana. How about we sit down?"

Nana crushed her tiny fist protectively to her chest, the electric cords to the television and lamp by the couch drooping from her hand like two, wilted poppies. "But the television, if we plug it back in while it's still storming, it'll blow!"

Gently, Dixie stroked the back of her grandmother's frail hand. "We won't plug anything back in until the storm is over. You can drop the cords."

Indecision knitted across Nana's brow. "I don't know."

"How about if I hold them for you," a low, masculine voice offered.

Dixie looked up. Wonder of wonders, Sam hadn't

slipped out the side door but now stood on the far side of the television, hand extended in help.

Sam saw the surprise in Dixie's eyes. Heck he'd surprised himself. He wasn't even sure if he helped or hindered. He knew only he hadn't liked the concern pulling Dixie's eyebrows together as she'd attempted to get her grandmother to give up the electrical cords. He didn't like that Dixie was alone coaxing her grandmother out from behind the TV set or that Ben had to witness his grandmother's dementia. Maybe it had been Mickey's spirit who'd pushed him to his feet and propelled him across the room where he offered Dixie's grandmother the palm of his hand.

Nana eyed him narrowly as she tilted her head toward Dixie. "Do I know him?"

"He's the Tin Man," Ben chirped from the couch where he bounced on his knees.

Okay. The kid didn't seem the least traumatized by his great-grandmother's confusion. But what about Dixie?

"This is Sam Ryan, Nana," she explained through a twitchy grin. "Michael's cousin. He's filling in for Carl. I told you about him this morning. Remember?"

Clearly she wasn't as overwhelmed by her granny's state as he'd thought. Given that fact, he could just imagine what she'd told her grandmother. *Michael's cousin, the loser who partied his way through a higher education, tramped around Europe while responsible people worked, and runs at the first hint of trouble.*

"Can we trust him?" Nana asked from the side of her mouth.

The old dame wasn't as confused as she appeared, at least not where he was concerned. Did

Dixie recognize that fact?

"I don't know," Dixie drawled, a devilish glint in her eyes. Or was that a dubious glint? "Can we trust you, Sam Ryan—" Dixie flicked the drooping heads of the cords. "—not to plug these things in?"

Devilish, Sam decided with relief. She was teasing him. Whether or not she should was another issue.

With a flourish, he drew his finger across his heart in the figure of an *X*. "Cross my heart and hope to die if I'm not telling the truth." *About the electrical cords.*

He added that last just in case someone almighty was listening. He wasn't ready to die over a slip of the tongue or a lie of omission.

Dixie nudged her grandmother. "How about it, Nana? Think we should trust him?"

Sam shifted his focus to the tiny woman with the mane of white hair. Behind him, Ben hopped from cushion to cushion, reciting in cadence, "Lions and tigers and bears, oh my."

Nana's watchful eyes narrowed further.

"How about we lay the cords over the top of the TV set?" Sam suggested. "You can keep an eye on them from anywhere in the room."

Something in the focus of the rheumy old eyes changed and Nana held up the cords to Sam. He drew them over the top of the set until their dark ends dangled against the blank screen.

Dixie settled her grandmother in one of the over-stuffed chairs and squatted in front of her, still holding her hand. "How about I make you some chamomile tea?"

Sam's eye strayed to where Dixie's jeans

stretched across her delectable behind.

"Let the chef do it," Nana said, her voice not nearly as tremulous as it had been seconds ago.

He blinked up from Dixie's backside and found Nana eyeing him.

"I'll make the tea," he said and ducked into the kitchen.

"Thank you, Sam," Dixie called after him. "That would help."

That would help. Golden words in his ears.

He actually caught himself whistling as he filled the tea kettle and set it on the gas burner.

"That can't be the tea pot whistling already," Nana said.

Sam stepped over to the opening between rooms and stuck his head around the corner into the living room. "No, it's me."

"Happy fellow, isn't he?" Nana commented to Dixie who now perched on the arm of the chair holding Nana's hand.

Not quite sure whether the old dame was criticizing him or just making an observation, Sam rummaged the cupboards for tea bags in silence.

By the time he fixed a tray with cups and saucers, milk and honey, scones and jam, steam whistled from the teakettle.

"Is that you whistling again Tin Man Sam?" Nana called.

"Nope," he called back. "This time it's the kettle. Just as soon as the tea steeps—" He poured the boiling water from the kettle into a ceramic pot. "—I'll serve it."

"Did he say he'd serve?" Nana asked in an incredulous tone.

"He sure did," Dixie said, a clear note of pride in her voice.

Sam smiled and added napkins to the tray. A man had to love a woman who appreciated a man in the kitchen.

Love? Oh yeah. Saucy, sexy, good-hearted Dixie Rae would be easy to fall in love with. No wonder Mickey had fallen fast and hard for her. Heck, who wouldn't love a woman like her?

Stuart Carrington.

Sam winced at the reminder of who'd sent him here and why. Would he do more harm sticking around, even a short time, than running the first chance he got?

He carried the tray of tea and snacks into the living room and set it down on the table next to the chair Nana and Dixie shared. Nana gave the goody-laden tray a wide-eyed once over and declared, "He's a keeper."

Then, as she spread jam on a scone, Nana hummed the wedding march. Dixie rolled her eyes and mouthed, "I'm sorry."

He bet she was. Good thing he had no intention of sticking around long enough for Nana to do any serious matchmaking. Best for Dixie if he went AWOL. But when he did, where would he hide from Stuart?

He could high-tail it back to Europe. He had friends there.

Friends who rode the shirttails of his trust fund…which Uncle Stuart would cut off a nanosecond after finding out he'd failed to nail the goods on Dixie.

Maybe the South Seas. The exchange rate on the

dollar could allow him to live a long time before the money ran out. He could bask in the sun and wander barefoot on the beach.

No. Too much idle time there to think.

Alaska?

Frostbite.

South America?

Snakes.

Maybe he could just ride the Ducati across the country. It was fun the last three times he did it.

Sam waited for the jolt of enthusiasm that would tell him he had a plan. All he got was a dreary *done that, been there.*

His gaze fixed on Dixie, the warmth in her eyes enveloping him. She'd made it clear he was welcome to stay at The Farmhouse. And hadn't he sensed Mickey had something to do with the storm preventing him from leaving? Or was that just wishful thinking?

But, she did need his help. Not that he could do much about her Gran, but he could at least be her chef, take that burden off her shoulders. He might even be good for Ben. In spite of their abundance of testosterone, his uncles weren't here nor could they teach Ben about his father the way he could. What harm could there be in sticking around The Farmhouse for a while?

Lightning strobed through the little room, its accompanying thunder more like a sign from Stuart than Mickey. What harm could there be in staying? The longer he stuck around, the more likely he was to find some dirt Stuart could use against Dixie.

CHAPTER SIX

Sam's voice drifted up the stairwell amidst the aromas of hot, maple syrup and percolating coffee. In spite of how well he'd handled Nana's entrance last evening, Dixie still wouldn't have been surprised to find him gone this morning, especially since the restaurant was closed for the day and his chef's talents not needed. But Sam, who had a reputation for running from responsibility, had stuck it out.

"Atta boy, Sam," she murmured and continued down the stairway.

She reached the bottom step just as Sam flipped a flapjack into the air and spun around to catch it in a frying pan behind his back. Ben, who sat on Nana's lap at the table under the steps, squealed with delight. But it was to her Sam's gaze strayed as she stepped off the last step.

"Mornin', Red," he said through an impish grin that made her own lips twitch. She liked that Sam Ryan, who grew up in a family short on showing affection, accepted sticky hugs from a four-year-old and didn't run at first sight of an old lady's dementia...nor from said old lady's intonation of the wedding march. Michael hadn't run from her nontraditional family, either. Likewise, Michael had blossomed to their offbeat way of accepting someone into the family, but he hadn't needed TLC to the extent Sam did. And that was all the attraction she dared allow herself where Sam was concerned.

They met mid-kitchen, Sam on his way to serve the flipped flapjack, she on her way to the coffeepot. She rose onto her tiptoes, planted a chaste kiss on his cheek near his ear, and murmured, "You're a useful man to have around, Sam Ryan."

"Useful? Me?" he said, drawing back from her. "First time anyone ever accused me of being useful for anything."

Poor, self-effacing Sam.

She laid a hand on his forearm, holding him a moment from fleeing all together. "Few men would cook breakfast for a high energy preschooler and a dysfunctional senior citizen."

Behind her, Nana and Sam broke into a chorus of "We're off to see the Wizard."

If only life were that simple. See Wizard. Get wish granted. Live happily ever after.

But, life was lived in the real world where happily ever after didn't always work out. Michael dying proved that—Michael whose affection-starved cousin stood in her kitchen not recognizing his own worth. Sam, who made her itch in places she wasn't sure she was ready to scratch.

Releasing him, she headed to the coffeemaker. She plucked a mug from the mug tree in the corner by the stove then glanced back at Sam. He was tipping the pancake from the frying pan onto Ben's plate, giving her a three-quarter view of his backside.

He was an underdog with a darn cute behind. She was doomed.

He was back at the stove by the time she filled her mug. She turned and watched him pour a new puddle of pancake batter into the frying pan.

"Heart shaped?" she questioned of the spreading

batter.

"For your grandmother."

"You're a sweetheart, Sam."

"Your grandmother's the sweetheart."

Dixie peered over the rim of her coffee mug at the little table under the stairs. Nana was cutting Ben's pancake into bite size pieces and telling him how she used to do the same for his Mommy.

"She's the quintessential nurturer," Dixie said quietly.

He gave her a sidelong glance. "Unlike you who moved back here to take care of her?"

Dixie stopped blowing on her coffee. "I was broke. I needed a place to stay. Besides, it's the sort of thing family does for its own."

"Not mine."

He nudged the bubbling edges of the heart-shaped pancake with his spatula, no longer looking at her. She wanted to smooth the hurt from his wounded brow. She wanted to hug the dejection from his shoulders.

She wanted to kiss the smile back onto his lips...which went beyond *Tender Loving Care*.

She turned to the refrigerator, opened the door, and let the cool air spill out over her. That would do the trick. It had to.

She plucked a fried chicken leg from a platter in the fridge and shook it at Sam. "Stuart is the one who'll lose in the end. You know that, don't you?"

Sam nodded at the leg she held and quipped, "First time I've ever seen anyone use last night's leftovers to make a point."

The playfulness may have returned to his voice and the devilish slant to his lips, but the truth—his skepticism—still crimped the edges of his eyes. She hip-bumped the fridge door shut, her gaze never wavering from Sam's sad eyes. "Stuart's rigidness already cost him a son."

"And a grandson," Sam said, smile slipping, eyes blinking away from her.

"Perfect example," Dixie retorted, careful to keep her voice low enough that the child in question couldn't hear. "Stuart's welcome to visit Ben any time he wants. I've made that clear."

She moved closer to Sam, so close she could feel the tension radiating from his elbow as he flipped the heart-shaped pancake. So close, she needed only to whisper her words. "But he looks at me and sees only the woman who took his son away from him."

"You didn't take Mickey away from anyone," Sam muttered. "Mickey was his own man."

"I know. But it's easier for Stuart to blame me than for him to face the truth of why he lost his son."

Sam looked at her through eyes that spoke volumes about loss. Loss of a father. Loss of nurturing, approval, and encouragement.

Loss of Michael who had been more brother to him than cousin. She'd heard the affection in Michael's voice whenever he'd spoken of Sam. She saw it now in Sam's eyes. It hadn't mattered that they'd been an ocean apart the last years of Michael's life. The bond had never broken.

She was half a second away from plopping the chicken leg into her coffee mug, setting the whole mess aside, and enveloping Sam into her arms when he broke into a grin.

"Too early in the morning to be maudlin, Red," he wisecracked and bit into her chicken leg.

She laughed even though she knew Sam hid his pain behind quippy comebacks and mischievous twinkling eyes. She laughed because he needed her to laugh. And she laughed harder when he came away with the major portion of the chicken leg caught between his teeth.

"Some gentleman." She waved the all but denuded bone in his face. "You didn't leave me much."

He sucked the meat into his mouth with a slurpy sound and mumbled around the mouthful, "Who said I was a gentleman."

"Whatever you are, you have grease on your chin." She set down the coffee mug and wiped his chin with her fingers.

His eyes darkened in the soft morning light of the kitchen. "Watch it, Red," he said in a low, husky voice. "A man could get used to being taken care of like this."

For an instant, only the two of them existed in that small space of a kitchen. Sam with his heavy-lidded eyes angled at her and her tilting her head in a way that invited him to keep looking. Then his bedroom eyes slid past her and he frowned.

"Why is that woman pointing a monkey at us?"

Dixie turned and found Miss Weston watching them from the stairway, hugging her ever-present, over-sized purse to her chest and clutching the neck of the stuffed monkey that seemed to be peeking out from the top of her purse. Leave it to Weston to cool a girl's libido as effectively as a cold shower.

"Lions and tigers and bears, oh my," chanted Nana and Ben from the table.

Reason number two for why the kitchen was the

wrong place to contemplate a lip-lock with Sam.

"Isn't she a little old to be carrying a stuffed animal around?" Sam whispered, his words a warm breath against her ear.

Dixie shrugged and her shoulder brushed Sam's chest, he stood so near. Damn but she wanted to lean into him. Sam—Michael's cousin. Reason three why Sam was off-limits.

"I can see why she freaks Ben out." Sam shivered and strode from her side toward the kitchen table, frying pan in hand.

By the time he'd dumped the heart-shaped pancake onto Nana's plate, Weston had skittered down the remaining steps to his side to Sam's side. Fastest Dixie had ever seen the woman move. And the closest she'd ever seen Weston stand to anyone. Slowly, Dixie chewed at the cold chicken leg.

Sam turned toward the black-clad woman and drew up short, holding the frying pan like a shield between them. "You want something?"

Weston's beady eyes darted between Sam and Dixie.

"Would you like some pancakes, Miss Weston?" he asked.

Weston blinked owlishly up at Sam. "Pancakes?"

"Yeah. Would you like me to make some pancakes for you?"

Behind Weston, Ben stood on the end of the bench and eyed the stuffed monkey peeking out from the purse. "D-does it have wings?"

Weston wheeled at Ben and grabbed him by the arm. Before Dixie could so much as utter a single motherly sound or take a single protective step forward, Sam had Weston by the wrist.

"Let the kid go," he said in a low, ominous tone.

Weston released Ben.

"Never," Sam growled, "touch him like that again."

Sam let go of Weston and she shrank back from him, nodding. Ben slid down in his seat, eyes hero-worship wide on Sam. Dixie knew exactly how her son felt. At the moment, she was feeling much the same way about Sam.

Without a word, Weston slunk off through the living room and out the back door.

Sam ruffled Ben's hair. "You okay, Buddy?"

Ben's syrup-smudged face split into a smile. "Okey-dokey, Tin Man."

"How about another pancake? I could make this one in the shape of an animal."

Ben frowned. "No monkey."

"No monkey."

He gave Ben's sandy hair a gentle stroke before heading back for the stove. Dixie's fingers flexed around the chicken leg. So much for *their* giving Sam TLC. Clearly, the man could give better than he got.

"My hero," Dixie murmured as he passed.

#

Hero?

The word echoed in Sam's ears as he cooked one last bear-shaped pancake for Ben. It nagged him as he wiped the griddle clean and served Miss Weston a plate of pancakes out on the side porch.

Just when he thought he'd gotten it settled in his head that Dixie's family was too perfect for him to fit into, she calls him her hero. He shook his head in dismay. Mickey's widow, thinking he was some kind of hero. He barely qualified as *useful*. This is the thanks the universe gave him for vowing to stick around long enough for her to convince her old chef to come back. He really needed to leave before she figured out what an impostor he was. Or maybe what he needed to do was confess before another day passed.

Dixie emerged from the screen door behind him, looped her arm through his, and guided him off the porch and away from the sulking Miss Weston. "Come on," she all but purred. "Time you got the grand tour."

This was good. They should be alone when he told her what a despicable person he was—that he was nobody's hero least of all hers. That should be enough to motivate her into getting chef Carl back on duty fast.

Back on the porch, the screen door banged open, Miss Weston shrieked, and Ben and Bear tumbled out across the porch and down the steps after them. Okay, confessions weren't for young ears. He'd have to wait until the little tyke was out of hearing range.

Ben skipped past them, kicking stones in the driveway between the house and outbuildings. At that speed, he'd soon be out of hearing range. But, he and Dixie would still be within viewing range of boarder Weston. For some reason that prickled the hair at the back of his neck, Sam didn't want Dixie's reaction witnessed on any level by that witchy woman.

Dixie hugged his arm against her side and drew in a deep breath. "I love how it smells after a good rain."

He sniffed the air, smelled the freshness of newly-washed earth and apple blossoms. He sniffed again and realized the scent came from Dixie's hair.

"Don't you just love the way a good rain freshens up everything?" she said, drawing another deep breath.

"Yeah," he murmured. "Love it."

She tilted her chin at him just as they stepped from the shadow of the house. The morning sun glinted in her raised eyes, shimmered across her smiling lips, and caught in the curls of her ponytail, turning them to spun gold. A man would have to be a saint to ruin a moment like this with a confession and he was no saint.

"The country air is one of the reasons I moved us here," she said.

"Your grandmother needing you was another," he returned, remembering how his uncle had insisted Dixie's motives for taking over her grandmother's farm were anything but altruistic. "You're a very noble woman, Dixie Rae Carrington."

"Noble?" Dixie huffed. "This is also a great place for a child to grow up. So you see, moving here was hardly for noble reasons."

Any reason you have for being here is far nobler than mine.

Ahead of them, Ben flung a stick for Bear to chase. The stick didn't go far and it hooked to the left. The boy needed someone to teach him how to straighten out his throwing arm. Mickey had taught Sam how to throw a ball. Maybe he could... No, he wouldn't be here long enough to pass along that lesson from the kid's father.

Dixie tipped her head against Sam's shoulder and sighed. "This place was the one geographical constant in mine and my brothers' lives when we were growing up. We could always came back to visit Nana."

He covered her hand with his. "Home, huh?"

She nodded, causing a little frisson of heat to travel down his arm from where her temple moved against his shoulder. "The farm gave us roots. Not that Mom didn't make any place we lived seem homey. She used to say, *home is where the heart is* and she could put heart into the dinkiest of quarters."

"You have a remarkable family, Red."

"Thank you," Dixie said, lifting her head and looking at him, her smile bright enough to light up half the city of Chicago—a smile bright enough it lit a path clear to his deficient soul.

Funny, in a lifetime of failing to live up to the standards of his family, he'd never thought about whether or not they lived up to his. He'd never before considered that pride could be a two-way street.

Not that he was particularly proud of himself at the moment. He harbored a secret from a righteous woman and coveted his cousin's widow.

He shook his head, attempting to focus on a less enticing landscape. Ben and Bear disappeared into the barn ahead of them and they followed. Dust lazily rode the shafts of sunlight that seeped in through cracks and fly-flecked windows. Even inside a dim, old building, sunshine found Dixie's curls—played in them as she gathered up an armload of buckets. Right or wrong, he wanted to play among those wisps of hair that had escaped her ponytail—to weave his fingers into their soft tangles and pull them fully free of their binding. He wanted to bury his face in those wild tendrils.

She bent and dipped a bucket into the grain bin, pulling his eye from her hair to the curve of her jeans-clad hip. He was hopeless.

"Here you go, Benj," Dixie said, handing the smallest bucket to her son. "You feed the chickens this morning."

Obediently, child and dog trudged toward the door they'd entered. Dixie called after Ben for him to be sure to spread the feed around. Then Ben and Bear were gone, and he and Dixie were alone in the barn.

Tell her now, whispered a little voice inside Sam's head. *Confess. Put an end to this charade before it turns into an all-out train wreck.*

Dixie filled two buckets with grain, handed one to Sam, and nodded toward a door at the far end of the small barn. "Follow me."

All the way down the yellow brick road.

She stepped out into the sunlight, her golden halo of curls all but blinding Sam. He followed, only vaguely aware of the sodden earth sucking at his feet and the loamy fragrance adding to the rain-washed fresh air. She walked in front of him, her hips swaying in gentle rhythm with the bucket she carried, her t-shirt slipping back and forth across her spine. She was an angel with the body of a mythological siren.

And he a weak and heartless mortal.

She veered to one side and he found himself eyeball to eyeball with a huge, rangy cow. Sam jumped back. From the long, wooden trough where Dixie emptied her bucket of grain, she called back to him, "Moo is quite gentle."

The huge brown eye blinked at him.

"Gentle?" Sam squeaked. "Compared to what, Godzilla?"

Dixie tapped the bottom of her bucket and Moo ambled off toward the wooden trough. Watching that long, brown body pass was like watching a time-lapsed video of a soufflé rising.

But this soufflé fell as the cow passed out of the way, revealing a sway-backed horse, a gray-muzzled pony, and a three-legged llama headed their way.

"What are you running here, Red, a retirement home for the walking wounded of the animal kingdom?"

"Something like that."

He joined Dixie on the near side of the trough, effectively putting the feed hamper between him and the animals. "Are you serious?"

"If I didn't take them in, they'd all have ended up as dog food." She handed him the empty bucket and took the full one from him.

"At least the cow gives milk, right?" he ventured as she poured the grain from his bucket along the bottom of the trough.

She shook her head and faced him, an impish tilt to her lips. "Too old to freshen."

"But—" He glanced at the pony, horse, and cow snuffling up the grain from the trough. He eyed the llama who imperiously eyed him back. What was he going to say, that these animals were useless and feeding them a waste of good money? Stuart had often enough implied the same thing about him. By contrast, Dixie had welcomed him into her fold.

"But what?" Dixie prompted.

"But nothing," he said and looked her deep in her eyes. "You have a big heart, Red; and I, for one, am grateful."

"Grateful?" Her lovely arched eyebrows lifted. "For what?"

"For that big heart of yours." *And hopeful that*

you'll find it in that heart to forgive me after I tell you
what I need so desperately to say— that Stuart sent
me to spy on you.

"Grateful for my big heart, huh?" she purred in
her smoky voice, then set about finishing her chores.

Much more of this and he'd lose what backbone
he had left and never confess. He glanced toward the
chicken coop beyond the pasture fence to make sure
Ben was still out of earshot.

"Dixie. About my being here," Sam started.

The cornflower-blue eyes lifted at him, narrowed
ever so slightly. They'd show him worse before he
was done. Could he bear it?

He lowered his head. He stared at the muddy
ground between their feet. Then he drew a deep
breath, bolstering himself for what he must say.

He'd barely opened his mouth when something
rammed him from behind with enough force to slam
him into Dixie. The next thing Sam knew, he was
sprawled face-down on top of Dixie.

She began to laugh, her sugared-coffee breath
sweet and warm against his mouth, her stomach and
all surrounding anatomy quaking against his
correlating parts. In that heavenly instant, his body
reacted, tightening in all the wrong places.

Trouble with a capital *T*. Even the animals knew
it. The cow blew, the llama spit, and the horse and
pony stomped.

Sam scrambled to his feet, clutching a feed
bucket low in front of himself. "I'm...sorry."

Dixie levered herself up onto her elbows, still
chuckling. "*My* goat rams you, and you're sorry?"

"Goat?"

She nodded toward the feed trough. There,

balanced on its tiny hooves on the trough's narrow lip, stood a diminutive Billy Goat.

"I should have warned you about Rocky."

The goat raised his bearded chin at Sam as if to say, "That'll teach you to get in my way at feeding time."

"Guess which bad habit Rocky's former owners were unable to break him of?" Dixie said.

"I'd say it's the same one you haven't been able to correct," Sam remarked dryly, rubbing his behind.

Dixie held out a mud-caked palm to Sam. Bucket firmly gripped against his groin by one hand, he helped her to her feet with the other. She circled in front of him, brushing at her backside...her deliciously inviting backside.

"I'm all muddy," she said.

Sam thumped the bucket against his thigh in an attempt to divert the blood flow to a less improper place.

"You, too," she said, brushing at his knees.

He stutter-stepped back from Dixie. Behind him, Rocky bleated, giving new meaning to the phrase *between a rock and a hard place.*

Swell. If he confessed why he was here now, she'd think he was a total degenerate.

#

Twenty minutes later, Sam stood in Dixie's bedroom doorway. She'd shed her muddy clothes, washed, and donned a blue, silk robe that clung to her curves like sin. He wanted her all over again. All the more reason to say his piece and hit the road, which he would do as soon as she was off the phone.

"But, Carl—"

Good. It was the chef who'd called. Confirming

he'd be back on the job tomorrow morning, right?

"Is it the money?" Dixie asked, pacing the narrow path between her bed and desk. "Do you need more money?"

Sounded like Chef Carl was holding out—working Dixie for a raise. Sam was liking Carl less and less by the second. He could throw a monkey wrench in the greedy chef's strategy. All he had to do is step forward and tell Dixie he would stay and cook for her.

But to stay, to sleep nights in the room next to hers and work daily elbow to elbow with Dixie would be more temptation than a weak-willed degenerate could resist. Then again, out there in the paddock, he'd come face to face with proof what she did with the broken and the castoff. She took *care* of them. And she wouldn't likely welcome a damaged man into her bed.

"What if I banned Miss Weston from the kitchen? What if I did all the cooking for her?" Her pleading made Sam want to take the phone receiver from her fingers and tell Carl to go to hell. But, could he bear living and working with a goddess who could never reciprocate his feelings?

"What if—"

There was a loud click in Dixie's ear, then dead air. She spotted Sam in the doorway in time to stifle the curse welling up in her throat. The last thing she wanted was to embroil him further in her crisis.

Flicking off the talk button, she set the phone aside, pasted on a smile, and bobbed her chin at Sam's crisp, new jeans. "If you throw the muddy ones in the laundry, I'll wash them for you."

He frowned. She wagered that surly expression

had nothing to do with her doing his laundry. More likely, he'd heard enough of her conversation with her *ex*-chef to be worried what she'd next impose upon him. If she didn't want him avoiding them in the future like the proverbial plague, she'd better do something quick to show him that she and Ben came without strings attached.

"Out in the barnyard before Rocky laid us out," she said, "you were about to say your good-byes, weren't you?"

He dropped his chin, breaking eye contact with her. "Not exactly."

She planted her hands on her hips. "Don't lie to me, Sam. I'd far rather hear bad news straight up than be blindsided."

His chin came up, the eyes meeting hers wide and beseeching. "I wasn't trying to say good-bye out there, not exactly."

She softened her voice. "It's okay for you to leave, Sam. We've had a nice visit. You saved Ben from Miss Weston's wrath and me from a disastrous Sunday brunch. What more could anyone ask of a houseguest?"

He huffed. "I thought we established yesterday that I'm not a houseguest, I'm family."

"So we did," she said.

He jammed his fingers into the front pockets of his jeans, hunched his shoulders, and peered at her through thick lashes. "You could ask me to stay and help."

She started to shake her head.

He cut her off with, "Carl isn't coming back to work for you, is he?"

Now what was she going to do, lie when the one

thing she asked of him was his honesty?

"I'm right, aren't I, Red?"

She sighed and nodded. "He got another job."

"Then you still need my help."

She wanted to tell him she didn't need him, but the truth was, "I could use your help. But, I'm not about to impose further on you."

His shoulders came down and his chin went up. "How many times do I have to say you're not imposing on me?"

"You stopped by for a meal and a passing howdy-do and the next thing you know, I've got you cooking in my kitchen. Not the most hospitable thing I could have done."

"You had an emergency."

"Through which you helped me out. I'm eternally grateful." She glanced at her watch. "And right now you can help me by excusing me. I still have time to email the local newspaper and get a want ad in tomorrow's edition."

"And until the want ad produces results, until you wade through resumes and check out references, what are you going to do for a chef?"

"Handle it," she said, sitting down at her computer desk and pulling up the Internet.

"How?" he asked.

"We'll rely on specials," she said as she logged onto the newspaper's web site. "I can cook, you know. Remember that beef roast sandwich you had night before last? It didn't kill you, did it?"

A crooked smile bent Sam's lips. "Are we having our first fight, Red?"

"Looks that way," she said as she began typing up her ad.

He leaned a shoulder against the doorjamb and folded his arms across his chest. "I'm just saying you don't have to *manage* or *get by*. I could stay and cook until you find a suitable replacement chef."

"And I'm saying that that's imposing a lot on you, Sam."

"Family helps family," he retorted. "Isn't that how your family works?"

She swiveled her chair toward him. "Yes, but..."

"Let me help you out, Red. I have nothing better to do. I don't even have a job waiting for me anywhere."

She wanted to jump at Sam's offer. She wanted to jump at him, throw her arms around his neck, and kiss and hug him and thank him. But, for all his good intentions, Sam Ryan was a man with a history of running out on responsibility. Michael had said enough for her to get that message, and she'd rather be prepared for no help than get left in the lurch on the brink of the dinner rush by a chef who impulsively hit the road because the whim struck him. She could not abide one more man abandoning her.

"If not for you, for Ben," he said.

"For Ben, huh?" *And Sam and yourself,* whispered a voice inside her head, a voice she hadn't heard aloud in over two years—a voice she never would hear aloud again. The voice of a man who'd abandoned her via his death.

She turned back to the computer, frowning. It was silly of her to still think of Michael's death as abandonment. He hadn't *chosen* to leave them.

She typed.

But Sam was another matter.

She proofread her ad one last time and hit send.

"Okay," she said, turning her full attention back to Sam. "I accept your offer…under one condition."

"Shoot."

"When you've had enough, tell me."

"Tell you what?"

"Even if I haven't found a new chef, when you've had enough, don't just leave."

He shoved his hands back into his pockets, his lips curling a sheepish grin. "Aaah."

"Tell me."

"In other words, don't take flight in the middle of the night." he said. "Don't skip out, take off, run away."

"Just be honest with me, Sam. That's all I ask."

#

Just be honest.

Sam stood just inside Ben's open bedroom door so he could watch for anyone approaching, the cell phone pressed to his ear. He hadn't kept time how long he'd been standing there like that, but his uncle must have been haranguing him for a full five minutes about not responding to his numerous voice messages.

"I'm at The Farmhouse now," Sam said when the old man finally took a breath.

"I know you are!"

How could he know that? Before he could explore the possibilities, Stuart was harping at him again.

"Have you found out anything?"

"I just got here night before last," Sam said. "What do you expect me to have learned in less than forty-eight hours?"

"It was enough time to bed the woman, prove her

immoral."

Sam scrubbed a hand over his face. "Stuart, you must know that me *bedding* Mickey's widow would hardly be reason enough for any court to take her son away from her...unless you already have a string of lovers to testify against her. In which case, I don't know what you need me for."

Silence filled the receiver and, for a moment, Sam thought the connection had been broken. Then... "Just stay there. Find something I can use against her. Does she drink to excess? Smoke pot? Do drugs? Does she leave the boy alone? Does she hit him? Take pictures of the bruises."

Sam rolled his eyes. "Oh yeah. Running around with a camera won't look too obvious."

"You have a damn cell phone. Use the camera feature on it!"

"Yeah. Sure," he said and the connection went dead.

Just be honest with me. At the moment he wasn't being fully honest with his uncle. But then, Dixie hadn't made him promise to be honest with anyone else. And what better place to hide-out than The Farmhouse, especially since staying was at Stuart's command.

CHAPTER SEVEN

Pushing the lawnmower across the yard, Sam inhaled. There was something about the scent of freshly cut grass that made him feel alive. Maybe because it *didn't* take him back to the Carrington estate where grass clippings were shot into a collection bag to be emptied onto some compost pile far from the manicured lawns. Maybe it was the fact that he, good-for-nothing Sam, was the guy pushing the lawn mower that made him tingle from his fingers to his shoulders. Stuart had once fired a gardener for allowing Sam to take a few passes with the riding mower.

Or maybe the reason Sam smiled even in the trail of exhaust fumes off the aged gas mower was because it was Dixie's lawn he cut. He liked doing things for her, loved how everything he did made her happy. He'd even made it through a full week working at her side and sleeping in the bedroom next to hers without breaking the promise he'd made himself, to keep his hands off her.

Of course he didn't manage that without a lot of distraction…like playing general handyman. Dixie had argued with him over every little task, insisting his being her chef was more than enough help. Granted, his handyman skills required reading a lot of self-help books. But at least she didn't have to wait until her contractor brother Roman visited to get her leaky kitchen faucet repaired, the loose floorboard in the front hall tightened down, or the bathroom drain snaked out.

But here it was Monday again, the one day of the week the restaurant was closed. He'd started today's distractions by helping Dixie tend her castoff critters and mending a broken fence. When he'd hauled out the lawnmower, she'd shaken her head.

"One of these days, Sam," she'd said, "the newness of all this will wear off. Then you won't find the endless maintenance that comes with an old house and a family so much fun anymore."

Was newness all there was to his enjoyment of doing such simple tasks as cleaning gutters, emptying trash, and mowing the lawn? Would he eventually tire of this place like she said—like he had every other adventure?

Not as long as Ben trailed him, calling him Tin Man and asking for horsey-back rides. Not as long as Nana kept pinching his cheeks and calling him "a keeper" or Dixie's cousin Annie regaled him with tales of her twelve-year-old twins' antics and her truck driving husband Lou's bewildered parenting skills as though he were part of the family.

Not as long as Dixie treated him like family.

Family. No wonder he was glad no one had responded to Dixie's ads for a chef. As long as she needed him to cook for her, he could pretend to be part of this family—Mickey's family.

The lawnmower sputtered, coughed a couple times, and died. The sweet aroma of cut grass was lost to a puff of exhaust; and that life-affirming tingle the puttering mower had vibrated up his arms turned into a prickling premonition.

All good things must come to an end.

"Some too soon," he murmured, thinking of Mickey—leaning on the handle of the stilled mower and surveying what his cousin had left behind.

At the back of the yard in an orange-plastic sandbox, Ben built sandcastles. Bear dozed nearby in the shade of a mature oak. Along the side of the house, Dixie with trowel in hand tended the flowerbeds that added to the charm of the Victorian era house. The quiet life. The simple life.

The kind of life Stuart would take away from Ben.

Sam shivered and glanced skyward as though seeking reassurance the sun hadn't disappeared. A single white cloud floated across a sky as blue as Mickey's eyes. For an instant, Sam swore he felt the weight of Mickey's arm on his shoulder.

Acceptance or warning?

From Mickey, acceptance. Always acceptance.

But he, Sam, had come to The Farmhouse to dig up dirt on Dixie for Stuart. Even Mickey would never have endorsed that.

But Mickey would know there was no dirt to be found that Stuart could use to gain custody of Ben. Just as Mickey, from his celestial perspective would have known Dixie would need a chef.

But, wouldn't Mickey also have known Sam came to The Farmhouse for his own selfish motives? Mickey would never have put his family's well-being at risk for the needs of a goof-off cousin…Mickey who'd always looked out for him.

Sam winced and gripped the handle of the mower, muttering, "All good things do *not* have to come to an end." *Not if I can help it, Mickey.*

Sam rolled the mower to the garage. Everything would be fine as long as he did nothing to give Stuart ammunition to take custody of Ben—as long as kept his hands off Dixie. He unscrewed the cap from the mower's gas tank and picked up the gas can. A soft hand covered his.

"Didn't anyone ever tell you never to gas-up a hot lawnmower," Dixie said in her smoky voice. "The gas fumes could ignite."

Sam sucked a quick breath, amazed the spark that had jumped between their flesh upon contact hadn't ignited the fumes. And therein lay his biggest problem. He still wanted to touch her every bit as much as he knew he shouldn't.

Dixie fought the impulse to pull her hand away from Sam's. Touching him made her tingle—made her want to be touched back by him. He brought a lightness to her heart that made her want more.

And Sam too needed touching—yearned for it. She'd seen it in the way he held onto Ben's hugs and in the way he leaned into Nana's pats on his cheeks. Felt it every time he jerked away when they bumped into each other as they rushed to fill orders in the restaurant kitchen.

"How about some lemonade?" she asked, lifting her hand from his.

He shook his head. "I'm fine."

"Water?"

He stepped back—stepped beyond her reach. "I'll just sit in the shade until the mower cools down."

In spite of the common sense screaming for her to leave him to himself, she followed him to the oasis of grass in the middle of the circular drive. He plopped down, his back to the apple tree. She settled

Indian style facing him.

"Thanks for keeping me from blowing myself up," he said, folding his arms across his chest as though he needed to block her presence. "Guess I'm not too practiced at manual labor."

"Could have fooled me," she countered, pressing—pushing him. "I no longer have to contend with iron stains in my sink from a drippy faucet or worry about a customer tripping in my entry hall."

"I didn't do anything any one of your brothers couldn't have done and a whole lot better than me. I cringe to think of Roman checking out my jobs."

"He's a contractor. He's looks at all jobs with a critical eye."

Sam's brow puckered. "Does he know about me…that I'm staying here?"

"Of course," she said. "I've told all my brothers about you."

He winced and looked away.

"Why do my brothers intimidate you?" she asked.

He snorted. "They are very capable men."

"Each in their own way," she conceded.

He met her gaze. "They're rock stars at what they do."

"And you aren't?"

"I needed self-help books, simple ones with lots of diagrams to do jobs most men learn in the course of growing up. My training in *handy work* fell more in the realm of notifying the estate maintenance man of any problem."

She couldn't help but chuckle. "It's actually a good thing to know who to call to get something done. As for self-help books, if every man or woman knew how to repair everything there wouldn't be so many of them being published."

He grunted.

"Sam, no man is a rock star at everything."

"I'm no rock star at anything," he said.

"You're an excellent chef."

"I'm a pretty good cook."

"If any one of my brothers tried to dice and slice anything with the speed and precision you do, they'd end up with much shorter fingers."

He shrugged. "Practice. Repetition. That's all that is."

"You won't find even one of them whistling a happy tune over a flattop."

"So I like cooking."

"You cook from the heart, Sam."

"I do *love* cooking," he conceded.

"What got you cooking from *your* heart?" she asked, pushing him—willing him to see how that passion gave him worth.

His smile turned sad. "I hid out a lot in the kitchen."

Ah, the heart *of his issue.*

"From what, or should I say from whom?" she asked.

"Uncle Stu." Sam flexed a sardonic smile in her direction. "He pretty much steered clear of the *helps'* domain."

"So you got to know the kitchen staff pretty well."

He bobbed his head, memories flashing across his eyes, contentedness smoothing his lips. "Real well."

"So they took the *master's* nephew under their

collective wing and taught him the love of food."

"Pretty much," he said.

His gaze slid off into the distance. There was so much more to the story. She knew. Michael had talked endlessly about Sam, love-starved Sam. Sam who'd found refuge in a mansion kitchen.

Sam who never recognized his own value.

"They were good people," he finally said. "Fun to be around. And they taught me how to be good at something. They taught me what flavors blended, what the different spices did to foods, and how technique elevated a dish. They taught me the beauty of presentation—how we eat first with our eyes."

She watched his face transform as he talked— saw him grow more animated. And she heard the passion in his voice as he spoke about what he'd been taught and the people who taught him—heard it as well in the silence when he paused.

"So that's why you became a chef?" she asked, when his pause stretched.

He waved her off. "I'm no chef. I played at learning the techniques. I cooked when the mood struck me. Mostly, I just wanted to be anything but a suit, much to Uncle Stuart's dismay."

Her heart ached for the little boy who sought solace in a sterile prep-kitchen.

No, that was wrong. The kitchen where he got his earliest schooling in food prep was anything but sterile.

"Whatever drove you into that mansion kitchen, Sam, you emerged with a passion—a love."

He grunted. "And just enough skill to be a cook."

"That skill pushed you toward culinary school."

He frowned and looked away. "Which I never

completed."

"Yet you said food is love."

"So I did," he conceded.

"No culinary degree can put love in food the way you do, Sam."

He stared at the ground, his brow puckered.

"Do you love cooking?" she asked.

"Yes," he answered without raising his eyes.

"Sam, do you know how many people work at jobs they hate?"

He shrugged.

"Don't you see what an accomplishment it is, not only to be good at what you do, but to be able to do what you love to do?"

His chin came up and his gaze met hers. "I never thought about it that way before. In the Carrington family, success is measured by money."

"There's more to life—to happiness than money, Sam."

Didn't he know it? For years, he'd made light of his failure-filled life with countless people. For most of his life he'd hidden his pain of failure behind false laughter. But there'd be no joking his way around Dixie. Dixie listened more carefully than other people—saw beyond the words. She fixed broken animals and wounded souls.

He closed his eyes. He didn't want to see the pity in her eyes, not from this woman for whom he longed.

"And so goes the story of my life," he said, forcing a lightness into his voice, opening his eyes but not meeting her gaze as he asked, "Getting any responses from your local ads for a chef?"

She shook her head. "I've placed more ads in

broader-reaching newspapers and on-line. Maybe one of those will pay off. How about you, Sam? You know anyone you could recommend? I know it's a lot to ask of anyone, to relocate to the land of the frozen tundra."

He gave her a sad smile. "I've been living in France for the past several years. I doubt anyone I cooked with there even knows where northeastern Wisconsin is."

Her cell phone rang. She pulled it out of her pocket and eyed the readout. "Business," she said with a resigned sigh and answered the phone. "Hi, Jim. What's up?"

After listening a moment, she replied, "No. I've got no problems with your meats."

"Your prices are fine," she said after another short pause. "You've always been fair with me. What's this all about?"

Confusion pulled her eyebrows together above the bridge of her nose. "That didn't come from me. Of course the order stands. Thanks for calling and checking."

She closed the phone. "That's strange."

"What happened?" Sam asked.

"My meat supplier received a cancellation of my order from my FAX number. But I didn't cancel my meat order."

"Is your FAX machine somewhere easily accessible?"

"Not really. It's in my bedroom with my computer."

"Does your FAX keep a history of what's been sent from it?"

"Only one way to find out," she said, popping to

her feet.

Sam followed Dixie into the house. Her bedroom door was open and Gran was plucking at the keys of her computer.

"Gran, I thought you were napping," Dixie said.

"I'm chatting with the most charming gentleman."

Dixie leaned over her grandmother's shoulder, examining the screen. "You're in a chat room."

"Mr. Dick has been trying to send me his picture."

"When did you learn to log onto the Internet?"

"Ben showed me."

"How did he learn to use the Internet?"

"From watching you," Nana said.

"I set him up with an on-line game now and then," Dixie said.

"Never underestimate the observational skills of kids," Sam said.

"Don't I know it," Dixie murmured, turning her attention to the combination printer-scanner-FAX machine. "So Gran, did you touch the printer this morning?"

"No. No." She tapped away at the keyboard. "Except when I tried to print out Mr. Dick's picture."

"What buttons did you hit on the printer?"

"Just about all of them. Nothing I hit would make it print Mr. Dick's picture."

Dixie groaned, her gaze locking on Sam's.

"She'd still need to have entered your supplier's phone number," Sam said, "not to mention inserted a paper instructing him to cancel the order."

Dixie shrugged, the look in her eyes one of sad resignation. A flash from the computer screen caught

Sam's eye. He moved closer to Dixie's Gran and read Mr. Dick's latest entry.

"Geeze," he muttered after reading the subject line of the image being transported to Dixie's computer. *My Sausage.*

He squatted beside the office chair and gently addressed Nana. "Do you know what kind of chat room you're in?"

"One where I've met a most charming gentleman."

Sam caught Dixie's eye and nodded toward the screen. Dixie leaned in and started reading.

Eyes rolling, she straightened. "You didn't give this guy any information about The Farmhouse, did you? You didn't give him our address or names, did you Nana?"

Gran's confidence melted. "I-I don't think so. Did I do something wrong?"

Sighing, Dixie shook her head. "Come with me. Ben's alone in the yard with Miss Weston."

Gran rose and tottered toward the door. Dixie hesitated, glanced between printer and computer.

"I'll take care of this," Sam said.

"Thanks," Dixie said and followed her grandmother out.

Sam sat down at the keyboard and typed, "You've been chatting with a fifteen year old girl, you perv. If you ever contact this email address again, I'll put the cops in touch with you."

Instantly, Mr. Dick signed off. Sam deleted Mr. Dick's anatomical image and read through the history of the correspondence. Once he was satisfied Gran hadn't revealed anything personally detrimental, he deleted the chat conversation, any coinciding cookies, and any history of the chat. There was history of a FAX to Dixie's meat supplier. The time stamp seemed to coincide with when he and Dixie were feeding the animals. But he could be remembering wrong and there was nothing to indicate who had sent the FAX. He was about to shut down the computer when an icon caught his attention.

Farmhouse Business.

He had no business snooping, but rules never being his strong point, Sam clicked on the icon. Slowly, the old computer opened to the financial statements of The Farmhouse and home.

Being more familiar with restaurant expenses, he studied those costs first. Receipts showed she bought locally as much as possible. Pulling up her menus alongside her food expenses, he saw she built her menus around seasonal vegetables and fruits, and did a pretty good job of cross utilization of ingredients. Saturday night's roast beef dinner became Sunday brunch's hot beef sandwich and Tuesday's stew. On the average, she'd kept her food costs respectably below twenty percent. Her staffs' wages were slightly above par for the area. But the restaurant was financially healthy. Still, it shamed him to realize the rent on his Paris apartment could pay her monthly bills three times over.

Even utility and insurance expenses weren't out of line, given the age of the building and that it doubled as a restaurant and home. Maintenance costs were surprisingly low. No doubt due to having a brother in the construction business. He found receipts for only the materials needed to construct the restaurant kitchen, secure the living quarters from the restaurant areas, convert a parlor into a small dining room, and freshen up the entry hall and old dining room. Having no labor expenses had been a huge cost saver for her. Yet, her grandmother had taken out a second mortgage on the farm to pay for the additional kitchen. What was wrong with this picture?

CHAPTER EIGHT

Sam lie on his back in Ben's little bed, staring at the patterns the moonlight cast across the ceiling. A little infusion of money into The Farmhouse would help Dixie. He had the money to do it...as long as Stuart didn't catch on to what he was doing with his trust fund allowance. Money was the answer to his taking care of Mickey's family and his escaping being tied down by responsibility—escaping the attraction of Dixie. But something still didn't sit right about his reasoning.

Sam rolled onto his hip and faced the open window over the bed as if the night air coming through the screen held the answer. But one word kept circling behind his eyes.

Money.

When he'd snooped through Dixie's accounts, he'd found far more than restaurant and household expenses. Given the hefty amount of Mickey's life insurance, a policy he'd seen himself thanks to one of Uncle Stuart detectives, there should have been more than a few hundred dollars in Dixie's saving's account. Add to the insurance payout the sale of the Chicago restaurant and she should have had a small fortune...providing the Chicago restaurant had sold for a profit. Even if the restaurant sale had broken even, there should have been enough by far to save her grandmother from having to re-mortgage her farm to turn the place into a restaurant for Dixie. Nor did the facts match the Dixie he'd come to know.

But then, how much did he really know about her? She cooked a mean beef roast, had three devoted brothers spread around the country, another a continent away, and two loving parents half a world away. Her customers liked her. She collected damaged strays. Being among that last category made him wince. Damn, but he wanted to be more to Dixie than a project to fix.

Then again, she was aces at charming the socks off him. Maybe the questions, all the prodding to face things had nothing to do with fixing him. What if she charmed him because he was a potential source of money?

Suddenly there wasn't enough air in the little room. Sam sat up and shoved the window open wider. The screen insert fell out, clattering onto the porch roof outside his window while a shrill whine sounded simultaneously through the wall from the adjoining room. Almost instantly, the whine halted and the door to the small balcony off the neighboring room opened. Dixie stuck her head out, whispering loudly, "Sorry about that. I should have disconnected the motion detector from Ben's window when you moved into the room."

He gave the window frame a quick scan and found the apparatus. At least she cared enough for her child to protect him from falling out a window...or be taken away through one. He flinched at what his last thought implied of Stuart.

"Hope I didn't wake the household," he said.

She glanced over her shoulder in the direction of her bed. "Ben barely stirred."

"Is it going to go off if I move the window again?"

She shook her head, her loose hair shimmering in the moonlight. *Not for your eyes.*

He reached for the errant screen.

"Don't," cried Dixie. But it all happened so fast she couldn't get her full warning out before the window dropped on his back.

A curse escaped his lips.

"Are you okay?" She'd stepped out onto the balcony, poised at the nearest railing should he need her aid.

In spite of his current doubts about Dixie, all he saw was her in baby-doll pajamas. They weren't the sheer, lacey type with panty bottoms. Hers were boy-cut shorts with a cap-sleeved top made of a far less filmy fabric. But cotton or lace, all he could think about was unwrapping her from those baby-dolls and seeing if the rest of her was as flawless as her long, naked legs.

Naked.

He groaned and blurted, "I'm fine."

He lifted the window off himself.

"There's a dowel on the sill that you can use to prop the window open," she said.

He nodded, withdrew and secured the window. With all the movement, the sheet slipped down his hips. He pulled on his jeans before going after the runaway screen again. Good thing he did because Dixie now perched on the balcony's nearest railing, hugging her knees to her chest.

She'd donned a thin robe. She still looked too damned fetching.

He turned his attention to the wayward screen.

"I like to sit out here on clear nights and watch the stars." Her soft voice carried to him as he hauled the screen off the porch roof. "I like to believe one of them is Michael."

Sam paused, half inside, half still outside his window. It was agony to be this close to her when mere feet and a few too many layers of clothes separated them. But, if he wanted to know where Mickey's insurance money had gone...

Hell, maybe Mickey even had a hand in setting off the motion detector and dropping the damn window on him. Maybe there was something here Mickey wanted him to expose and what better time to raise the question than when his widow was in a pensive mood.

Sam tossed the screen inside onto his bed, raised the window further and settled it on his shoulder as he sat straddling the sill. "Nice, to believe he's up there watching over you and Ben."

"Yeah," she murmured, eyes lifted to the heavens. "It's comforting."

Damn but the seductress had an angelic profile. He knew which he wanted her to be. But the fiscal facts of The Farmhouse Restaurant and that her grandmother had mortgaged the farm for the improvements when Dixie had been the beneficiary of Mickey's ample life insurance wasn't adding up.

"Must have been hard to give up the Chicago home the three of you shared...and the restaurant."

He watched her closely for her reaction. The sad smile that shaped her lips had to be a trick of shadows, right?

"Actually," she said, "I think he bought the restaurant more for you."

"*Me?*" He all but choked on the word. This wasn't the direction he'd expected the conversation to take.

She looked at him. "He asked you to be his Head Chef, didn't he?"

"You knew about that?"

"Of course."

"I was still in culinary school. I hadn't the kind of experience required to be a Head Chef." Sam snorted. "Making an unproven like me head of any kitchen at that time would have guaranteed failure."

"The restaurant failed anyway," she said.

That was a fact Uncle Stu had failed to mention. But, would Mickey really have let her run the business into the ground?

"Mickey the Golden Boy never failed at anything," he said.

"You've got to know what the odds are of a new restaurant succeeding, Sam," she said.

"Yeah. But Mickey had an MBA and you had the restaurant management degree."

"And, like you, little experience," she said. "Michael and I also disagreed on what kind of restaurant we wanted. I wanted low-key and homey. He wanted high-end gourmet."

So the perfect pair had their differences.

"Then came Ben and Michael took over managing all aspects of the restaurant while I immersed myself in motherhood."

"But Mickey never failed at anything," Sam repeated, still unable to accept that Mickey might have failed at something.

"Michael wasn't perfect, Sam. He was as mortal as you and I, and he let love blind him to reality."

Was she about to admit she'd duped him just as Stuart had insisted?

"He built a restaurant for you and me," she said, "because he thought it was what we both wanted— because he loved us and wanted to take care of us."

Sam swallowed at the lump in his throat. "And I rejected his offer to be his Head Chef."

"You knew you weren't ready."

I knew I would mess up, run when the pressure got to me, and screw things up for him.

"And I never wanted a high-end restaurant," she said. "I just wanted a little place where people could gather for good down home cooking."

"Like The Farmhouse."

"Yes."

"Seems in the end Mickey gave you what you wanted."

She sighed. "I'd rather have had a lifetime with Michael."

"Yeah. No doubt." *If it was the truth.* He badly wanted to believe it was. One way to find out. "At least he left you a life insurance policy that enabled you to turn your Gran's house into the restaurant you wanted."

A half snort—half laugh escaped Dixie.

"That sounds like sarcasm," he said.

"I didn't spend Michael's life insurance money to start over here."

Here it comes. The answer he'd been waiting for.

"I spent it fighting Stuart for custody of Ben."

This time, the sarcastic snort came from Sam. He should have guessed—should have known. Nothing in Dixie's persona suggested she was the type to squander an inheritance...or use another person.

"We've got an early morning," Dixie said and excused herself from the balcony with, "Better sleep while we can."

Like he would be able to sleep after learning all he had. Motherhood personified, this woman who'd been forced to spend hers and her son's financial security on a high priced lawyer who could fight Stuart's battery of attorneys. It was the kind of mother he wished he'd had—the kind of mother who wanted her son enough to fight for him. *His* mother's response to his young tears when she'd married a man who didn't want him had been to chastise him and remind him he would be financially secure with his uncle. But there was no love in money, only escape and even that was fleeting.

But money could wipe away The Farmhouse's second mortgage. All it would take was a few months allowance from his trust fund.

He looked up at the stars. *Mickey, Mickey. Is that why you're keeping me here, for the financing I can provide?* Sam shook his head. *But, I give her one dime and Uncle Stu will cut me off.*

One particularly bright star pulsed.

You know he'll find out. He always does. And you know what a coward I am.

CHAPTER NINE

Dixie entered the restaurant kitchen, reading the order off the guest ticket in her hand. Sam gave his usual "got it," response. But, when she glanced up to tuck the ticket into the carousel, she saw Sam wasn't alone.

From the far side of the prep table, the twins giggled.

"Who's watching Ben?" Dixie asked

"He's napping with Nana."

"Still, you girls know you're not supposed to be in the restaurant kitchen," Dixie said. "Out."

They began sliding off their stools. Sam turned, jabbed a spatula at them, and commanded, "Stay."

Dixie blinked at him. "We have health regulations as you well know. Besides, it's too dangerous for them to be in here, for them as well as you."

"And our customers," Sam said, giving the girls a meaningful look...at which they giggled.

He met Dixie's gaze. "I caught them trying to add sugar to my salt bowl."

Dixie folded her arms across her chest and leveled a no-nonsense look on the girls. "You two know better than to mess with my restaurant."

"We weren't really going to do it," said Lulu.

"We knew Sam would catch us," said Lola, all but batting her lashes in Sam's direction.

Dixie bit the inside of her cheek to keep a smile from escaping. So this was about the girls having a crush on Sam—about trying to get his attention. But the no unauthorized personnel in the kitchen rule was a serious one. She raised an eyebrow at Sam. "They pull their shenanigans on you and you let them stay in the kitchen for it?"

As he assembled two club sandwiches, he called over his shoulder of the girls, "What did I say when I caught you?"

In unison, they answered. "If you wanna play you gotta pay."

"And how are you two paying?" Sam asked.

Through a Cheshire cat grin, Lulu said, "He's making us peel potatoes."

Dixie moved to Sam's side, her voice barely more than a whisper. "You know they have a crush on you."

The look he gave her was incredulous. "They're twelve. I'm an old guy to them."

"A cute old guy," she murmured.

"You think I'm cute?" he asked through a crooked grin.

She thought of the first morning he'd been at the farm when she woke him while getting Ben's toys from his room and had called him cute. There'd been a lot of innuendo in their flirtations that day, flirtations she wouldn't have minded pursuing. But Sam had pulled back in the days since and she could only assume it was for the same reason she'd cooled things between them. Michael.

Whatever the reason, teasing him seemed safer these days. She slanted a crooked smile at him. "Don't get a swelled head over it."

Still, to be on the safe side herself, she turned her attention to the bowl of peeled potatoes.

"What are these being used for?" she asked Sam.

"Boiling for mashed," Sam said.

Dixie scrutinized the spuds in the bowl. Much as she wanted to praise the girls for their work—encourage them toward more productive occupations like peeling potatoes, this was still a working kitchen.

"*All* the peel needs to be removed," she said, pointing out several small patches of potato skin still clinging to the spuds.

The twins groaned.

Dixie turned back to Sam, her voice once more lowered. "Please tell me you made them wash their hands before they started handling the food."

"You touched your nose," Lulu said.

Sam winked at Dixie. "Listen and you'll have your answer."

"Did not," Lola countered.

"Did too."

"What's the first rule of the kitchen?" he called to the girls.

"Wash your hands," they said in unison.

"What's the second rule of the kitchen?"

"If you touch your nose, your eyes, your mouth or anywhere on your person, wash your hands again."

"Lola, go wash your hands," Sam said.

Lola groaned but slid off her stool and went to the wash sink.

"And that's another dollar for Lulu," he said.

"All right!" hooted Lulu.

Dixie chuckled. "Quality control Sam Ryan style?"

"You got it," he said.

"I'm impressed."

#

So she was impressed with him. That Dixie thought well of him made Sam feel good. But, at the same time, he was still trying to figure out how to help her without Stuart finding out—without him losing his only means of support. That last—that selfish part of him negated Dixie's high regard for him as he saw it.

From the narrow staircase at the back of the house, he saw Dixie sitting cross-legged on the living room floor, Ben in her lap and red slippers on her feet. What was with the red footwear? First the high-tops then the rubber boots now these fuzzy slip-ons. She never wore anything else red. She didn't even decorate with red.

Not that he had any right to explore her penchant for red foot gear. He shouldn't have even been here long enough to discover she wore red slippers. She should have kicked him out on his wayward butt the night he arrived, not invited him into her home.

Yet, she had. And now the sight of mother and son so close together spread a toasty warm feeling through Sam that had little to do with the fresh jeans and gray turtleneck he'd donned following his cold shower. Cold showers seem to have become the norm for him lately.

He'd have given anything not to be the loser he was—to be somebody Dixie didn't need to *fix*...somebody worthy of her. He should tell her now, tonight, that he'd had enough. That he was leaving. Especially given the latest call from Stuart. The old man was growing ever more impatient.

Dixie whispered something in Ben's ear and the

two of them giggled. He couldn't remember the last time his mother had invited him into her lap. Heck, he couldn't remember his mother ever sitting on the floor with him.

Ah, Mickey. No wonder you fell for her.

No wonder I want to be more than a cause to her.

No wonder I can't make myself leave her.

As though they had a mind of their own, his feet carried him into the living room. Dixie looked up from the game board spread on the floor in front of her and Ben and smiled that come hither smile of hers that hooked him every time.

"Wanna play with us, Sam?"

Does duck and orange sauce go together? Oh yeah. He wanted to play all right. But the game he had in mind had nothing to do with a game board and definitely didn't include a four-year-old.

"What's the game?" he asked, nodding at the game board on the floor in front of the pair.

Ben tipped his head back against his mother's shoulder. "Candyland."

Dixie wore another of her fuzzy sweaters, this one with a deep *v* neckline that the kid's movement pulled wider. All that creamy skin did not evoke a motherly image for him. Didn't the woman own anything other than fitted sweaters? Yes, she did. Tailored-to-her body camp shirts and tightly-cinched aprons.

"I don't know how to play Candyland," he said.

"You never played Candyland when you were a kid?" Dixie asked in an incredulous tone, the tilting of her head making the burnished gold curls dance around her head. His fingers itched to test which would be silkier. Her hair, or the pale skin exposed by the wide *v* of the sweater.

Not here. Not now. Not ever.

"Nope," he said.

"And here I thought you were the one with the privileged childhood."

Her tone teased. But he heard the underlying pity in her words. He wanted to tell her he didn't want to be her cause—that she and Ben were supposed to be *his* cause. That he was here to protect them because he owed it to Mickey who'd looked out for him all those growing up years under Stuart's watchful eye.

"Haul your deprived behind down here on the floor, Sam Ryan," Dixie ordered good-naturedly, patting the floor beside her. "Time you find the kid in yourself."

He grunted. "Most people would say I need to grow up."

"Most people? Or just Stuart?"

He winced. "Anyone ever tell you, Red, you have a tendency to get right to the point?"

She laughed and patted the floor again. "Get down here. We need a third player."

And you need a chef. Why can't that be enough?

He folded down next to Dixie. "Okay. How do I play?"

"It's easy enough a four-year-old can teach you," Dixie said through that hundred watt smile she kept turning on him—a smile that he never wanted to see fade. Yet, here he was an agent of Stuart's and he was bound to ruin that smile.

Ben handed him a plastic gingerbread man playing piece—the yellow one. Appropriate, thought Sam, recalling how often he'd been tempted to take his usual coward's way out with them—how close he'd been to sneaking off without so much as a good-bye after brunch that first Sunday at the farm. Maybe he should have left Monday morning and shown Dixie then and there his true colors.

Dixie elbowed him in the ribs. "Don't look so grim. We don't play for blood."

He forced a smile. "Whew. That's a relief. For a minute there, I thought I might have to get cross-matched for blood type in case I needed a transfusion."

Dixie laughed, the sound lyrical and full bodied as bamboo wind chimes. He could easily lose himself in that low, breathy melody. *Too easily.*

"What do I do first?" he asked, plunking his game piece down on the game board's starting point.

Between chubby fingers and thumb, Ben held up a card with a colored square on it. "You take a card and then—" The kid slid his game piece along the colored squares. "—And then you move your gingerbread man to the color on the card."

"Got it. Now, how do we start?"

"We already did," Dixie said.

He looked at her in silent question.

"Rule number one," she said. "The youngest always goes first."

"That's me," Ben chirped.

"But of course," Sam said. "What was I thinking?"

In short time, the three of them left Plumpa the troll and his gingerbread plum tree behind, passed Lord Licorice, and traversed the peppermint forest. The first hitch came when Dixie took a shortcut through Gumdrop Pass.

"Nobody told me about any shortcuts," Sam said.

"You didn't land on any of the squares that would have let you take advantage of the shortcuts."

"I see," Sam said. "Anything else you haven't told me about this game?"

"It's a game of chance, Sam."

Chance. Yeah. Like he believed there a chance in hell he could fix Dixie's problems and escape without her learning what a louse he was by coming to the farm to spy on her.

Sam eyed the game board, noting things he hadn't before, like shortcuts, pink spaces with pictures on them, and other colored squares with black dots.

"What are the dots for?" he asked.

"You get stuck if you land on them," Ben said.

"Stuck, huh?" *Like he seemed to have gotten himself stuck at the farm with Dixie and Ben and Nana.* Sam eyed Dixie.

She shrugged. "You'd have found out if you landed on one."

"Yeah. Sure. You want to tell me how I get *unstuck* if I land on one of those dots? Or is your strategy to keep me in the dark."

"Like I said, Sam. There is no strategy to this game. It's pure chance."

She sounded a little too smug for his liking. "Nothing's pure chance, Red. Give me the whole scoop."

She gave him a wily smile and a quick overview as Ben took his turn.

"Is that everything?" Sam asked.

"Everything *I* know about this game," Dixie said.

"I picked you a card, Tin Man," the kid said, clearly impatient with the adults and their chatter holding up the game.

"Thanks, Buddy." Sam said, moving his yellow gingerbread man forward.

Then Dixie drew a card that stuck her in the gooey gumdrops.

"So much for your shortcut, Red," Sam said, raising his eyebrows at her.

"A temporary setback," Dixie said. "Merely temporary."

Another turn and Sam was a scant two spaces behind Dixie.

He leaned in close to her. "That's my breath you feel on your neck, Red."

"You haven't caught me yet."

He and Ben were rounding the first bend by the time Dixie freed herself from the gumdrops. One more turn of good luck and Dixie jumped ahead of them both to Gramma Nutt's peanut brittle space.

She laughed and tickled Ben. To Sam she said, "Eat my dust."

"You are a competitive woman, Red."

"*Moi*? Why I haven't a competitive bone in my body."

"We'll see about that if I draw a skip forward card to Princess Lolly's lollipop."

He drew a card off the top of the pile, making a great show of palming it so no one else could see it—which sent Ben into a giggling fit. Dixie smiled at her son in her lap and then at Sam. He wanted to freeze the moment. He wanted to spend the rest of his life basking in the warmth of that smile. But that was impossible. He was nothing more than her current cause and one she would inevitably learn had deceived her. And once she learned the truth, she'd never smile his way again.

Sam peeked at the card in his hand and whooped.

"You didn't," Dixie said, clamping onto his forearm and forcing him to reveal the card he held in his palm. No pink square with a lollipop picture on it for him, no skip forward card.

Dixie swatted him playfully on the arm. "You're a big tease, Sam Ryan."

"Not a competitive bone in your body, huh?" he teased back.

Dixie snorted and drew her next card, only to break out in laughter. "It's a double blue. I'm lost in the Lollipop Woods."

"What a shame," Sam said.

"You could come find me," she purred.

If only she meant it the way it sounded. He'd gladly rescue her from the Lollipop Woods. Better yet, lose himself with her in that land of fantasy and never again have to face reality.

Not going to happen. Never.

"Dream on," he said, letting loose with a sinister laugh. Ben and I are going to trample you in our race to the finish."

"Don't trample Mommy."

Ben lifted watery eyes at him. Swell, he'd reduced Mickey's kid to tears.

Awkwardly, Sam ruffled Ben's hair. "Hey, Bud. I was just kidding."

Still, the kid gave him a wary look...which didn't lessen as they came out of the last turn from the Ice Cream Sea, Sam in the lead.

"Looks like Sam might win." Dixie flexed her knees, making Ben bounce in her lap.

But the kid didn't giggle. He just frowned. He clearly wasn't happy about that probable outcome.

Sam thought back to a time when he'd moped over something he'd wanted. How had Stuart handled it? Oh yeah. Stu had said, "Cater to the child's ploy and you weaken his character. Failing will teach him character."

A groove creased Sam's forehead and Dixie wondered what had put it there. He'd seemed to be having a good time, caught up in the fun of the game. He'd seemed relaxed.

Until now. Sam stared at the game board, the thought line in his brow deepening.

She took her turn, moved her game piece the requisite spaces to the color square on the board that matched the color square on the card she'd drawn. A mere two spaces. She sighed. "I can't catch a break."

"Can't catch a break," Ben mimicked as he studied the card he drew.

Then it was Sam's turn again. His long fingers slid the top card off the deck. He palmed it as he had the one he'd pretended catapulted him to the Lollipop Woods and studied the card in the cup of his hand. What did Sam Ryan see in that child's playing card that he appeared to be rubbing away with his thumb?

"If we were playing with a regular deck, I'd accuse you of trying to rub the spots off it," she said.

"Spots. Yeah," he murmured, his thumb stilling against the face of the card he held close to his chest as his eyes scanned the game board on the floor in front of them.

Then, an amazing transformation took place before her eyes. The lines crimping the outer corners of Sam's eyes smoothed and the groove in his brow disappeared. Even the tightness around his mouth mutated into a cockeyed grin as he announced,

"Seems I've been sent to the Molasses Swamp. I'm stuck."

Ben was the first to reach the Candy Castle and win the game. At which time, Sam fell onto his side, "Now I'll never get out of the Molasses Swamp."

Ben giggled.

"I'm stuck in the molasses," wailed Sam, rolling on his back and flailing his arms. "Help meeeee."

Ben scrambled out of his mother's lap, grabbed Sam by the hand, and tugged. But Sam pulled Ben down with him, tickled him in the ribs, and cackled like a demented crone. "Now you're stuck with me, my little wizard."

Ben giggled and Bear barked. Dixie watched them frolic as she gathered up the game pieces. When she picked up the stack of game cards, she turned them over. She'd kept track of how many cards had been played since Sam's hapless detour into the Molasses Swamp. She counted back from the bottom of the deck to the card that had been Sam's. It didn't match the *stuck in Molasses Swamp* square. Sam had let Ben win.

Damn, but the man was lovable…in far too many ways.

#

Sam sat on the porch roof outside his *borrowed* bedroom, back against the house beside Dixie's balcony, an arm dangling over his bent leg. He wished Mickey really was one of the stars above in the night sky. Maybe he'd have an answer to how he could move part of his allowance monthly into Dixie's account without Stuart catching on. He had to make sure Ben stayed with Dixie whose mothering was the kind any boy would flourish under. She was the kind of mother whose love a boy could be secure in.

The door from Dixie's bedroom opened and she stepped out onto the balcony.

"Evening," he said.

Wordlessly, she hitched a hip onto the balcony rail nearest him, her slick robe settling against her skin...like his hand longed to. "I know what you did."

He went cold despite the warmth of the night. Had she finally figured out Stuart had sent him?

She looked down at him, a smile curling across her lips. "You let Ben win the game."

He shrugged to cover his shiver of relief. "Ah, yeah. Four is too young to deal with the losing-makes-you-tougher lesson."

Her smile stretched at one corner. "And the creative way you handled the twin's discipline today... You're going to make a great dad someday."

Was she beginning to see him in a different light than that of one of her rejected animals? Was she beginning to see him as he saw her? He wanted to go to her, pull her into his arms, and take that kiss he'd wanted from the beginning. He wanted to promise to stay forever and take care of her and Ben. He wanted to declare his love.

Never going to happen.

The voice in his head was right. His promises weren't worth the breath it took to voice them and he was too much a coward to declare anything. He was no good for them. And when Dixie found out Stuart had sent him here, she'd know it, too. Now all he had to do was head off whatever feelings Dixie might have begun to entertain toward him. No sense letting the hurt become worse than it would already be for her.

"Thanks," he said, "but I'm hardly a good example of parenthood."

She started to protest but he cut her off.

"Remember, Red, I'm the guy who didn't show up for his cousin's funeral, a cousin as close to me as a brother."

"Sam..."

He raised a hand, silencing her. "You must have wondered why I wasn't there. And your wedding..."

"None of the Carrington side of the family showed for our wedding."

He grunted. "Fit right in with the rest of the snobs, don't I?"

"You're not a snob, Sam."

Sam gazed up at the sky. "He wanted me to be his best man. I couldn't even manage that."

"You were in Europe. It costs a lot to..."

"Pocket change for a Carrington," he cut in, keeping his gaze trained upward so he wouldn't have to see the disappointment in her face—in her beautiful eyes.

"Then what?" she pressed.

He swallowed hard. "I was afraid."

"Of what?" she asked, her voice quiet.

He stared at one particularly bright star. Did he tell her the truth; that he was afraid to be around that much happiness knowing none of it would ever be his?

He lowered his head and gazed into the darkness of the yard below. "I knew what Stuart thought of yours and Mickey's union. I was afraid of disappointing Stuart yet again."

"And Michael's funeral," she said, an odd edge

creeping into her voice, "were you afraid coming for the funeral would also disappoint Stuart?"

He closed his eyes and shook his head. "Now you're getting the true picture of me, Red. I'm nobody's role model, nobody's hero. I'm a coward."

A soft hand came down on his shoulder and he opened his eyes. Quietly, she said, "If you're going to lie, Sam, keep it consistent."

"I don't know what you're talking about."

"If you were trying *not* to disappoint Stuart, you'd have been at the funeral. Stuart was there. Besides, given all Michael told me about you, you were never much into to pleasing Stuart."

He turned his face away from her, his voice barely a whisper. "Like I said, I'm a coward."

Her fingers flexed against his shoulder. "I don't buy it."

He grimaced. "I failed Mickey in so many ways, most of all by staying away for so long. And then… Then, he was dead. After all the ways I'd disappointed him, I couldn't face his funeral—couldn't make myself look at him in a casket. I failed him even in his death."

Her fingers tightened on his shoulder. "Ah, Sam. I'd have given anything to be anywhere else that day, too."

CHAPTER TEN

She was supposed to be repulsed by his weakness—his cowardice. Instead, she'd empathized. That was enough to leave Sam sleepless through most of the night. The gray of false dawn had lit the sky by the time he'd finally fallen asleep. Then the cell phone in the pocket of his jeans he still wore vibrated.

Sam groaned. He could ignore it. But Stuart would just keep calling back, making it impossible for him to sleep. Besides, a glance at the alarm clock told him he was due in the kitchen shortly.

"Yeah," he grumbled as he answered the phone.

"I haven't heard from you all week," Stuart said without preamble. "Haven't you dug up something on that woman yet?"

"There's nothing to *dig up,*" Sam said through a yawn.

"What about the chat room stuff?"

Sam swung his feet to the floor and sat up, suddenly awake. "What chat room stuff?"

"The sex chat room where she was talking to the sausage guy."

"That was her addled grandmother. And how do you know about it anyway? You got someone hacking into her computer?"

"I don't care who it was doing the chatting, it was done from her computer. There's no way she can prove it wasn't her in that chat room."

He knew better than to tell the old man he'd been there, that he could testify Dixie wasn't the person chatting it up in a sex chat room. He sighed. "One conversation in a sex chat room won't make her an unfit parent in any court of law."

"There might be more," Stuart said. "Keep an eye on that woman, boy!"

"I'm definitely doing that."

"And didn't you just call her grandmother addled?"

Sam winced at the thought of having given his uncle any ammunition. "Maybe."

"Well, is she or isn't she?"

"What?"

"Addled!"

"Look, she's old. Her husband died a year ago. She's a little confused at times. The normal stuff."

"Is the child ever left alone with the grandmother?"

"He's with babysitters when Dixie works." *For the most part.*

"But there are times she leaves him alone with the grandmother, right?"

Sam opened his mouth, ready to out-right lie to Stuart. But something in the way his uncle phrased his question warned Sam a lie at this point would only damage his credibility with Stuart and he'd lose what little leverage he had to help Dixie.

"Yeah," he said, thinking of the few minutes he stayed with her each day before the twins arrived, of how it was normal for the twins to leave Ben in Nana's care on her good days, of how often Nana and Ben napped together.

"Document every time she leaves the boy with

the grandmother, if the grandmother falls asleep while watching him or wanders off and leaves him. Whatever could be construed as neglect or child endangerment."

"Will do," Sam said, scrubbing a hand down his face as if he could wipe away the lies—the deception—the dilemma he faced. If only he could tell Dixie what Stuart was doing. But to warn her would require he reveal how he knew what Stuart was up to. And that meant revealing why he'd come here.

#

It didn't feel cold enough. That's what Dixie was thinking as she stood in the walk-in cooler. One look at the salad greens and she didn't even have to step back out and check the temperature gauge to know the cooler had stopped working.

"No," she groaned out. "No," she said, her hands balling into fists. "Noooo," she wailed, raising her fists in the air.

The door whipped open behind her and Sam was halfway into the cooler before he stopped. "What's wrong?"

She dropped her fists in defeat. "Cooler went out." She shook her head. "The cooling system is the one place I didn't skimp. It's all new components. How could this happen?"

Sam stepped past her, opened the freezer door, and checked several packages. "It should be colder in there, too. But nothing's thawed."

"Yet," she said, slumping down on a stack of crates.

"Hey," he said, closing the freezer door and facing Dixie. "Where's that eternal optimist I've come to know?"

She smiled weakly up at him. "Sometimes she gets tired of keeping it all together."

Sam pushed the cooler door open, giving her shoulder a squeeze as he passed. "Maybe it's just a blown circuit."

"We can hope." A blown circuit breaker didn't fix ruined food, but his touch nudged her normally optimistic self, reminding her how nice it was to have someone else to face a disaster with her.

That he was back in the cooler before the door fully shut told her he didn't have to go to the circuit box to find their problem. "The controls were turned off. I turned them back on."

She jerked upright. "That can't be."

But as she said the words, she heard the cooler system kick in.

She looked at Sam. "Were the twins in this part of the kitchen yesterday?"

"I never noticed them skulking around the cooler area."

"Ben's too short to reach the controls," she said.

"And he wasn't in here."

She sighed. "Maybe Nana…"

"Figuring out who and why we can deal with later," Sam said, pulling a small notebook and pencil from his t-shirt pocket. "Right now we've got to figure out what we need to replace for breakfast."

"Yeah," she said, circling the small space scanning the racks of ruined perishables. "Eggs and milk for sure. All dairy and greens. The prepped fruits need to be tossed."

"The un-cut fruits are fine," Sam said. "Same for the whole vegetables."

"It's too early to call a supplier. I'll have to hit the

all night grocery. Maybe Harry will sell me some supplies wholesale."

Sam raised an eyebrow at her. "Harry?"

"The manager. My older brothers hung out with him when we visited Nana and Pupa."

"Red," he said, giving her a side-long look. "Given your charm, I have no doubt Harry will give you wholesale price on whatever you buy from him and not because he hung out with your brothers."

She waved him off. "I believe you catch more flies with honey than vinegar. Besides, we both know one man who doesn't buy into my *charm*."

"Stuart," Sam said.

"Let's get the spoiled stuff out of this cooler." She started to reach for a tray of eggs.

"No." He handed her the list he'd made. "You shop. I'll clean out the cooler. I'll also call Annie and see if she can come in early to help prep."

Another couple pounds of stress fell from Dixie's shoulders. It really was nice to have a partner.

As if she didn't have enough proof of that fact, when she returned with eggs, milk, cheeses, greens, and whatever else they'd determined unsafe for restaurant consumption, she found a kitchen buzzing with activity.

"Eggs," Annie all but squealed, running to her and snatching a tray off the stack Dixie carried. "Girls," she said to the twins, "help Dixie bring in the groceries."

The girls promptly put down their pairing knives amidst the unruined fruit they'd been cubing, rinsed their hands, and joined her in restocking her perishables. She gave them a "well done" and several "thank yous", biting her tongue when she really wanted to ask the usually devilish now turned angelically helpful girls if their change in persona had anything to do with turning off her cooler.

"Is that cinnamon I smell?" Dixie asked as she paused on one pass to the cooler.

"Cinnamon rolls are proofing," Annie said.

"How'd you manage to make rolls without milk, eggs, and butter?" Dixie asked.

Annie's eyes slanted in Sam's direction. Without breaking his rhythm of breaking eggs into a big bowl, Sam glanced up at her. "I used canned milk, thawed some of the frozen butter, and, as luck would have it, Annie had just bought an eighteen count carton of eggs. It was enough to set one batch to rising."

"A carton of never-been-opened eggs out of my fridge isn't going to get us in trouble with the health inspector, is it?" Annie asked, her usual bluster absent.

"All the inspector looks for is graded eggs and, if they came from a store, they were graded. Better yet, I have a chef, a cousin, and a pair of second cousins who jumped in when I needed help to insure my customers are served the same quality food I always serve them. Thank you, all of you."

But the eyes she looked into were those of the one who'd taken charge when she'd been on the brink of a minor melt-down—the one who'd prompted her into action and organized her ever ready supporters for further help. Sam.

#

Sam stepped from the shower, grinning. He'd been a grinning fool all day and all because, when Dixie had thanked everyone, she'd looked at him like he was her hero.

Sure, she'd looked at him like that before, had even called him her hero. But he was actually beginning to believe he could be her hero. Hadn't he taken over the disaster of the turned-off cooler, sending her for supplies while he cleaned up and summoned the troops? And he had stepped in between Weston and Ben without a second thought the day the woman had grabbed Ben for touching her monkey. He'd even volunteered to be Dixie's chef until she found a replacement. Best of all, he hadn't run when the going got tough. And it'd gotten tough a couple of times.

Whistling, he toweled himself dry. The restaurant had run like a finely oiled machine the rest of the day.

He squeezed the excess water from his hair, swiped the towel across the steamed up mirror, and looked himself in the eye, something he hadn't done in some time.

"Yesiree, Sam my man. You are finally doing someone some good."

He shaved, slipped on his jeans, balled up the rest of his clothes in his fist, and stepped into the hall. Dixie's door was open. He'd have to pass it on the way to his. He smiled.

But the sight of Dixie slumped forward in her desk chair, chin propped in an upraised palm as she stared at the computer screen chased away his good spirit.

"Pretty late for you to be working on the books," he said from the doorway.

She glanced up and the worry lines eased some from her forehead. "Couldn't sleep anyway," she said.

Here he'd been feeling good all day for being her hero while Dixie still had to deal with the loss of spoiled food. He wanted to do something to lift her spirits, but he had nothing.

He glanced at her empty bed. "Where's the Wizard?"

"Bunking with Nana for the night."

"Aaah." His gaze ricocheted from her empty bed to Ben's bedroom door and back to her. "Guess I'll get to bed then."

He took a step away from her door only to stop in mid-stride. There was something that might help. He turned back to her. "I was thinking... Not that I want to overstep... Not that this is the right time to even bring it up."

She swiveled her chair toward him and gave him a patient smile. "Just spit it out, Sam."

"You've got your menu pretty well streamlined, but I've got some ideas on how you can make some of the dishes more cost effective."

"I'm always open to suggestions, especially from someone who's worked a professional kitchen. What do you have in mind?"

"For example, your tuna, crushed pineapple, and chopped pecan salad could be served as a scoop on the side instead of already loaded into the croissant. It'll elevate the look of the plate as well as shave off a bit of prep time for your chef."

"Great idea," she said. "Let's sit down tomorrow and go over all your ideas."

She swiveled back to her computer screen, the message clear. *Thanks for the help but I have more immediate concerns to deal with.*

"Goodnight then," he said.

"Night," she said, giving him a finger wave.

He should move on—go to bed. But... She

looked so worried—so alone in front of that computer screen.

"Is there something I could help you with now?" he asked.

"Not unless you can squeeze more from a nickel than I've been able to," she said.

"Mind if I take a look?"

She glanced up and smiled. "Fresh eyes are welcome, Sam. Come on in."

He stepped to the side of her chair and scanned the screen in front of her. He already knew what he'd find in her bank accounts. The benefits of his earlier snooping.

"I need money to pay for this morning's ruined supplies," she said. "And, as you can see, my available cash isn't much."

"Insurance?" he queried, reaching over her and scrolling through her accounts just in case there was something he'd missed earlier.

"To save money, I went with a higher deductible," she said, bringing him back to her reality.

He nodded and pulled up the payroll screen. He could think of one place where she could find the money she needed right now. He scrolled down until the cursor flashed on his name. "Here's one expense you can skip."

She looked up at him. "Are you suggesting I put off paying you, Sam?"

"No," he said, looking her in those incredible blue eyes he'd been avoiding. "I'm suggesting you don't pay me at all."

The eyes flashed surprise and she all but sputtered, "I can't *not* pay you, Sam!"

He straightened—backed a step, needing to put

space between them before he hauled her to her feet and into his arms and begged her to take what he had merely by virtue of being a Carrington. "I don't need the money."

"But you worked for that pay. You work harder than any chef I've ever had. You deserve it."

"Nice of you to say. But I live off a trust fund, Red. I don't need the money."

"That's not the point."

He placed his hands on the chair's armrests and leaned close. "I know. But it's one way I can help."

"You already helped by stepping in when my chef walked out on me. You helped keep me from totally losing my cool today."

"Believe me, Red, money is the easiest way in the world I can help you. In fact..." he tightened his grip on her chair as though anticipating she would try and flee at what he next said. "I want to wipe out your debt. I may have to do it in installments..."

"You're going to do *what*?" She leaned at him, but didn't seem to be in flight mode. Of course not. That wasn't how she operated. That was his modus operandi.

He released the chair. "I'm going to wipe out your debt. I can't do it with one big check. That'll red flag Stuart. But smaller amounts..."

"I can't let you do that," she said.

"You can't stop me."

"No. I can't—I won't take a handout."

"This is no handout, Red. This is Mickey's screw-up cousin trying to make things right for his family. You wouldn't be so strapped if you hadn't had to fight Stuart over Ben."

She shook her head. "I don't feel right about

taking money from you."

"From me? Or from anyone with Carrington blood in his veins?"

"What are you implying, Sam?"

"I'm implying nothing, Red. I'm saying you're gun-shy about taking anything from any member of Stuart's family. I'm saying you're afraid it'll feed into his impression of you."

"I don't care what Stuart thinks of me."

"Yes, you do. You care because he's Ben's grandfather and because he was the father of the man you loved."

He'd hit the nail on the head. He could see it in her eyes. But there was more.

"And you're afraid taking money from me might give him fodder in his case to prove you unfit to support Ben."

She swallowed hard.

"Don't look so scared, Red. He'll never get Ben away from you because there's no way in creation anyone could see you as anything but the best mother in the world."

She sank back in her chair, tears glazing her eyes. "Oh, Sam. What do I say?"

"Say 'Yes. Thank you.'"

She shook her head. "I'll give-in on the paycheck, but I can't let you pay off my debt."

"Why?" he asked.

"I have to make a go of this on my own."

"Which you would easily be doing if not for Stuart fighting you."

An indulgent smile lifted her lips. "Life is great for handing us lemons, Sam. Our choices are to let the lemons sour us or to take those lemons and make lemonade out of them."

"Don't let pride get in the way of accepting my help, Red," he pleaded.

"I'm a mother, Sam. I need—I want to set a good example for Ben. It's all about integrity."

Integrity. Something he had none of. No wonder he found it hard to accept her reasoning. But he could still help her on some level and that was something.

"So, it's a *no* to wiping out your debt, but a *yes* to my not taking a paycheck."

She nodded. He sighed.

"You drive a hard bargain, Red."

#

Was she being overly proud, not to take his handout? This was the family homestead, Nana's home on the chopping block if the restaurant failed. The farm wasn't hers to lose. Then there was Ben's future, his security.

Sam set a plate of quiche in front of her, a beautiful spring greens salad beside it lightly dressed with raspberry vinaigrette.

"Beautifully plated," Dixie said, and glanced at Nana and Ben across from her on the bench of the little table under the back stairs. They were already digging into their quiche.

"I'm thinking we could add quiche to the Sunday brunch," Sam said. "Start it as a special. See how it goes over. It's cost effective to make, especially if we offer a fruit of the season cup in place of the salad for those who'd prefer fruit to greens."

She took a bite of the quiche, chewing slowly so as to take in every nuance of the dish.

"It could eventually replace one of the omelets on the menu, thus cutting down on chef labor," Sam said.

"The flavor is divine. But a quiche is a more involved dish to make than an omelet," she said.

"But it can be made up ahead of time," Sam said, spinning the lone chair from under the end of the table and sitting straddling it. "Or, during the slow periods between services."

She nodded. "Thus relieving my chef's duties during the busy times."

"That's the idea."

"And the more quiche served, the more time my chef has to cook made-to-order orders and the quicker my customers get served."

"You got it," he said. "So, what do you think?"

"I think I'd like another piece," Nana said, holding up her empty plate.

Sam grinned, Ben crammed another bite into his mouth, and Dixie laughed.

"My Sunday brunch clientele are the type who'd like quiche," she said. "Add it to the weekly lunch menu and I could increase my lunch clientele."

"I've got half a dozen winning quiche recipes already picked out for you."

"Whoa," Dixie said. "Let's not go overboard."

"We won't as long as we feature just one a day."

"*We?* You planning to stick around and bake quiches for a while, Sam?" She raised a questioning eyebrow at him.

He blinked away and shrugged. "Whatever the future holds, you'll at least have an arsenal of quiche recipes that'll keep your customers coming back for more."

Not quite the answer she'd hoped for. But ever grateful for whatever good came into her life, she placed a hand on the back of his. "That's very generous of you, Sam."

"Just trying to be helpful."

She smiled at him, willing him to see how valuable his help was. "You've gone above and beyond anything I could have, or even should have expected of you."

He shifted in his seat, shrugged, and muttered something about it being the least he could do.

The least he could do? He made it sound almost like he owed her.

"I better put together a tray for Ms. Weston and bring it up to her," he said, removing his hand from under hers.

"I'll do it," she said, sliding off the bench.

"You've been on your feet all day," he said, rising from his chair.

"And you haven't?" she retorted, turning to the cupboard.

"I'll do it," Nana said, scooting around them and collecting a plate from the cupboard.

Sam placed himself between Nana and the quiche on the counter. "No. I can do it."

"Of course you *can*," Nana said, sidestepping him. "The issue is I've got a slice of that quiche in my belly while you have eaten yet."

"But—"

"Not to mention you both have worked your backsides off all day while I pretty much laid around."

"Nana, please," Dixie said, from beside Sam, her chest tight with pride in how readily he'd jumped to help with Nana.

Nana shook a finger at her. "I'm addled girl, but I can still walk and carry things. And if a bit of milk gets sloshed onto the salad, it'll serve that cantankerous biddy right for expecting to be waited on hand and foot."

Dixie exchanged a look with Sam. He raised questioning eyebrows at Dixie. Under his breath, he asked, "Does she get like this often?"

"This is new."

They watched Nana plate the quiche, salad, and a muffin. Plate, glass of milk, silverware, and napkin added to a tray, Nana headed toward the steps. From the bottom of the stairway, Dixie and Sam watched her climb the stairs. When she climbed out of sight, they listened, on the ready should they hear a crash.

A couple door rattling knocks echoed down the stairwell.

"Is she kicking the door?" Sam asked.

Dixie clapped a hand over her mouth to keep from laughing and nodded.

"Here's your supper, you lazy cow," Nana said, her voice reverberating down the stairwell.

Dixie fell against Sam, burying her face in his chest to muffle her laughter. He hugged her, laughing into her hair. It was a fun moment, a release of tension. As long as they could still laugh, Dixie knew everything would be all right.

#

Holding each other and laughing at the bottom of the stairs was a moment Sam wished would never end. But, in his experience, all good things came to an end. Stuart's phone call that night had proven it. The volume of the old man's rants at his failure to yield anything useful to him had been so loud, he'd drawn Ben's Pooh Bear bedspread over his head in fear Dixie would hear Stuart from her bedroom.

So, here he was, torturing himself by tossing bales of hay from a loft in a dusty old barn just to be near Dixie.

"That's the last of them," he called down to her.

"Great," she said. "For once I won't be scrambling at the last minute to clear my loft for the early hay harvest, thanks to you, Sam."

He smiled, Dixie's words crowding out Stuart's and infusing him with super hero energy. All puffed up with pride, he grabbed the uprights of the loft ladder and vaulted from the loft, booted feet gripping the outer edges of the uprights. But, as he slid toward the barn floor macho hero-style, something went wrong. A stab of reality, courtesy of an old wood ladder.

He hit the floor with his heels. The next thing he knew, he was flat on his back on the straw strewn floor, too embarrassed to utter a single *ouch*.

Dixie was instantly on her knees at his side, hovering over him as he lay there. "Did you hit your head?" she asked, fingers sliding through his hair and across his scalp. Searching for bumps, no doubt.

"There's nothing wrong with my head except for it making some stupid decisions," he said, sitting up, breaking contact with her fingers in spite of how much he enjoyed their exploration.

"How about your back?" she asked, running a hand down his spine.

He pushed himself up onto his feet, grumbling, "The only thing hurting is my ego and my hand."

"Your hand?" Instantly she had the hand he'd waved cradled in both hers.

"It's only a sliver," he said, attempting to pull free only for her to tighten her grip on him.

"What were you doing, sliding down the ladder like that?"

"Trying to impress you."

She poked around the sliver and he jumped. "You impress me every day, Sam."

He grunted.

She glanced up at him. "I'm beginning to think you keep playing that poor Sam card just to get me to say nice things to you." She released his hand and headed toward the door facing the house.

Bereft of her letting him go, he went after her. "I didn't. I don't. If I do, I don't mean to."

She stopped just short of the open door and faced him, a soft smile on her lips. "I was teasing, Sam."

She lifted a first-aid kit from a shelf by the door. She hadn't been leaving at all.

"Come stand in the light, Sam."

He moved to the doorway. She stepped in front of him, her back to him, and tucked the arm of his wounded hand against her side. "Can't take a chance my favorite chef's hand will get infected."

"Favorite chef?" He laughed. "I'm your only chef."

"At the moment," she said, gripping the sliver with the tweezers from the first-aid kit and easing it from his palm.

She stepped away from him, leaving his body cool in the places where hers had touched his.

"Someone answered one of your ads?" he asked.

"We've got two to interview," she said, returning with a bottle of peroxide and motioning him to hold out his hand.

"This'll be cold and bubbly, but shouldn't sting."

"Shouldn't?"

She peeked up at him through her lush lashes. "Even if it does, I can't risk my favorite chef's hands to infection."

Favorite, but soon to be replaced chef. Soon to be no longer needed by her. Her with hair the color of sunshine and a smile that could warm a man clear to his soul. What would he do once she no longer needed him? Where would he go?

Who could replace her? No woman on earth. Dixie Rae Carrington was a one of a kind, standing there holding his hand—blowing on his palm where a splinter had once been. He knew, in that moment, he couldn't leave without knowing what those lips felt like against his.

Gently, he knuckled her chin up until her eyes met his—until he saw in them she understood what he was asking her. Her lips parted and she leaned in, lifting her mouth as he lowered his toward hers.

He'd meant to take just a sampling. Just enough to create a memory he could dream of for the rest of his misbegotten life. But she rose into the kiss, pressed back—parted her lips further.

Their tongues met, tasting, teasing, each inviting the other into the ancient dance of two people in need. Her fingers wove through his hair, holding them in the kiss. His hands stroked down her back, holding them in close embrace.

When their mouths broke for breath, she let her head fall back, baring her throat to him. Without hesitation, he accepted her invitation. He tasted her sweet, dust-coated flesh. Small gasps escaped her and he traveled lower into the *v* of her t-shirt, kissing and nipping his way, listening for response.

She moaned.

He slid one hand up her side and stroked her breast with his thumb. Her breast rose with a deep breath as she inhaled a throaty, "Yes."

He ached for more of her and, if the way she slid one leg up the outside of his until they were crotch to crotch was any indication, she wanted everything he did. He recaptured her mouth and half carried, half rolled her onto the hay bales he'd thrown from the loft that now littered the aisle of the barn.

Somewhere in his lust drunk mind the prickliness of the hard-packed bales registered. But she'd wrapped her legs around his waist and held him close, all tongue and soft curves beneath him.

Later, they'd fix that less than comfortable problem of scratchy hay, their bodies seemed to say as they wrestled their way behind a pile of bales. She was on top of him now, legs splayed to either side of his hips, thick lashes fanned across her cheeks from her closed eyes. She removed the clip from her ponytail, her hair falling about her shoulders like golden fire. She moved her hips, the pressure almost painful for him, but the guttural groan rising from her throat—the scent of her need made it worth it.

Then she reached down, gathered the hem of her t-shirt and peeled it up over her head. He cupped her high, round breasts, weighing the bounty within the slick fabric of her bra.

"You're beauti—"

She pressed a finger to his lips, silencing him, and slid her hands under his tee, pushing it up. Leaning forward, she laid her cheek against his bare skin, her breasts tightening against his stomach as she inhaled.

He stroked her hair. She purred and rolled her

head, her tongue tasting his skin, her lips nipping at his nipples. Her fingers slid up his sides and her arms pressed into him as though she couldn't get enough of his flesh. He wanted more, too.

He sat up, taking her mouth with his, drawing her legs around his hips. Her heat enveloped his throbbing core. He cupped her behind and her arms tightened around his neck. They moaned into each other's mouths. Fingers scrabbled for fasteners and bells went off.

But the bells weren't inside his head. The vibration against the palm cupping her behind confirmed the source of the ringing.

"Your phone," he panted against her lips.

"Ignore it," she panted back, fingers struggling at the snap on his jeans.

"We have to separate to get these pants off," he said, nibbling his way to her neck.

"Yes. No. Not yet," she said, hugging him to her. "Hold me for a moment."

He drew his arms across her back in spite of the need tearing at him.

"I haven't been held by a man like this since..."

He understood why she let her words trail. He knew whose arms had last held her like a lover. He didn't want *him* here between them at this very moment.

He tightened his hold on her, his lips pressed to the tender skin just below her ear. He stroked her back and shifted between her legs just enough to remind her she was a woman well desired. She rolled her hips—rolled her heat across his throbbing ache. They both groaned and she began to move back, her hand reaching down between them.

"Mommy, mommy."

Dixie was off him before he even fully registered Ben's voice.

"What, sweetie?" she asked, head raised above a hay bale.

"Uncle Roman's on the phone. He said he called you on your cell phone and you didn't answer."

"Tell him—" She looked at Sam who remained out of sight from Ben in their would-be love-nest, a bevy of emotions rolling across her face. "—I'll call him back."

Sam held up her t-shirt, mouthing, "Go."

CHAPTER ELEVEN

It had taken a full five minutes to convince Roman nothing was wrong; and her body hadn't stopped tingling the entire time. As soon as she hung up she wanted to run back to the barn and take up where she and Sam had left off. But she had questions.

She took out her cell, ducked into one of the restaurant dining rooms where she'd have privacy and hit the quick dial for her most frequently called number.

"Annie, can you talk?"

"Sure."

"He kissed me."

"He who?"

"Sam. And I kissed him back."

"All right!"

"Is it, Annie? Is it right?"

"Let me see. He's cute. He's fun. He's warm-blooded. Duh!"

"Come on, Annie. He's a cousin."

"Only by marriage and you're not married anymore."

Dixie twisted the wedding band still on the third finger of her left hand. *Not married any more.* She'd come to grips with that fact long ago. She'd even had an erotic dream or two in recent months. But the lover in those dreams had been faceless. Sam Ryan wasn't faceless. He was…

"He's Michael's cousin."

"And you want me to play Dr. Freud," Annie said.

"Something like that," Dixie said, gazing across the room, through the window at the barn.

She heard Annie send her girls out to play before continuing. "Did he drool?"

"What?"

"When he kissed you, did he drool?" Annie asked.

"No!"

"Did he mash his teeth against yours? Did he draw blood? Did he leave his eyes open?"

"No. No. And I don't know. I closed my eyes."

"Okay. We've established that you were into it."

"Annie! I wouldn't be calling you if I wasn't having a problem with this."

"Aaah, to have such a problem."

"Knock it off. Lou worships the ground you walk on and you love it."

Annie sighed. "Yeah."

"Annie, are you fantasizing about him right now?"

"Just a minute."

"He's been home from a run for a week. You shouldn't have to fantasize."

Was that a kissing sound she heard?

"You're not fantasizing. You're kissing him right now, aren't you?" Dixie demanded more than asked.

Annie panted out, "He leaves tonight on his next cross country haul and, for some reason, every time I send the kids outside he thinks—"

"I get the picture. Just tell me what to do about Sam and I'll let you off the phone so you two can take it to the bedroom."

"Go for it."

"But—"

"But nothing. Michael loved you and would want you to be happy, right?"

"Right."

"And, from everything you've told me about Michael and Sam, Michael loved his cousin and wanted him happy, right?"

"Right."

"If you and Sam getting together makes the both of you happy…"

"But Sam's not an in-it-for-the-long-haul kind of guy."

Annie's voice turned serious. "Is commitment what you want from him?"

"I-I don't know. I just don't think I can rely on him to stick around."

"Then let him be your transition guy."

"Transition guy?"

"The man who comes between the love of your life and your next serious relationship."

"I know what a transition guy is," she said, but tasting the two words on her tongue and finding them less than sweet.

"Have some fun."

"I have fun."

"Not the *adult* kind."

True.

"Let Sam take a little of the pressure off. Use Sam to get back in the saddle, so to speak."

"Yeah, thanks," she said, slow to disconnect, knowing this issue was far from resolved.

She'd never been the *fling* sort of girl. But then

she'd never before been attracted to a fling sort of guy. Maybe it was time. Maybe it was serendipitous that Sam came along when she needed him and not just to be her chef. Hadn't Michael always said, "Wait until you meet, Sam. You'll love him?"

#

"What the hell am I doing?" Sam asked himself.

The hay bales on which he sat pricked the backs of his legs and his body still tingled everywhere Dixie had touched him, and even some places she hadn't. She was Mickey's widow. He had no business kissing her. Maybe she'd had the same thought in the moment reality intruded on them…when she'd pushed herself out of his arms.

But the fact remained, he had kissed her.

And he wanted to kiss her again…everywhere.

That's why he'd fought the urge ever since coming to the farm. He'd known, once he let his lips have their way, the rest of him would want equal opportunity. And since one kiss was not going to be enough…

Sam groaned. "Now what am I going to do?"

The old barn creaked around him. He lifted his chin and peered up through the dusty sunbeams, past the patchy hayloft, at the ceiling high above. "What am I going to say to her, Mickey? I want you in every way a man wants a woman?"

Sunlight streamed in through the cracks between the ancient boards and around the hay doors just under the peak of the roof casting the trusses in an ethereal haze.

"Damn it, Mickey. I know she's your wife. But she needed kissing and you weren't here to do the job."

A tomb-like silence answered him.

Sam blinked. "Okay. I wanted to kiss her."

More silence.

"This can't be what you intended when you looked at me through the kid's eyes and made me stay."

The barn groaned.

"And don't give me that business about her and the kid needing my help. They've got family. Lots of family. Family that's already helping them, watching out for them. Family that will be here come July 4th. Just a few weeks away. What if they take one look at me and see me for what I am?"

Sam listened for some sign that Mickey agreed. But he heard nothing in return except the settling of old timbers.

"I'm no good for them," he argued. "You know I'm the family screw up. The Carrington black sheep. I run when the going gets tough."

Something skittered along a truss overhead. A mouse? A squirrel?

The ghost of a brother-like cousin?

"Okay, it's been tough around here and I haven't run...yet."

Why, the old barn whispered around him?

"Because I owe you, Mickey."

Why, creaked the aged timbers?

"Because I promised her."

Why, whistled the wind through the cracks between boards?

"Because... Because..."

A memory of Ben running to him when he'd been frightened by a shadow in his sandbox wrapped itself around Sam. It made him feel warm and...needed.

Sam scanned the silent rafters. "He needed me only because his macho uncles weren't here at the moment to chase away an imaginary flying monkey."

He squinted through the dusty air at the highest peak of the roof. "And Dixie needs me only because her jerk of a chef ran out on her."

He peered into the deepest shadow where roof and walls met, waiting for Mickey's answer.

What came to him was the image of Mickey's eyes looking back at him from Ben the night he'd arrived at The Farmhouse. What bounded across his brain was Checkers the bunny and Bear the dog hopping one after the other beneath the apple tree in the grassy oasis in the middle of the circular driveway the day he'd tried to sneak off. What made him swipe from his brow raindrops that weren't there was the memory of rainfall that had come along at the very moment he'd needed an excuse to stay at Dixie's farmhouse.

Had all that been about only Ben?

Sam thought about the way he'd peered up at Dixie from the ground that day before the rain had begun. Mickey knew him better than anyone else. Mickey would have known what he was thinking…on the ground…staring up at Dixie.

And still, Mickey had sent the rain to keep him here.

Or had he?

Sam shook off the doubt. Of course Mickey would do whatever it took to keep him from leaving, because noble Mickey put his family ahead of all else.

Mickey who had loved him like a brother.

Who entrusted him with the tasks of watching out for his son and taking his place with his widow.

There was a thread out of place in the tapestry of Sam's reasoning, a wispy, blue angora-like thread that curled into a fuzzy ball in the corner of his brain like a bad dust bunny. But he didn't want to see the flaw in his conclusion, that the rain—that all of it was likely nothing more than coincidence…or his own wishful longings.

He folded his hands behind his head and flopped back into the hay to contemplate a happily-ever-after future with Dixie. Instead, he came face to face with the grizzle-bearded Rocky staring down on him from the next tier of hay bales.

Sam bolted upright, faced the goat, and reflexively rubbed his backside where the ill-mannered goat had butted him the first time they'd met. He'd argued why he should leave. He'd explored all the reasons why he should stay. But, what stared him in the eye right now was the one reason he had no business considering a forever after with Dixie.

Softhearted Dixie who'd given a home to a blind pony, dry cow, and three-legged llama had also rescued a goat because no one else wanted to deal with his butting bad habit. She'd taken them all in and cared for them. The used up. The unwanted.

And the outcasts like Rocky…and him.

Poor Sam. She'd spoken those words to him the day a run-away rabbit had thwarted his attempt to sneak off. They echoed through his hollow chest now.

Poor Sam. Abandoned by his father. Ignored by his mother. Cast out by his uncle. How could he have forgotten that he was just another of her causes.

It crossed his mind to argue that, when he'd kissed her, she'd kissed him back—that a woman doesn't kiss a man like that out of pity. But surely a young widow starved for passion could have easily gotten caught up in the moment. Maybe her was yet no more than answer to another need of hers.

He peered deep into the goat's unblinking eyes, his suspiciously blue eyes. Mickey would have known it all, too. Mickey the responsible one. The noble one.

The one who had looked out for him most of his growing up years.

Sam looked deep into the blue eyes watching him, eyes that suspicious cool shade of Mickey-blue. "Did you plan this? Did you think poor Sam needs them as much as they need...*someone*?" He thought of the restaurant Mickey had bought for Dixie with plans to make him Head Chef.

"Damn it, Mickey. There's only one thing worse for me than making them dependent on me and that's making me need them."

The goat bleated.

"You're planning my life for me, Mickey. Just like your father tried to do."

Deftly, the goat hopped from one hay bale to the next.

"If you think this will make me stick around and take care of Dixie and Ben for you, forget it!"

The goat bounded several tiers to the floor.

"This isn't fair to me."

The goat lowered his head the way he did when he was about to butt something. Mickey driving his point home?

Sam fisted his hands at his sides. "Damn you, Mickey. This isn't fair to her."

As if an omen, Rocky raised his head, turned, and hopped out the Dutch door into the paddock.

#

Dixie was halfway through the living room when she saw Sam crossing the yard toward the house, his shoulders forward, his strides long. She'd never seen Sam move with such purpose. Had he grown impatient waiting for her to return? Was he coming to finish what they'd started in the barn? Her stomach did a little flip and her lips tingled at the idea of more kisses.

She pushed the screen door open and stepped out onto the porch just as his foot hit the bottom step. She met him at the edge of the porch as he cleared the top step, their gazes locked.

She wanted to trace his set jaw with her fingertip. She wanted to tease apart his lips with her tongue. She wanted to sink her fingers into his thick, dark hair and pull his face into her cleavage.

She settled for plucking a shaft of straw from his temple.

"Don't," he said, catching her by the wrist and stilling her hand.

The tightness, the hoarseness of his tone confused her. "Sam?"

His gaze shifted to the side. She followed its trajectory and found Miss Weston hunched in a wicker chair, her ever present bag of a purse in her lap and its resident stuffed monkey pointed in their direction. So, he was concerned about what other people might think. Dixie peeked up at Sam through lowered lashes.

"I was only removing a piece of straw." She twirled the shaft in front of his face then flicked it away.

He wheeled around and towed her down the steps toward the far side of the house. She liked the firmness in his grip and decisiveness in his stride. She liked that he'd taken command of the moment—that, for a change, she didn't have to be the one in the lead. She'd missed this about Michael...even though he'd had a tendency to take charge too often.

She tripped around the corner of the porch after Sam, brushing at the hay chaff dusting the back of his t-shirt. "I didn't think we'd rolled around enough to cause this."

He released her just long enough to peel the shirt off over his head. The skin of his back wasn't bronzed the way Michael's had been, Michael who'd spent his summer leisure hours boating on Lake Michigan and his winter vacations diving in the Caribbean...before he'd married her. But Sam had sturdy shoulders and a strong, straight spine. She touched that track of backbone with a fingertip.

He groaned and glanced across the backyard toward where Ben played in his sandbox. The next thing she knew, he was ushering her ahead of himself through the service door to the restaurant kitchen, his hand warm where it touched her on the shoulder, her elbow, the small of her back. She wanted to lean into that contact. But, his hand moved with a nervous energy, not lingering on any one part of her body long enough for her to sink into its support.

Inside, she laughed, faced Sam, and placed a hand on his forearm. "What are you so nerved up about, Sam?"

He brought his hand down on the back of hers, pinning it from moving further up his arm, and he said, "We need to talk."

There were deep lines crimped around the bittersweet chocolate-brown eyes. Dixie sobered.

"Because Ben almost caught us kissing? Because I jumped out of your arms when Ben burst in on us? I was startled." She leaned into Sam, close enough to smell the musty, masculine scent of barn and man. "That's all."

"Red—"

"Really, Sam. It isn't going to hurt Ben to see us kissing," she said, taking him by the hand and drawing him deeper into the kitchen. "It would be good for him to see how a man and a woman show affection for each other."

He blew an exasperated sounding sigh and let go of her. Maybe she was reading him wrong. Maybe Sam didn't want to *talk* about anything at all. Maybe he wanted to find some place private as badly as she did.

"I can think of better places to finish what we started in the barn, Sam," she said, turning in front of him and leaning back against the prep table.

His gaze dipped to where her hip contacted the stainless steel table and he groaned. She raised an eyebrow at him. "Has my chef been harboring lascivious thoughts about the use of his kitchen?"

She caught him by the belt buckle and tugged him closer. He folded both his hands over her fist and held himself away from her.

"We can disinfect everything when we're done," she all but purred.

Still, he resisted. "I shouldn't have kissed you."

The little electrical charge tingling up her arm sputtered. He really did want to talk and she was beginning to think she knew about what. Or, more specifically, *who*. Good thing she'd called Annie with the same concern and had the answer to Sam's dilemma.

"Why, Sam? Because I'm Michael's widow?"

Sam winced. Why did she have to sound so reasonable, so gentle...so sexy?

"Sam?" she probed in that foggy voice that made his nerve endings beg for more. "Do you believe Michael loved you?"

He grit his teeth. "Yeah."

Hand still on his belt buckle, she pulled him closer. Why couldn't she just accept that he shouldn't have kissed her and let him go?

"Don't you think he wanted you happy?" she murmured against his chin.

Damn.

"Sure."

"Do you believe he loved me and would want me to be happy?" she whispered against his cheek.

"Yes, but—"

"Didn't kissing me make you happy?" she purred against the corner of his mouth. "It made me happy." She breathed the words across his lips in a way that made him want to accept the invitation of her parted lips—to tip his head, part his lips, and fit his mouth to hers. It would be so easy to stop fighting the press of her breasts against the backs of his hands—to sink into her warmth.

To slide his hands around her, take her in his arms, and—

Her lips brushed his...so like how his had hers that first tenuous testing touch...in the barn. He jerked back from her.

"Damn it, Red. I can't make you happy. Not the way Mickey wants you happy. I'm not the kind of guy who sticks around for the long haul."

One corner of her mouth twitched and she tilted her head in a way that made her have to peer up at him through her thick lashes. "Is that the problem, Sam? You think I'm expecting a commitment because you kissed me? I'm not."

"You're not a one-night stand sort of girl, Red."

"You don't know that," she countered. Still, that flirtatious smile of hers ratcheted down a notch. Whether she realized it or not, she wanted more from him than a fling.

He wheeled away from her. Just looking at her was more than he could bear. "Damn it, Red, I'm not your hero!"

"Sam Ryan, you are a fraud."

Finally, she'd figured him out. She'd caught on to what he was. He was glad he wasn't facing her—that he didn't have to see the disappointment cloud her beautiful eyes. He could just walk through that swinging door between the kitchens and out the back door to the garage where his bike waited for him. He could be gone in less than sixty seconds. He took one step toward the door.

"You call yourself the family black sheep," she said behind him, "but you're not nearly as bad as you'd have people think."

"Not nearly as bad?" He pivoted on his heel—faced her. "You have no idea how bad I can be."

"Stop buying into what Stuart would have you thinking of yourself."

He shook his head. "You have a blind spot where I'm concerned because you see good in everyone—everything. I'm just another of your damaged rescues."

"There is good in everyone," she said, advancing

on him.

He shook his head.

She took his face in her hands, held it so he had to look her in the eye. "Did I kiss you like I thought you were damaged?"

He scowled. "Sooner or later I'll disappoint you."

"That's life, Sam. We all disappoint at one point or another now and then. A person works through those moments."

"I don't. I run away from them. Always have."

And to make his point, he reeled back from her, turned, and escaped through the door between kitchens, leaving her alone with her arguments.

Leaving himself still wanting to scoop her up and carry her off to bed.

CHAPTER TWELVE

Sam had made it clear. Corner him and he'd run. She didn't want him to run. She wanted him to stay and for reasons far beyond his chef's skills.

So she'd kept her distance...as much as a restaurant owner could from her chef. But she hadn't stopped trying to figure out how to convince him there was nothing wrong with their feelings for each other. At least interviewing two potential chef candidates forced them together. It hadn't taken much to convince Sam she needed his input in evaluating them.

The first candidate, an experienced cook, had come in yesterday at end of day's service. The second, a young man fresh out of culinary school, came in today. The young man had just finished demonstrating his knife skills with an onion.

"Looks uniform to me," Dixie said as she looked overt the pile of chopped onion. "What do you think, Sam?"

Sam stepped closer and poked through the pile, all business. He nodded. "Good. Uniform."

"Okay," Dixie said. "Let's try some cooking."

She leaned back against the dish-washing station next to where Sam had settled so as to give the kid space to cook. She could feel the heat of Sam's body, smell the scents of herbs and spices clinging to him. The man didn't need aftershave, not as long as he had a kitchen.

He moved away from her. Because he too felt the draw? Because it made him uncomfortable?

Or did he move just to get a better view of the young man working her flattop. She'd given the chef an order that would test his time management skills as well as how he did with one her menu mainstays. French fries, cheeseburger with toasted bun, and fried onions.

She watched the kid cook, but it was Sam her attention fixed on. He had spoken little to her since their *talk*. Avoided her. And he no longer laughed, at least not with her. She sorely missed the old Sam.

The kid placed a plate on the prep table in front of them, his hand shaking.

"Nicely arranged," Dixie said, eyeing the plate.

"The fries are dripping with oil," Sam said. "Your oil wasn't hot enough."

"I realized that too late," the kid said.

Dixie lifted the top of the bun. "The cheese is perfectly melted."

"Nice caramelizing on the onions," Sam said.

But before she even cut the burger in half, she knew the kid had grilled the life out of it. She sighed. She favored the kid over the experienced cook they'd interviewed the day before.

"Jessie, the burger is overdone—dry. I take pride in serving juicy burgers."

"I took too much time trying to brown the fries." He glanced in Sam's direction. "Because I didn't have the fryer hot enough. It threw off my timing and, as a result, my burger was on the grill too long." The kid hung his head. "Guess I blew it."

"Don't be too quick to write yourself off, Jessie," Dixie said. "You took responsibility for your error and I appreciate that."

The kid's head came up. "You're known for your omelets, too. I make great omelets. Give me a full breakfast order and I'll prove I can cook to your standards *and* manage my time."

"Sounds like you took the time to learn our menu," Sam said.

The kid glanced between them. "Isn't that what anyone applying for a chef's job should do?"

"Yes," said Dixie, exchanging a glance with Sam. Their first chef candidate hadn't known anything about The Farmhouse before arriving for his interview.

"So," the kid ventured. "May I cook an omelet for you?"

"Sure," Dixie said. "Cook us an omelet…and a sunny-side up egg, pancakes, and sides of bacon, sausage links, and hash browns."

The kid grinned, turned, and threw himself into the task of preparing her order. She gave him props for fighting for this job. If only she could get Sam to fight for what he needed…wanted.

#

After Jessie left, they sat at a table in the empty dining room, Dixie with the application of the two chef prospects and her notes, Sam with his regrets.

"What do you think?" she asked him.

I think I want you more than breath. But you want—deserve a man who will take responsibility for his errors. A reminder of her standards, thanks to her comment to Jessie.

"They both have their strengths and weaknesses," he said. "The kid has the skills but no practical experience." He tapped the other chef's application.

"He's got the practical experience."

"In a burger joint," she said.

"He needs refining but he knows how to run a kitchen."

"The kid cooks with love, Sam. You know what love adds to food."

He looked at her—looked her in the eye for the first time in two days. He didn't want to address love in any form with her. "If we—you go with Jessie, I'll need to stick around until he learns how to run a kitchen."

"The other guy needs to be brought up to speed on cooking just about anything beyond a burger and fries," she said. "Either way I could use your help training my next chef—would appreciate it if you'd stay a while longer and do the job."

He drew a deep breath, a mistake as it pulled in the scents that he would always equate with Dixie...apples and cinnamon. "Looks like either one you choose, I still have a job to do."

"Only if you're willing, Sam."

He snorted. "Just don't sneak out on you, huh?"

"Just tell me you've have enough and you're free to go," she said.

Sounded good. Problem was he wasn't *free.* Never would be as long as the memory of Dixie Rae followed him. He shook his head.

"I won't bail on you." *Not until I've seen to it you have the right chef running your kitchen.*

"Thank you, Sam. How about each candidate cooks with you, one each of the next two days?"

"Works for me."

#

Which brought them back to the same table at

end of Friday service two days later.

"I want to hire Jessie," she said.

"I knew all along you'd hire him," Sam said, feeling an odd sense of regret that had nothing to do with which chef she hired and whole lot more to do with his time at The Farmhouse running out.

Seeming to misread his silence as disagreement, she leaned toward him and thumped a finger pointedly against the tabletop. "He's got the passion for cooking."

"Agreed."

"He's trained in the basics."

"Agreed."

"He's eager to learn. He's like a sponge," Dixie said.

"Agreed."

"He needs this job."

"They both need the job," Sam said, even though he knew she needed the upscale chef more than a run-of-the-mill cook who could run a kitchen—knowing she'd handle the kitchen business just fine on her own.

"But Jessie needs that first job to get him started," she said.

And there it was. What worried him most where Dixie was concerned.

Sam leaned forward, bracing his forearms against the table. "*Started* being the key word here. You'll mentor him, teach him. He'll build a resume on your little restaurant and then move on."

She lifted a wobbly smile at him. "I know. It's what I do."

He slumped back in his chair. Of course she knew that about herself. Still, he couldn't just leave her guiding herself by her big heart.

"And when he leaves?" he asked.

"*Before* he leaves, he'll train my next chef."

"And then you'll let your little chick fly and you'll start over with another one."

"I suppose that's what I'll do."

"Is that what you've been doing with me?" Sam asked.

She huffed. "Training *you* as a chef? Hardly."

"You know what I mean. Fixing me so I can fly off like the rest of your little rehabbed chicks."

She frowned. "I guess it sort of started that way."

"Sort of?"

She slanted a crooked smile at him. "My first thoughts upon seeing you pressed against my leaded glass door that first night had nothing to do with rehab."

"What were your first thoughts?" he asked..

A bit of the flirtatious Dixie glinted in her eye. "You cut a dashing figure, all flattened out before me. Kind of incited carnal thoughts."

"Carnal?" He swallowed. No wonder he hadn't been able to keep his hands off her. With her being attracted to him, he'd been fighting a losing battle all along. But then, she hadn't known who he was— hadn't known about his wounded soul.

She shrugged, a sheepishness dulling her flirty edge. "At least I had thoughts at that moment I hadn't entertained since Michael died."

Sam winced. "You smartly pinned my ears back that night when I got too fresh with you."

"You were Michael's cousin" she said.

"And it didn't feel right, did it?" he stated more than asked.

"Among other things."

"What else did there need to be?" he asked, belatedly regretting his question.

"That first night, I was leery of why you came to The Farmhouse."

"Aah." He leaned back in his seat. The root of the problem, the real reason he'd declared her hands off.

"Why did you come here, Sam?"

He should tell her Stuart had sent him. He should confess his deception—end this charade right now. But she still needed his help and, if he revealed what a snake in the grass he was, she'd send him on his way.

Wrong. He couldn't confess because he couldn't face seeing how she'd look at him afterwards. He was coward.

"Why, Sam?" she pressed. "Did you need something and you thought it might be us?"

The possibility that she was right cut through his chest with the ease of a finely honed knife through Prime grade filet.

She took his hands in hers. "If you need us, Sam. We're here for you. We'll always be here for you."

Us? She didn't get it at all. He needed her.

"I won't press you about the kiss. I won't talk anymore how Michael wanting you and me to be happy could translate into you and me together."

"And what about you, Red?" he asked, wanting badly to slip his hands from hers and stroke her cheek the way she needed it stroked. "What do you need?"

She released his hands, blinked. "I have my family. They're everything I need."

She actually believed family was all she needed— that she'd be okay sacrificing her own needs to make him feel comfortable in her home.

He shook his head. "Red, you're so busy taking care of everything and everyone else, you don't even think about what *you* need."

#

Twenty-four hours later, Dixie still couldn't stop thinking about what Sam had said to her. Absently, she dropped a napkin-rolled place setting onto the very dining room table where he'd accused her of not thinking about her own needs.

Annie came up to her waving one of the wrapped sets of silverware. "Since when do we set five places at a table for four?"

"Huh?"

"Get it together, Cuz. We'll need all our wits to handle tonight's wedding reception."

"Yeah. Sure," Dixie said, smoothing a wrinkle from the tablecloth, wanting everything to be perfect for the young couple who'd chosen her humble establishment for their modest reception.

But it had already been a tedious day, but not because Saturday pretty was much a dawn to dusk workday what with dinner service added. The tension crackled between her and Sam whenever she entered the kitchen even with Jessie there to act as buffer between them. If Sam had thought calling her out on her penchant for putting everyone's wellbeing ahead of her own would end her attraction to him, he'd badly miscalculated the effect. She ached all the more for him because *he* was what she needed.

Annie slung an arm around Dixie's shoulders. "You're not your usual perky self, Dix. What's up?"

"Nothing really," Dixie demurred. "It's just, last evening, Sam said something that's got me thinking."

Annie gave her a squeeze. "And that is?"

Dixie tipped her head against Annie's. "He said I take care of everyone else before myself."

"You do."

"But it makes me happy."

"I'm sure it usually does," Annie said. "But you haven't been your chipper self ever since you called me about kissing Sam. What went wrong?"

Dixie dropped into a chair, her basket of silverware in her lap. "He said it wasn't a good idea, him and me. That I wasn't a one-night stand kind of girl."

"How…responsible of him." Annie pulled out the chair around the corner from Dixie's, set her tray of coffee cups on the table and sat facing Dixie. "Did you tell him you knew he wouldn't be around forever—that even good girls can handle a one-night stand now and then?"

"Yeah, but…"

"You want more than a one-night stand," Annie stated. "You want Sam to be more than a transition guy."

Dixie nodded. "And he clearly saw that."

"And you think he's afraid of commitment?"

Dixie slumped. "Sure. He's not a guy that sticks around anywhere too long. He's made that clear."

"He's stuck around here for nearly a month and, you've got to admit, The Farmhouse isn't five star in anything but food and good, loving family."

Dixie grunted. "I also think he's hung up on me being Michael's widow. He kept saying things like he wasn't the right guy for me."

"And you're accepting that?"

Dixie shrugged. "You'll recall I pretty much had

the same questions about him and me and Michael."

"So you're not even going to give him a chance?" Annie asked.

Dixie blinked at her cousin, confused. "A chance for what?"

"To come to the same conclusion you did, that Michael would readily give you two his blessings. To realize he, Sam, is doing the same thing you are, sacrificing his own happiness to protect the person he loves."

#

If there was the slightest chance Sam held her at bay because he thought he was protecting her, they had a lot more to talk about. That's how Dixie saw it. But they couldn't talk until after the restaurant closed, and the evening reception seemed to last forever. Then came cleanup, Jessie and Sam scrubbing down the kitchen, Annie and she clearing the dining rooms, and the twins running dishes through the washer.

Dance music still played on the speaker mounted iPod, lending a lively beat to work to. Soon, the last dishes had been washed, the kitchen cleaned for next day service, and the rugs vacuumed. Everyone lent a hand setting up for Sunday brunch, the festive mood of a wedding reception yet lingering.

A particularly good dance beat blasted from the speakers and Annie grabbed Sam and danced him around the tables. The twins joined in. Nana and Ben emerged from the private quarters wanting to know what the commotion was all about and were soon dancing.

Laughing, Dixie looked at Jessie. "Shall we?"

He replied by boogying them to a space where they could move unencumbered.

They all danced through a second song. The third was a slow number and Annie cut-in, taking Jessie from her. Dixie sighed, turned and found herself facing Sam. She slipped her arms around his neck and hugged herself against him, giving him no option but to put his arms around her.

"What are you doing, Red?"

"Snuggling in where I belong."

"I'm not what you need," he said.

"Shhh. It's just one dance."

To Dixie's relief, he settled into their embrace, his arms warm, strong around her. They swayed in rhythm to the music—in rhythm to each other. They felt so right together. Did he feel it, too?

"Sam," she said.

"Yeah," he said, his tone full of uncertainty...regret.

She looked up, looked into his sad eyes. "Yesterday you asked me who took care of me. It seems, Sam, that it's you."

Sam's stomach dropped. This was so wrong. He tried to ease back from her. But she wouldn't release him.

"You are my strength," she said.

He couldn't let her believe that of him. "You were strong enough on your own to fight off Stuart, move, and start a new business before I ever came along."

"Since you came to The Farmhouse, everything's been easier for me."

Much as he wanted to be the man she thought him to be, he wasn't. "I'm not reliable."

"I've never seen that in you."

"Didn't Mickey warn you about me?"

"You've been reliable with me, Sam. What does that tell you?"

Without thinking, he drew her close and swayed to the music for several beats before responding. "You and Mickey are the only two people who never demanded I be something I wasn't."

"That's good, right?" she asked.

He pressed his temple to hers. "I still let Mickey down."

She started to shake her head. He lifted his and looked her in the eye.

"Mickey wanted me to be his best man at your wedding and for me to run his restaurant kitchen."

"You knew better about the restaurant," she said, "and he understood about the wedding."

"Nobody should have to be *understanding* of my failings, Red, least of all Mickey or you. You need someone you can depend on."

She gazed up at him, confidence shimmering in her eyes. "You've been dependable for me, Sam. You stepped in when I needed a chef. You stayed way longer than I had any right expecting you to. You stayed when things didn't go right. You even took over when I was having a melt-down and kept my kitchen running in top form."

He laid his cheek against hers and whispered in her ear. "I'm a coward, Red. I couldn't even face Mickey's funeral."

"You faced down Miss Weston when she laid hands on Ben," she said, her breath warm and reassuring against his ear.

"What do you want from me, Red?"

"I want you to give us a chance."

He swallowed hard. "You need more than a guy

passing in the night."

"You're right," she said, pressing her cheek into his. "I need you to stay and be my strength and for you to let me be yours. We're good together."

"I'll disappoint you, Red."

"There'll be times I expect you will, as I will you," she murmured, her lips brushing his jaw. "But that's part of life. We'll work through those times."

"What if I hurt you?"

"I've survived a lot of bruises, Sam."

He rocked her against himself. "But I don't want to be the one bruising you."

She lifted her head and peered up at him, her eyes full of determination. "And I don't want to let you go and wonder for the rest of my life if I made a mistake."

"Red…"

She rose onto her toes and brushed her lips across Sam's.

"Be careful what you invite," he said. "I've wanted you more than anything from the moment I saw you."

She smiled and pressed her lips to his. He sucked a breath, parting his lips, accepting the full ardor of her mouth—accepting all she offered him. Everything he ever wanted could be his. *She* could be his. All he had to do was let it happen.

The music changed to something more upbeat, stealing away mood—his fantasy. Self-conscious, he glanced about. To his amazement, they were alone.

"Where'd they all go?" he asked.

Dixie chuckled, her arms still around his neck, her body still pressed against his. "Home. To bed. Wherever. Most importantly, I doubt we'll see any of them until tomorrow."

Afraid to read too much into the flirtatious invitation of her voice, he murmured, "Okay. Now what?"

She raised her eyes to the ceiling—toward the bedroom above.

"What about Ben?" he asked.

"Knowing Nana, Ben is already bunked in with her."

"Are you sure about this, Red?"

"So sure I'm about to throw you across one of these tables and have my way with you right here."

He scooped her up in his arms, carried her up the wide front stairs, the music still playing in the distance. He carried her into her bedroom, kicked the door shut behind them, and tossed her onto her empty bed. She laughed.

He grinned, toed off his boots, and jumped onto the bed beside her. There was no thought to how they removed their clothes, just action driven by need.

They explored each other in a frenzy of hands, mouths, and tongues. He took her to the moon first with his mouth. Then sank into her hot wetness and took them both to the stars.

Afterward, he savored the feel of holding her until they both fell asleep, curled into each other's embrace.

Sometime during the gray hours of false dawn, something woke Sam; a sound, a stirring of air. He couldn't place what. But it was enough to remind him he shouldn't be caught in Dixie's bed by Ben.

He looked down on her, head pillowed in the crook of his arm. With her hair in disarray about her head and her full lips puckered ever so slightly, she looked like a wanton angel. A well satisfied wanton angel.

He smiled and brushed his lips across hers. She stirred and her lips curled around a throaty purr. She looked up at him through dreamy eyes.

"I better get back to my room before Ben wakes up and comes running in here," he said.

She slid a hand around his neck, her fingers threading into his hair. "Not yet."

"Keep that up and we'll have a repeat of last night."

"I like the sound of that," she said in a sleepy voice.

"But you wouldn't want Ben to walk-in on that, would you?"

Her fingers slipped from his hair. Elbowing herself up, she pulled his face down to hers and gave him a long, sweet kiss.

"See you later in the kitchen," she said when their lips parted.

#

After Sunday brunch, Sam and Dixie cleaned up the barn, teasing each other and stealing kisses. Later, while she and Nana put the house to order, Sam played with Ben in the sandbox. For supper, they opted for leftovers from the restaurant kitchen. Come evening, they watched a movie on TV, Ben snuggled up with Nana, Dixie and Sam on the couch surreptitiously holding hands.

It all felt so perfect to Sam, maybe too perfect. But he was determined not to think beyond the moment.

When Ben fell asleep, Sam carried him upstairs. When he turned down the hall toward Dixie's room,

Nana stopped him. "Put the boy in with me."

"You had him last night."

"And a warm little bundle he was. Felt good against my arthritic back."

"Arthritic back, right," Sam murmured under his breath. He'd seen the twinkle in Nana's eye. She was still playing matchmaker. He smiled. Fine with him.

He rejoined Dixie on the couch for the end of the movie. This time, though, they skipped the hand holding and snuggled into each other, his arm around her, her head on his shoulder. She slid a leg over his, settling her slippered foot just below his knee.

The crimson scuff seemed to wink at him, reminding him of how the red high-tops she worked in had winked in and out of the folds of her long skirt the first night he'd followed her upstairs—the night he realized what a fool's errand Stuart had sent him on. He chuckled.

"What's funny?" she asked.

Not wanting to ruin things by bringing up Stuart, he asked, "What's with all the red foot-gear? First the high-tops, then the rubber barn boots, and now the fuzzy slippers."

She waggled her crimson covered toes in the air. "Christmas gifts from my brothers."

"And they all decided on red footwear why?"

"As a joke."

He may lack her brothers' machismo but humor he understood.

"Let me guess," he said. "Your stunt riding brother Renn gave you the boots for mucking out stalls."

"Wrong. Roman's gave me those."

"Of course, the practical brother."

"Renn gave me the high-tops. He believes a person should always have fun while working."

"Okay. Does that mean Mr. Hollywood gave you the slippers with the flash and dazzle?"

"Now you're catching on," she said.

He thought a moment before venturing further. "There seems to be a pair of footwear missing. What did Jake give you? Or are they top secret given they're from Mr. Seal?"

She smiled widely. "Jake gave me ruby red, four inch heels."

"The most impractical footwear of all from the Navy Seal?"

"Former Seal, and yes."

"I wouldn't have guessed that one in a hundred years," he said.

"He wasn't being impractical...or funny." Her smile grew wistful. "The note he sent with the shoes read, *"For when you're ready to dance again."*

It hit Sam then that Mickey had died two years ago in January. The joke footgear had been meant to lighten her spirits her first Christmas without him. Jake's had been meant to remind her she had a future to look forward to, one beyond being a mother, a care-giver, and restaurant proprietor—a future in which she would wear ruby red high heels.

But, was he the man for whom she should— would wear those shoes? When they headed up to bed themselves, he paused in the hall outside her bedroom, no longer certain of where he fit into the grander scheme of Dixie's life.

When she looked at him expectantly, he shrugged. "I didn't want to assume—"

She yanked him into the room and shut the door

behind him. Maybe he was the man for whom she'd wear the, *for when you're ready to dance again,* shoes.

#

Monday was idyllic. Ben riding the pony, Dixie leading the animal, Sam carrying a blanket and picnic basket with Bear bringing up the rear, they headed for the woods across the pasture.

They played hide and seek among the trees, Dixie making sure Sam always found her first so they could sneak a kiss before heading off to find Ben who always hid with Bear beneath the draping branches of the same evergreen tree. Though they pretended not to notice, drawing out the game until Ben's giggles gave him away.

Dixie and Sam fed each other cold parmesan baked chicken and sweet seedless grapes while Ben munched on home-made chicken fingers, occasionally sharing one with a drooling Bear. They drank chilled apple cider and ate thick slices of lemon Bundt cake for dessert.

They watched Ben and Bear search for pollywogs in the shallows of a pond, while they sat on the blanket, Sam with his back to a tree, Dixie between his spread legs with her back to his chest. Sam pressed his lips against the strip of skin behind Dixie's ear.

"You know that drives me crazy," she said.

"Yeah," he murmured against the back of her ear.

Playfully, she pushed him away. "There'll be none of that here."

He came back for a quick nip of her earlobe. "Never say never."

She tipped her head back against his chest and

peeked up at him. "Not with Ben here."

"Didn't you once say it would be good for Ben to see us kissing?"

"Kissing yes, but—"

He closed his mouth over hers, silencing her, while he trailed his fingers down her throat, over her collarbone, and into—

She caught his hand before it went any lower. One errant fingertip traced a soft circle against the tender skin just above where her v-neck t-shirt dipped between her breasts. Her giggle rippled across his tongue and vibrated against his lips. Then, for a moment, her laughter stilled and her hand came up to stroke the side of his face. He threaded his fingers through her hair and cupped her head, holding her in place.

"Mommy, mommy." Ben's voice rushed at them all excitement and wonder.

They broke from the kiss and Dixie straightened on the blanket between Sam's legs just as Ben stopped in front of her, water sloshing from the plastic cup he carried.

"Look," he said, thrusting the cup at Dixie. "I found a pol—pollywog."

Sam looked over her shoulder at the lone would-be amphibian squiggling through the water in the cup.

"You sure did," Sam said.

"Amazing," Dixie said with all the enthusiasm of the nurturing mother she was. This was the kind of mother he would want for his children.

His children.

He'd never before thought about having children. Wrong. There'd been a kernel of a thought when he played with Ben in his sandbox, or when he'd pick up the kid and he'd throw his arms around his neck, or when the kid fell asleep on the couch and he'd have to carry him up to bed. He'd felt responsible in the best of ways, involved and included. He'd felt like part of something much bigger than himself. And it struck him now, that if this was what it was to be a parent, he wanted it.

"What do you want to do with it?" he heard Dixie ask.

"Take it home and watch it turn into a frog," Ben said.

"I don't know that the pollywog would like that," Dixie said.

"But I would," Ben said.

Feeling parent-like, Sam interjected, "It probably won't survive without its pond."

Ben frowned.

"We can come to the pond and visit your pollywog here," Sam said. "Watch him grow."

"What do you say, Ben?" Dixie asked.

He shrugged. "Okay."

And he trotted off toward the pond, cup in hand.

Dixie peered over her shoulder at Sam. "That was very good, Sam."

"Was it fatherly?" he asked.

She studied him a couple long seconds before answering. "It was the response of a very good father."

Something inside his chest swelled. A heart? Maybe he had one after all.

With Ben back pond-side, Dixie reclined back into Sam's arms once more. She sighed. "I've been thinking. What am I going to do with two chefs?"

Sam grinned, liking that she still thought of him

sticking around even after hiring a new chef. Still, he teased, "You're assuming a lot?"

"What am I assuming?"

"I promised only to stick around until a new chef was trained."

Dixie ratcheted up so fast she nearly clipped him on the chin. "You aren't really going to leave when that boy is trained, are you?"

So she still harbored some uncertainties where he was concerned.

"Where's my *you-can-leave-anytime* Dixie?"

She studied his face. "You can't be serious."

He sobered and gathered her across his lap. "No. You are everything I could ever want, Red. You and this family."

She smiled. "I knew we were what you needed."

Her words should have heartened him, but that she still saw him as a *cause* didn't sit right with him and he murmured, "I bet you did."

But, whether she saw it or not, she and Ben also needed him. "So," he ventured, "how about making this thing permanent?"

She gaped at him. "Are you proposing to me?"

He smiled but not as widely as he would have had there not been a note of panic underlying her question. "Yes, but relax," he said. "I'm not proposing what you think."

She raised an eyebrow at him.

"A business partnership," he said. "The restaurant could use an infusion of capital."

"You know how I feel about handouts."

"A partnership isn't a handout. I expect to be able to live off my investment."

She eyed him long and hard.

"You know Stuart will cut me off as soon as he finds out we're together," he said.

"Been there," she said.

"Mickey."

She nodded.

"And, if I can remain the grownup you seem to have inspired me to be, this is going to be a permanent partnership."

"Don't put too much pressure on yourself, Sam. Give what's going on between us time."

What is *going on between us,* he wanted to ask. Instead, he said, "No matter what, I'll still need to make a living." He looked her in the eye, but not too deeply for fear of what he might see...or *not* see. "Partners?"

She shook his hand. "Partners."

She snuggled into the cradle of his arms. "Sam?"

"Yeah?"

"We need you in more than financial ways. You realize that, don't you?"

Did he?

"Nana seems sharper since you came along, like you inspire or challenge her in some way. Ben adores you. And you've been my knight in shining armor."

Not quite the endorsement he hoped for.

"That's me, good old uplifting Sam."

She peeked up at him. "I'm afraid to say more, Sam—afraid what I really want to say will scare you off."

He grimaced. "I do scare easy, don't I?"

"We're good together, Sam. We're good for each other. Somewhere in there, there is love."

Love. She'd just offered him everything he ever wanted. Why did he feel like the ground had opened up beneath him?

"You looked horrified, Sam. Does the word *love* scare you that much?"

He shook his head.

"Is it my brothers' and parents' impending visit?"

The Fourth of July celebration. He'd forgotten all about it.

"Are you afraid their upcoming visit will make me want more of a commitment from you than you're ready or willing to give? That's not the case. I just want them to meet you."

And when they did meet him, one if not all of them was bound to see him for what he was. There was the fly in the ointment. Time to run?

No. Not when he'd just promised to be her partner.

But way past time to confess why he'd come to The Farmhouse in the first place. Now he just had to figure out how to do that without making her want to kick him out. Best if he waited until he'd at least invested in the business, bound them together at least in that way.

CHAPTER THIRTEEN

Sam peeled off his sodden t-shirt as he strode from restaurant kitchen through household kitchen.

"Is that blood?" Nana asked as he passed the table where she and Ben ate their afternoon snack.

"Tomato sauce," he said, heading up the stairs to change. "Had an accident while opening an industrial sized can and got splattered."

As he hit the top step, he heard giggling coming from Weston's room. Impossible. Weston was downstairs occupying her usual chair on the back porch. He'd caught a glimpse of her through the living room window on his way upstairs. Maybe she'd left her television on. He rapped on the door just to check. The giggling halted abruptly. Something wasn't right here.

He opened the door and found the twins standing between the desk and window on the back side of the room. "What are you girls doing in here?"

The girls exchanged looks and both spoke at the same time.

"She has two cells phones."

"We were playing games on her computer."

"Yeah," rushed out the first. "It's a rad gaming computer."

He glanced at the laptop on the desk beside them. It looked like a top of the line gamer. He frowned at the girls. "I strongly doubt Miss Weston gave you two permission to play with her computer, let alone be in her room."

The girls glanced at each other, guilt written all over their faces.

"Out," he said, stepping back, motioning them likewise into the hall. "And don't let me ever catch you girls in this room again."

They nodded and fled down the stairs. He continued on to his room where he found his cell phone vibrating on the dresser. He knew who called without even looking at the readout. The same man who'd been calling repeatedly ever since he'd taken the cell phone out of his pocket and left it on the chest of drawers two days ago.

Sam dug out a fresh shirt without checking the cell. He wasn't going to let Stuart ruin his happiness. But, somewhere in his subconscious, an old fear haunted him. *All good things must come to an end.*

#

The beginning of the end came the following day after Wednesday service. Annie and the girls had set up the dining rooms for the next day then went home. Jessie had cleaned the kitchen and headed out. Dixie had spent a little one-on-one time with Ben before heading up to her room to check emails and change into her barn clothes.

Much as he'd liked to have followed her and helped her out of her restaurant clothes, Sam joined Ben in his sandbox where they rearranged sand piles with the dump truck and frontend loader Sam had bought the kid the last time he'd gone to town. By summer's end, Sam intended to have filled the sandbox with every imaginable construction vehicle there was for Ben.

By summer's end. The notion of still being at the

farm come fall made Sam smile. He still needed to survive the Fourth of July visit by Dixie's brothers and parents and keep her from finding out Stuart had sent him here. His smile slipped. It was a big order.

The dust churning arrival and screeching halt of Annie's car in the driveway broke into his thoughts. Something major had to be wrong for Annie to come barreling back to the farm after her shift was finished—to make her practically vault from car to porch and race into the house.

Slowly, Sam rose from the sandbox. "I gotta go, Kid." Ben looked up at him, apprehension filling the blue eyes the kid raised at him. The kid sensed trouble, too. Sam could tell. As a kid, he'd learned the hard way to read when something was wrong, too. He'd be damned if he'd let Ben know it to the extent he had.

Sam forced a smile. "Time I change into my barn clothes. I'll be back to check on the progress of that mountain we're building."

The kid grinned. Reassured he'd diverted Ben's concerns, he headed for the house, pausing only long enough by Nana in her rocker to get a, "Go. I'll keep an eye on Ben," from her.

Dixie's bedroom door was closed, hers and Annie's voices agitated, their words muffled. He raised his hand to knock. But Dixie had called Annie, not him. He should leave them to their girl talk. Then he remembered Dixie had said she was going to check her email.

A chill slithered up his spine. He went into his room—went straight to the cell phone on the bureau, thinking it might hold the answer to what trouble had Dixie and Annie so agitated next door. As though it

were a poisonous snake, he picked the cell up and
called up the list of messages. They were all from
Stuart, of course, most cursing him out for not
answering his phone. But it was the last one that
chilled him to the bone, not because there was a
detached tone to the message that others from Stuart
lacked, but because of the words.

*Implant the attached file on her computer and
upload it from* her *computer, to as many social
networks as you can.*

Something told him he didn't want to see what
was on that file. But, that same niggling premonition
told him the file had everything to do with why Annie
and Dixie were closed up together in Dixie's
bedroom...even though he hadn't uploaded it.

He opened the file. The first still picture to pop
up on the cell phone screen looked familiar. Dixie and
him kissing in the open doorway of the barn. But
there was something not right about the tiny picture,
something he couldn't quite decipher on the small
screen. The second shot left no doubts about their
purpose. Dixie arching beneath him on her
bed...naked. Then He scanned several more shots.
Convenient how his head was never in frame. Even
the shot of them framed in the open barn door had
showed only the back of his head.

He ground his teeth together—wanted to shout,
to throw something. Damn, he hated seeing their most
intimate moments caught by someone. Someone with
an agenda and a camera with a powerful lens. No one
had gotten that close to them.

He flipped back to the shot of them together in
the open barn door. That first magic kiss ruined by an
interloper. Even the shots taken of them in her

darkened room were pretty clear. He knew who could afford such high end equipment. The same man who had ordered him to upload the pictures to the Internet from Dixie's computer.

He closed his eyes against the realization he'd been used by the old man to ruin Dixie. Naïve to have believed Stuart had depended on him alone to dig up dirt on Dixie.

Teeth gritted, he opened his eyes, the barn picture on the cell screen sharply detailed. He was about to punch the phone off when it struck what it was that was not quite right about that shot. Small as the cell phone screen was, he could barely make out the error. Dixie's shirt was missing. She hadn't taken it off until they were behind the hay bales. This shot was doctored and he could testify to that fact before any judge. He might yet be able to keep Stuart from making Dixie out to be a woman with morals too low to raise a child.

But he couldn't just burst into her room and announce what he'd just learned. To do so, he would have to reveal the file on his phone—reveal that he was part of Stuart's latest plan to discredit her. She'd kick him out before he could explain he hadn't loaded the pictures onto her computer.

But clearly someone had.

If not him, then who?

A hacker?

Why had Stuart even bothered to order him to upload the pictures when he could get any number of computer whizzes to hack into her system and upload them? Or maybe what was going on in the room next to his had nothing to do with these pictures.

Silently, he slipped out his window and over the

railing onto Dixie's balcony. He hunkered down beside her door, his ear trained on the sounds inside her room.

Whatever had upset Dixie enough for her to call Annie, he had to fix.

#

Dixie sat on the edge of her bed, Annie's arm around her shoulders, her cheeks wet with the tears she'd shed. "I still don't understand why anyone would plant a file like this on my computer."

"Not *anyone*, Stuart," Annie said. "Who else wants to hurt you?"

"Does he think invading my privacy like this will make me appear to be an unfit mother—to persuade some judge to take Ben away from me? Does he think it'll embarrass me enough that he can blackmail me into *giving* him up? He doesn't know me at all if he thinks embarrassing me would ever make me give up Ben."

Annie's arms tightened around her. "This is embarrassing, but it's not enough for a judge to rule you an unfit mother."

"But it can still hurt my reputation—hurt the restaurant."

"Your regulars won't abandon you."

"I was just beginning to expand my clientele base, people like the Hostettler sisters. Hortense hears about these pictures and I can kiss any expansion ideas good-bye."

"Maybe they won't find out about them. Maybe Stuart had the pictures uploaded to your computer as a warning—that they're not already out there in cyberspace."

"I don't get it," Dixie said. "Stuart's threats have

always been very straight forward. This—this subterfuge, I don't understand."

"He's a wretched old man."

"I never dreamt he'd stoop so low to get custody of Ben."

"Dix, you realize he had to have someone upload those pictures to your computer."

Dixie stilled, reluctant to ask Annie what she suspected. "What are you saying?"

Annie's arms loosened a bit. "Do you think...could it be possible...?"

"No," Dixie said, pressing her head against Annie's shoulder, knowing what—who Annie was suggesting was behind this.

"The cancelled meat order," Annie continued. "The cooler getting turned off. Equipment breaking down on you."

Dixie lifted her head from Annie's shoulder, quick with a defense. "I bought used equipment for the most part. It's not surprising it should break down."

"Did you ever find out who fiddled with the gauges on the cooler?"

"I assume—"

"Don't assume anything. Put it together. Somebody FAXed a cancellation of your meat order from your number. Do you really think Nana could have accidently done that?"

Dixie shook her head. "No, but—"

"These incidents aren't coincidence. There've been too many of them in too short a time. And if Jim hadn't called you about the meat order and you hadn't discovered the cooler issue soon enough, they could have been major catastrophes for you—for the restaurant."

"The cooler was a major catastrophe as it was. I had to replace most of the produce and all of the dairy."

"Every one of those equipment breakdowns cost you."

"Which means someone here is doing the tampering." Dixie slumped against Annie, knowing she no longer had a choice but to face Annie's suspicions.

"Has it occurred to you that all these incidents have happened since Sam arrived?" Annie asked.

Nausea rolled through Dixie's stomach. "It can't be Sam," she said even though she could read the evidence as well as Annie. "He's been helping me. He's loaned me the money to cover the costs of my losses."

"Who has access to your computer?"

"Anybody who's ever been in the house."

"You don't really believe some customer or delivery man could have gotten past you into your private quarters, not when Ben's safety is at stake."

"Maybe Miss Weston…"

"She was here a good month before Sam arrived. Were there any problems during that time?"

Reluctantly, Dixie shook her head. "But not Sam. He-he's—"

"Your lover?" Annie gave her a squeeze. "I like Sam a whole lot. I don't want it to be him, either. But you've got to consider all possibilities and he's one of them."

#

Sam heard the whisper of a door opening and closing. Annie leaving the bedroom? Both of them leaving? He was feeling too dejected by what Annie had said about him to listen for further sounds. So, when the balcony door opened…

He started and looked up. Dixie looked down on him, more somber looking than he'd ever seen her.

"How long have you been sitting there, Sam?"

"Long enough to know something terrible has happened. Long enough to know Annie suspects me to be behind everything bad that's happened here this past month."

In two strides, Dixie was at the front of the narrow balcony overlooking the driveway and outbuildings. While sitting outside her room, eavesdropping on her and Annie, he'd noted how limited a view anyone on the highway or even in the parking lot out front had of the balcony let alone into Dixie's bedroom. And though he could hear Ben calling for Nana to come see what he'd done in the sandbox, the angles and abutments of the Victorian era house blocked any view of the backyard from the balcony and vice versa. Besides, those pictures had been taken straight on.

He rose and stepped up alongside Dixie. The scent of apple blossoms drifted up from the tree occupying the oasis between the lanes of the circular drive. It was hard to see anything clearly through the branches of the tree and, presumably, even for the long lens of a camera to see them. He wanted to point out that fact.

But to bring up the pictures would mean admitting he knew about them. Then he'd have to confess how he knew about them—how they got onto his phone and why they'd been put there.

"Tell me you didn't have anything to do with any

of this," Dixie said before he could work out whether or not he was still too much a coward to confess.

The words he knew he should speak stuck in his throat.

Coward.

Or maybe he believed telling her he had nothing to do with the troubles plaguing her would be a lie since Stuart had sent him here. He could, however, answer her with what truth he knew. He faced her.

"I didn't cancel your meat order. I didn't turn off the cooler. I did nothing intentional to hurt you."

"Nothing *intentional?"* She faced him. "What does that mean, Sam?"

The weight of what he'd allowed to happen pulled at his mouth—at his eyes. "It means I would never do anything to hurt you, Red. Please believe me."

"I believe you," she said, lifting her fingertips to his cheek, their caress no weightier than a breath. Yet her touch stung as though she'd slapped him. It was what he deserved and he wanted to shout *"You're too trusting, Red."*

"Come," she said, taking him by the hand and turning toward her bedroom door.

He let her tow him inside—sat when she motioned him into her computer chair. "Something new has come up," she said.

Bringing the computer out of sleep mode, she pointed at an odd icon almost hidden among the others. "That wasn't there yesterday."

He tensed, knowing what the newly added file contained.

She tapped the icon twice and thumbprints of a dozen or more pictures filled the monitor screen. She clicked on one, enlarging it then another and another until he pushed her hand off the computer mouse.

"Enough," he said, clicking shut the folder.

"Is this why you didn't want to make love to me—why your carefully worded denial, that you would never do anything to *intentionally* hurt me?"

The pain of his complicity rolled through him and came out in a groan. "If I hadn't been here, Red... If I had kept my hands off you..."

"Did you know this is what would happen?"

He looked her deep in her trusting eyes, his answer truer than anything he'd ever told her. "No."

Her pained eyes softened on him. "No one could have anticipated this."

"No one," he murmured, utter misery creeping through him.

"Tell me you had no idea Stuart would stoop this low to get Ben away from me?"

He closed his eyes and shook his head. "I don't want to believe he would be this hateful." He looked Dixie in the eye. "But, he's a bitter old man who's lost his only son. He wants a second chance. He wants Ben to replace Mickey. I don't know any more what he's capable of."

She exhaled. "Okay. But you still know him best. Assuming he's behind the pictures, do you think he'll go further than to threaten me with them?"

Upload them to every social media site you know of...from her *computer.*

The last order issued from his cell phone drained Sam of all warmth. The old man wanted that file uploaded *from* her computer not to embarrass her but to prove her moral unfitness. He couldn't prove immorality based on her having multiple partners, but he could paint her as a woman with an exhibitionist fetish and that could well be just as damaging.

Sam reached behind the computer and disconnected the cable cord.

"What are doing?" she asked.

"A precaution," Sam said. "Clearly, someone hacked into your computer and put that file there."

"And you're afraid they'll do something worse," she said.

He looked deep into her worried eyes. "I'm going to drive into Green Bay and get the best scrubbing software and security program I can find. Then I'm coming back here and we are going to clean your computer and make it impregnable. Don't plug it back into the Internet."

She hugged him, murmuring in his ear, "Once again you come to my rescue."

#

So she still thought he was her hero. He could have bought it if he wasn't part of the problem. At least he'd been able to scour her hard drive clean of any *implanted* files—made her computer nearly impregnable by installing the best security software on the market. He'd even purchased a tablet from which he'd checked Dixie's Facebook page for any sign of the pictures. After checking other social media and a few porn sites that specialized in posting "*home* pictures," he was satisfied her pictures hadn't been spread around...yet. Important as it seemed to the culprit that the pictures be uploaded from Dixie's computer, there was no guarantee they wouldn't be uploaded from another computer. Desperate people often took desperate measures, as evidenced by the pictures themselves.

He and Dixie spent that night in her bed, drapes closed tight and doors locked. They didn't make love. He simply held her, sharing her fitful sleep. Neither met the next day with their usual enthusiasm. Both threw themselves into restaurant work, keeping themselves busy even though it left Jessie poking around for jobs to do. They both waited for the proverbial second shoe to drop.

But when it dropped during the lull between breakfast and lunch crowds, neither saw it for what it was.

Miss Weston burst through the door between private and restaurant kitchens, shrieking. "My monkey is missing!"

"It's not in here," Sam said.

"What's she talking about?" Jessie asked.

"She carries a stuffed monkey around in that big bag of hers," Sam said, slicing a chicken wrap in half.

Weston stepped further into the kitchen. Dixie blocked her before she got within a foot of the prep table. "Get out of my kitchen."

"My monkey is missing."

"So go look in your room."

"I have. It's not there. And it's not in the dining rooms or the living quarters."

"You're not searching my kitchen," Sam said, not hiding the fact he yet held a knife. "You even being in here is against health codes."

"Then I'll just have to search everyone's bedrooms," Weston said.

Sam dropped the knife and followed Dixie as she dogged Weston into the private quarters, shouting, "You will not go rummaging through anyone's bedroom."

"What's the ruckus?" Nana asked, coming in from the back porch.

"Weston lost her monkey and thinks she's going to search our bedrooms," Sam said.

Nana crossed her arms over her chest. "I'll make sure she keeps her nose out of people's private business even if I have to sit guard up in the hall."

"You're watching Ben," Dixie said.

"The girls are with him. They'll keep him out of mischief."

"Mischief." Miss Weston sniffed. "That boy of yours has always had an interest in my monkey."

"He's afraid of it, thanks to you," Sam said. "He wouldn't touch it."

"Maybe it fell out of your purse on the porch or in the yard," Dixie said on a shuddering breath.

With a huff, Weston wheeled toward the back door.

"Don't know what she's so hot about that monkey for anyway," Nana said. "It's the mangiest stuffed animal I've ever seen."

"Yeah," Sam said, wondering about the woman's attachment to what most would consider a children's toy.

#

The restaurant had been closed barely ten minutes when a scream reverberated through the house from the upper level. Dixie nearly dropped the pitcher of milk on the table and Ben scrabbled back into the furthest corner of the bench under the stairs.

"What the hell?" Annie asked, sliding the plate of cookies onto the table between where her girls sat across from Ben.

Sam bolted from the restaurant kitchen where

he'd been cleaning up into the family quarters just as Miss Weston appeared on the stairs from the second floor. She shook a ragged strip of fake fur in the air.

"It's his tail," she shrieked.

"Didn't find it in any of our rooms," Nana said, appearing on the steps behind the ranting woman. "I've been sitting in the upstairs hall ever since she come back in the house."

Weston descended into the kitchen. Sam advanced on her, putting himself between her and the others. Weston dangled the monkey tail in his face.

"It's my monkey's tail and it was in my room with a ransom note."

At a loss for a response, Sam glanced back at Dixie and Annie. But they were looking at the floor, struggling to suppress snickers.

"It's not funny," howled Weston.

A barely composed Dixie faced Weston. "Of course it's not." But she nearly lost it again when she asked, "What did the monkey-nappers demand?"

Sam had to bite the inside of his cheek to keep from laughing.

Weston squared herself. "They demanded my smart phone."

Dixie, Annie, and Sam sobered and all looked at the table under the stairs around which the children sat. Ben huddled in the corner, eyes wide while the twins munched cookies, exchanging fleeting glances.

"Girls," Annie said. "Do you have something to tell me?"

The twins giggled.

Annie snatched the cookies out of their hands and hauled them out from behind the table. "Where's the rest of the monkey?"

"We were just having a bit of fun," the girls said in unison.

"Besides," Lola said, pointing at Weston, "she got two smart phones."

Sam flashed back to the day he'd caught the girls in Weston's room. One of them had mentioned the phones, but the other diverted his attention by bringing up the computer with all the bells and whistles. But he wasn't pondering how the twins had duped him but rather why Miss Weston needed such an elaborate computer. For photo shopping photos maybe?

"What do you teach?" he asked Miss Weston, while Annie confronted her girls with, "You took something that didn't belong to you then damaged it."

"Math," Weston sputtered, her attention clearly torn between him and what was happening with the twins.

"And how'd you two leave a ransom note in Miss Weston's room without me spotting you?" Nana asked while Sam considered how math and computer science went hand in hand.

"Easy," said Lulu to Nana's question. "We just climbed onto the porch roof to the back balcony."

"Next stop," Lola finished, "Ms. Weston's room."

While the twins led their mother to the location of the kidnapped monkey, Sam revisited his theory about someone using a long lens to take the damning pictures of him and Dixie. Someone on the inside wouldn't have had to deal with tree limbs and leaves—wouldn't have needed a long lens to capture intimate moments in Dixie's bedroom. *She* would merely have had to enter Ben's empty bedroom, climb out the window onto the porch rood, then over the railing onto Dixie's balcony as he had often enough done. And that person wouldn't even have had to hack into Dixie's computer to upload that file of pictures.

The twins returned with the tailless monkey, singing, "We know why she's so freaked out about her monkey going missing. She's got a camera in it."

All eyes turned to Weston.

"Why would you hide a camera in a stuffed animal?" Dixie asked.

"That's nonsense." Weston reached for the monkey

Sam was quicker, though, snatching it before she could take it. It didn't take a leap of faith to envision the diminutive Westin sneaking through Ben's room and slipping out his window to take photographs from Dixie's balcony. But she wouldn't need a hidden camera for that. Still, he'd caught her pointing the damn thing at them more than once.

A closer look revealed a tiny hole in the monkey's nose. He turned it over and tore at the loosely sewn back seam.

"What are you doing," shrieked Weston. "You're supposed to be working with us—with your uncle!"

Weston working for Stuart didn't come as a surprise to him. But it was to everyone else in the room...as was Weston's revelation about him.

Sam looked up from the tiny camera he'd taken from the monkey and found all eyes on him. But the only pair that mattered were cornflower blue. They looked at him with confusion.

"Sam?"

"If you'd uploaded that file I sent to your phone like I told you to," Weston wailed on, "I wouldn't have had to sneak down the hall this morning and do it myself and those wretched girls wouldn't have gotten into my purse and taken my monkey. We would never have been found out if you'd done your part."

"My part?" he asked, his voice hollow in his ears.

Weston snorted. "You're the one who has unlimited access to her bedroom. No one would have questioned you being in her room. I damn near got caught—had to sneak off before I could upload the file from her computer onto the Internet."

"Uploaded *from her computer* so there'd be a trail that would make it look like she posted the pictures herself," Sam murmured, realizing the full purpose of the deception. To make Dixie look so uncaring of her son's well-being that she'd post indecent pictures of herself where all the world could see them.

As though through a long tunnel, he heard Annie saying something about issuing punishment later as she ushered her daughters out the back door, that it was time to go home…and that she was taking Ben with them. Nana said something about helping Ms. Weston pack and making sure she didn't leave with anything that didn't belong to her. That last brought him out of his paralysis.

Sam charged up the steps after Nana and Weston—bolting past them into Weston's room. He grabbed her over-sized purse off the nightstand and emptied its contents onto the bed.

"No electronics leave with her," he said, focusing on a problem he could do something about immediately.

"Those belong to me," Weston shrieked as he picked up two cell phones, an electronic notebook, and a flash drive from the pile on the bed.

"My guess is they belong to Stuart Carrington," he said, piling the electronics on the laptop on the dressing table-turned desk. He caught a glimpse of Weston framed in the mirror above the table and a long ago memory of his last visit to Carrington Corporation surfaced—a memory of a dark-haired woman with mud-brown eyes framed in the opening of an office cubicle. No wonder Weston had seemed familiar to him the first time he saw her in the restaurant kitchen.

He rummaged through desk and dresser drawers. "My guess is there's a camera with some very special low-light features somewhere in this room."

Nana retrieved a suitcase from the closet as Weston snarled, "You're supposed to be helping expose her!"

Dixie's voice lifted behind him, lost and bruised sounding. "What did she mean, Sam, when she said 'you're supposed to be working with us—with your uncle?'"

Nana shoved the suitcase into Westin's hands and nudged her toward the bed. Sam grimaced and, with a fancy camera in his hand, faced Dixie.

"She works for Stuart. Comes from his IT department. I didn't recognize her until just now."

Nana dumped a drawer full of Weston's belongings into the open suitcase on the bed. Weston started to protest but Nana cut her off with a silencing finger.

"And Stuart planted her here to spy on me?" Dixie said more than asked.

"Yeah."

"Did he send you to spy on me, too?"

Sam winced and looked into Dixie's bruised eyes.

"I believe his orders for me was to dig up dirt on you."

"And did you find any *dirt* on me?" she asked, her voice tight.

Weston's head snapped in their direction. Nana uttered an attention getting, "Shoes," and tossed a pair at Weston who juggled to catch them.

"Red, I figured out within twenty-four hours of arriving I'd find no dirt on you."

"Yet you stayed."

"I tried to leave."

Nana zipped the case shut, shoved it into Weston's arms, and prodded her toward the doorway muttering, "This is one conversation you're not eavesdropping on."

Dixie didn't speak again until the bedroom door closed between them and Nana and Weston. "And you never told me he'd sent you."

"I tried to a couple times but we always got interrupted."

"Is that why you said *we* weren't a good idea?"

"No, that was about me not being good enough for you."

She flinched as though he'd touched her when she didn't want him to. "When you found no 'dirt' on me, did Stuart ask you to create some?"

"I never wanted to hurt you, Red."

Her eyes fixed on his. "Did he order you to create dirt on me?"

He wanted to tell her no. But the way she looked at him, he knew she'd see through the lie. He closed his eyes. "Yes."

"And did you?"

He opened his eyes. "No."

"Were you responsible for any of the sabotage?"

"No. My guess given the events of today is Weston is responsible for all those problems."

"Did you know about the pictures?"

"I found out about them pretty much when you did."

"What do you mean by *pretty much when I did*?"

"I got a message on my phone with a file attached. I ignored it—didn't open it…until you and Annie were holed up in your room together."

"And you were supposed to upload that file to the Internet through my computer, leaving a trail that would make me look like…"

He nodded. "But I didn't. I never would have. My only regret is I didn't open the message earlier. If I had, I might have been able to head off Weston before she did and saved you a lot of hurt."

She turned her face aside as if she couldn't bear looking at him.

He threw the camera across the room, shattering it against the wall. "I didn't want to hurt you, Red. I never wanted to hurt you. That's why I tried to keep my hands off you. I knew anything between us could never end well."

He reached for her. She flattened a hand at him, stopping him. "I need to think all this through."

"What do you want me to do?" he pleaded.

"Give me space," she said.

"Okay. I can do that," he said.

When Dixie looked up, the room was empty. He'd left. She dropped onto the edge of the bed.

How long she sat there, words and emotions a tornado churning through her, she didn't know. Not until she heard the rev of his motorcycle engine did the tears come. Then silence filled the room and she curled into a fetal position, sobbing. Not since the night the police came to her door and told her Michael was dead did she cry so much and so hard—not since Michael left. And now Sam was gone, too.

CHAPTER FOURTEEN

"No! You listen, old man." Sam rounded the desk, grabbed the armrests to either side of Stuart, and leaned in close. "*You* don't deserve to have a relationship with that boy."

The old man sputtered with indignation even as he strained back from Sam. "She's not fit."

Sam jabbed a finger in Stuart's face. "You're the one who's not fit, not as long as you want to take Ben away from his devoted, loving mother."

Stuart pushed Sam's hand aside. "That uncultured—"

"Uncultured? Is that your problem with her?" Sam straightened, towering over Stuart as he never had. "She's traveled the world with her parents, who were in the Foreign Service as your background check no doubt revealed. She's met world leaders. Dixie has experienced more culture than you, Mickey, and me combined."

"She's a gold-digger," Stuart stubbornly argued, though with less conviction.

"Let me tell you what that gold-digger, as you call her, did with Mickey's substantial life insurance policy. She spent it all fighting you for custody of Ben."

Stuart shook a finger in his face. "I never said she wasn't smart. She's after the bigger prize, the trust fund, and, when I'm dead, the entire estate."

"Then leave your estate to charity and retain control of the trust."

"Do you know the legalities of establishing such conditions?" Stuart turned his face away from Sam as though even he knew how lame his reasoning was.

"No. But you do. You've controlled Mickey's and my trust funds all our lives. You cut Mickey off when he married Dixie. You'll no doubt cut me off after today."

Stuart scowled up at him. "Without the allowance I provide you, you won't make it to the end of summer."

The end of summer.

There'd been a day when Sam had actually thought he could still be with Dixie and Ben come summer's end. Like there'd ever been a chance of that. Not for a wolf in sheep's clothing…not for a man made of tin without a heart.

He returned Stuart's scowl. "Is that what you thought cutting off Mickey would do, make him needy enough he'd leave his wife and come running back to you—beg you to put him back on the dole?"

"He wasn't on the dole," Stuart said, his voice thick with indignation. "The trust was his."

"If that were true, you wouldn't have retained control of it."

"He'd have blown the money if I didn't," Stuart fired back.

"On what, Stuart? A wife he loved? His son?" Sam shook his head with disgust. "You might not believe Mickey turned out a success, but success is measured in more ways than by how much money a man makes. Michael loved an amazing woman. They were building a successful life together; and I'm not talking about any restaurant. I'm talking about a family.

"Ben." The old man murmured.

"Michael was happy," Sam said. "If there's anything I learned in the past month, it's that that's success."

The old man's eyes grew moist and, when he spoke his voice cracked with emotion. "I lost my boy."

Sam sighed. "And you think Ben can replace him."

Stuart slumped in his chair, looking smaller, grayer, and frailer than Sam had ever seen him. "*She'll* never let me near him, not after what Weston did."

"You ordered Weston to ruin Dixie's reputation."

"I ordered her to dig up dirt on her, just as I ordered you to do."

Sam brought his fist down on Stuart's desk, making the old man jump. "But I didn't find any dirt on her, just as Weston didn't. So you ordered her to create some, like you ordered me to do."

Stuart scrubbed a hand over his face. "I didn't know Weston would take things so far."

"You ordered her to create dirt on Dixie," Sam repeated, determined not to let Stuart off the hook for making life so hard for Dixie...and Mickey and Ben and anyone else who loved her.

A tear slipped down Stuart's cheek. "I was desperate. I made a mistake."

Sam had never seen the old man shed a tear. Silently, he cursed. He wanted Stuart to pay for the damage he'd done. He wanted him to suffer. But he no more had it in him to hurt Stuart than did Dixie have it in her to be vindictive.

Sam squatted in front of Stuart and looked him in the face. "You can have a relationship with Ben. You *can* be part of his life. You can be an influencing factor in his growing up and tell him far more than even I can about his father."

Stuart flipped a dismissive hand. "She knows what I've done. She'll never let me near Ben."

"You're wrong again, old man. Dixie wants you in Ben's life. She always has."

"But I tried to ruin her."

"She has the most forgiving heart of anyone I've ever known. If you'd taken the time to get to know her, you'd know that, too."

Stuart looked up at him, hope bright through the cracks of his despair.

"Let her forgive you," Sam said.

#

When she saw the email from Stuart, Dixie nearly deleted it. But the subject line stopped her.

To Mrs. Carrington

Stuart had never before referred to her by her *married* name. She opened the email.

First, my deepest apologies for all I've put you through. I've been a foolish old man. Sam tells me you have a forgiving heart. If you can find it in your heart to forgive me enough for a conversation, I'd like to talk with you. Please name a time and day when I may call.

She sat back in her desk chair, thinking. For days, she'd performed her duties as though she walked the fringe of Oz's intoxicating poppy fields, numb with loss. Thank goodness for Jessie, Annie, and Nana. Given time, she'd be her old self again.

She'd done it before…after Michael's death.

But, staring at Stuart's email, seeing Sam's name only reminded her Sam's absence wasn't like Michael's. It wasn't permanent. But, like Michael, he left and hadn't returned. Reconnecting with Stuart would only complicate that issue…if Sam had truly run away from her.

She hit the reply button and typed, "Now."

Within minutes, her phone rang. She answered.

"What do you want to talk to me about, Stuart?"

"I've made a big mistake regarding you. Because of it, I lost my son long before he even died."

"You lost out on a lot, Stuart," she stated.

"So Sam has already told me," Stuart said.

Sam.

She closed her eyes, the emotions she'd been holding at bay flooding her heart. She'd told Sam she needed time to think things through. She hadn't meant for him to go away forever. Had he too thought things through, decided he didn't deserve her and Ben— didn't deserve the happiness they'd shared? Had he run away? Her heart ached for both herself and Sam.

On the other end of the line, Stuart cleared his throat. "I was wrong to have pursued sole custody of Ben. I was wrong to have sent Miss Weston into your home to spy on you—wrong to have ordered her to get dirt…and create dirt when she found none. But, I swear I didn't mean for her to take it as far as she."

"Did you order Sam to do the same thing?"

There was a long pause before Stuart spoke again. "I did. But, unlike Miss Weston, he proved you to be the best parent for Ben."

"Does this mean you won't be pursuing custody any further?"

"Yes. I was foolish to do so in the first place. Foolish and grief stricken. I'd lost my only son…"

She heard his voice falter. "I understand, Stuart."

"Sam said you would."

Sam. The mere mention of his name made the ache in her chest grow.

"You've been a good influence on the boy," Stuart said.

For a moment, Dixie was confused as to whether he was talking about Sam or Ben.

"He faced me and pinned my ears back—made me see the error of my ways."

Sam.

"He did, did he?"

"The boy grew a backbone in the short time he was with you. Told me what I could do with his trust fund in quite graphic terms."

She smiled in spite of her ache. "He did?"

"Is there a chance…could you find it in your heart to let me visit Ben?" Stuart asked.

"Of course, Stuart. You are his grandfather. He should have you in his life."

"Thank you," his said, his voice thick with emotion. "Sam told me you had a forgiving heart."

A tear tumbled down Dixie's cheek. "Will you do something for me, Stuart?"

"Of course. What?"

"Remind Sam of my forgiving heart."

CHAPTER FIFTEEN

"We're pregnant."

Dixie dropped the paper plates on the picnic table, rose onto her toes, and threw her arms around her brother's neck. "I'm so happy for you."

Roman whispered in her ear. "I wish you could be as happy."

"Don't you dare ruin this wonderful moment with any of that," she whispered back and released him.

Turning to her slim, dark-haired sister-in-law, she pulled Tess into her arms. "You've made him a very happy man."

"I'm happy, too."

Dixie drew back but kept hold of Tess's hands. "You are glowing, but—"

Tess laughed. "You're worried the girl who vowed never to marry is going to regret getting pregnant within a year of the wedding?"

"No. I worry that Roman pressured you into this so soon. I know him and his five year plans."

Tess pressed her forehead against Dixie's as if her words were for Dixie's ears alone. "He didn't have to pressure me at all. Sometimes even a stubborn girl like me needs to just plain give in to her heart."

Dixie gave Tess one more quick hug before stepping out of the way so the rest of the family could congratulate the soon-to-be-parents.

The sun shown down upon them from a cloudless

sky and a light breeze stirred the aroma of grilling burgers and brats around them. It was a Norman Rockwell Fourth of July gathering...except for those missing.

Even as her heart swelled with happiness, it couldn't push out the ache. Of course Michael would always be missed. But there was another she missed—another who should be here.

Giggling pulled her back to the present. She smiled at Ben pushing one of the twins high on the swing while her sister snatched at her flailing feet and Bear loped circles around them. But even all that happiness couldn't hold her long in the present, not when the very swing set they played on reminded her of Sam. It had been barely a week ago he'd worked late into the night assembling the set so it would be waiting for Ben when he got up the next morning. She wished Sam were here with them enjoying the fruits of his labors. She wished...

The throaty rumble of a motorcycle from the side of the house jerked Dixie's attention to the driveway circling between yard and outbuildings. Her heart lodged in her throat as a familiar silver and red bike rolled to a stop at the edge of the yard.

"Is that him?" Roman asked, stepping close to her like any protective big brother would.

She nodded. "That's—"

"Sam," shrieked Ben, launching himself across the yard toward Sam.

Sam dismounted from the bike, dropped his helmet, and caught Ben in his arms. The kid's arms tightened around his neck. He'd missed hugs like these...and the laughter and participation in all things family, real family. Above all, he'd missed Dixie.

Love, longing, and regret tore at him.

She stood no more than a dozen steps from the back porch, all leggy girl in her Daisy Dukes and ripe femme fatale in her form-fitting tank top—all angel with her sun-gilded halo of loose hair. He ached for her acceptance—for her love. She took a step toward him. Just one away from the protective cluster of her family. Annie and Lou were there on the fringes, Annie looking worried. Nana was barely visible amidst the knot of towering men surrounding Dixie. There were a couple other females he recognized from pictures, namely her mother and sister-in-law.

He set Ben on his feet, let the kid take him by the hand, and tow him toward Dixie and her phalanx of family. They all watched him—looked at him like they expected him to call down on them an army of flying monkeys. He wanted to shout that he wasn't the witch. He was the Tin Man, his only crime he lacked a heart.

This was the point where the old Sam would have made his excuses and run. Hell, the old Sam wouldn't even have shown up. But he wasn't that man anymore. This Sam had returned to fight for a place in Dixie's life—to fight for her.

Hopefully, he hadn't damaged her forgiving heart beyond repair, the heart Stuart had said she'd asked him to remind Sam she had. He'd taken the message as an invitation. But she wasn't smiling. He hoped he hadn't gotten the message wrong.

Ben stopped them in front of Dixie.

"Look, Mom," Ben said. "Sam's back."

"I see that," she said, her voice barely louder than a whisper.

"Hi, Sam," crooned the twins in unison, pushing

their way to the front of the group, all flirtatious greeting.

At least there were three here happy to see him. But only one truly mattered.

He gazed into the cornflower blue eyes full of uncertainty, an uncertainty he'd put there. An uncertainty that was a mere blink away from disappointment and disappointment was the last thing he ever wanted those eyes to look with upon him.

Run.

No.

"You asked for time and space to sort all this out," he said. "I gave it to you."

"So you did," she said, her voice still low.

"I thought I was doing the right thing for Ben, when I first came here."

"You were," she said, all understanding.

"When I saw how well he was cared for—loved, I tried to leave."

"So you did."

"Then you needed me," he said.

"That I did," she said.

"So I stayed."

She nodded.

He glanced around the faces watching—studying him. Did they believe him, this family that knew he'd hurt Dixie? Even if she forgave him, could they? Family was important to her—what they thought of him important to her.

Maybe today had been the wrong day to face down his demons, this day when she was surrounded by loving, supportive family. Maybe she'd had second thoughts since having Stuart deliver the message about her forgiving heart. Maybe he shouldn't have returned at all. Maybe should give her up—leave her to find love with a worthy man.

"I just wanted you to know I loved—I love you, Red. That is the truth."

He started to turn away.

"Wait," she said.

He stopped, looked at her. But she was facing her brothers.

"Don't let him leave. I have something for him that'll make everything clear."

With that, she fled up the back porch steps, her flip flops slapping at her heels. As she disappeared into the house, a big hand cupped his shoulder.

"I'm Roman St. John," its owner said. "One of Dixie's *big* brothers."

Tentatively, Sam shook the hand Roman offered him, stating, "The contractor from Michigan's Upper Peninsula."

"Right."

"I'm Dane St. John," a second brother said through startlingly white teeth, also offering a hand.

"The action movie star," Sam acknowledged.

"And I do all my own stunts," Dane said, his grip on Sam's hand tightening.

The third, and clearly youngest, gripped his hand with a calloused one. "Renn here, stunt rider."

The fourth and only dark-haired member of the St. John siblings simply stood behind his brothers, arms folded across his chest.

Sam nodded in greeting. "That would make you Jake, the former Navy Seal."

The Seal gave Sam a clipped nod in return.

"So how's this going to go down. You each taking a turn at punching me out or are you all going to jump me at the same time?"

"Don't punch Sam," Ben said from the vicinity of Sam's knees, all round-eyed concern.

He'd forgotten the kid was there. It seemed so had his uncles.

Roman released Sam's shoulder and ruffled Ben's hair. "Nobody's going to punch Sam."

Nana pushed her way between her grandsons, giving them each a pointed look. "Not as long I have anything to say about it."

Check off another friendly among the picnickers, he thought as Nana herded Ben and the twins off to the sandbox in the back corner of the yard.

Sam shoved his hands into his pockets, muttering, "Though I deserve it after what I did to Dixie."

A woman who shared Dixie's flirtatious lips stepped forward. "Dixie said you stepped in and took over the kitchen when her chef bailed." The woman sandwiched one of his hands between her warm pair. "I'm Sarah St. John, Dixie's mother.

"I see the resemblance," he returned. "N-nice to meet you." *He hoped.*

A man with Dixie's eyes stepped forward, hand extended. "I'm her father, Mathew St. John."

"Sir."

"She said you invested in the restaurant," Dane added.

"Ben said he saw you kissing his mom," Jake said in an ominously flat tone.

Sam swallowed.

"I hear you talked Stuart Carrington to give up his fight for custody of Ben," Renn said.

"That can't be all she told you about me," Sam

said.

"No. It's not all she told us," Roman said.

"Are my brothers tormenting you, Sam?" Dixie said, from the porch.

"Just getting to know each other," Roman said, his eyes still fixed on Sam full of meaning.

"Is that smoke I see rising from the grill? You four had better get back to grilling duty before every last burger and brat is incinerated."

"Come along, children," Dixie's mother said, gathering her brood of men.

Roman nodded, but not without a final warning look that belied his amiable sounding, "Good to meet you, Sam."

Likewise, the other brothers followed Roman's suit. Though Jake, the oldest, took his time studying his sister before letting his mother herd him off toward the grill.

"They don't like me," Sam said.

"They don't trust you," Dixie said.

He looked up at her still behind the porch railing, not surprised. They had no reason to trust him and she was too honest not to state the truth for him.

"Give them time," she added. "Give them a chance to get to know the real Sam and, as Michael used to say, *wait until you meet Sam, You'll love him.*"

"Can *you* love a heartless bastard?" he asked.

She tipped her head to one side. "Oh Sam. Whatever made you think you were heartless?"

"The first night I was here, Ben called me the Tin Man. It struck me then that agreeing to do Stuart's bidding was heartless—that, like the Tin Man, I didn't have a heart."

"Silly Sam. Don't you remember how the story of

The Wizard of Oz went?"

"I remember the Tin Man went to Oz to get a heart."

"But when he got there, he found out he had a heart all along, just as the cowardly lion already had courage."

"And Dorothy was already home," he said.

Dixie stepped out from behind the porch railing, stopping at the top of the steps. The flip flops she'd been wearing when she went up those steps replaced by a pair of ruby red, four inch heels, the high heels her oldest brother Jake had given her *for when she was ready to dance again.*

The air went out of Sam, almost dropping him to his knees.

Up on the porch, Dixie clicked her heels together repeating, "There's no place like home."

When she stopped, she looked around wide-eyed as though she'd only just arrived at The Farmhouse. With an *oh* forming her lips she looked at Sam and said, "Why Sam, I think we're home."

"We?" he asked, his voice little more than a hoarse whisper.

"You got it Tin Man," she said, launching herself down the steps.

He caught her in his arms, her momentum twirling them around once, twice, three times. When he settled her feet, she placed a hand on his chest and smiled up at him.

"Do you feel that, Sam? It's your heart beating. The heart you always had."

"You always believed I had one, didn't you, Red?" he said.

She hugged him close. "Never a doubt in my

mind."

He clung to her and all she meant to him. "I love you, Red."

"And I love you, Sam."

the end

Addendum

You are cordially invited to the wedding of
Sam and Dixie…
in Book 3 of the St. John Sibling Series.

Excerpt from KELLY'S HERO: St. John Sibling Series, Book 3 by Barbara Raffin

"OMG, you're Dane St. John," squealed the teenage girl from the boat's bow seat, letting the tip of her fishing rod dip into the lake.

"Holy crap," hooted the younger boy on the middle seat of the small craft. "You're Hawk!"

"Watch the language Boy," the father said from the back bench seat, absently holding out his fishing license to Conservation Officer Kelly Jackson.

But his gaze sharpened on the man sprawled in the bow of her boat, muscled arms draped over the gunwale, legs so long he'd propped them on the center seat. He'd assumed that pose when she'd refused to allow him to help her launch the boat from shore. She was, after all, as capable of handling a boat by herself as any other Conservation Officer. Still, the indulgent grin of the newest action star to come out of Hollywood researching his next role in the remote Upper Peninsula of Michigan had taunted her all morning.

"You that that actor all the kids are crazed over?" the father asked.

"Mom likes him, too," said the boy through the wide grin he'd fixed on *Hawk* a.k.a. Dane St. John.

Kelly took the license from the father's fingers, not even bothering to glance Dane's way. She knew he'd be flashing his pearly whites for his *fans*. He'd done so at every boat they'd stopped. And if their passengers weren't fans already, a wink from his brook-blue eyes won them over. Somehow, she'd managed to remain immune to his charms. Maybe it was his longish hair or the smug way he watched her through his Ray Bans…which he removed whenever they pulled up to another boat. Couldn't pass up an opportunity to show off those famous blue eyes. Though, judging by *Daddy's* frown, maybe she wasn't alone in that immunity.

"OMG," the girl squealed again, this time dropping her fishing pole into the bottom of the aluminum boat and producing a cell phone from the purse on the seat beside her. "No one's going to believe this unless I get a picture!"

"Me, too," said the boy, likewise discarding his pole and jumping to his feet.

Their boat rocked and Kelly shifted her attention from license to overall situation. "Sit," she commanded.

The boy obeyed and the father added, "And mind your poles. What if you get a bite?"

The boy had plopped his backside down on the bench nearest the DNR craft, which left the small fishing boat listing to one side.

"OMG! OMG!" the girl kept repeating, raising her phone in front of her face, and twisting in the bow to get herself and Dane in the same frame, her movement adding to the already precarious tilt of their boat.

Dane grabbed the neighboring bow and tucked it in close to the larger DNR craft, holding it steady...all the while posing practically cheek to cheek with the girl while she snapped pictures with her phone.

"Teenagers," the father grumbled.

Kelly smiled at him. "Bet she's begging you for car keys all the time."

"Not a chance of that for another couple years," the father said through a sigh of relief, and Kelly ticked off any necessity to check for further licenses. A good C.O. didn't always have to ask direct questions to gain information...like whether or not the teenage girl was old enough to need a license herself.

Having given the father's fishing license a cursory once-over, Kelly handed it back to the father.

"I see you've got one of Sven Maki's boats."

"Renting a cabin from him, too," the father said.

"My turn," the boy said, rocking the boat again as he leaned from his seat toward Dane.

A muscle popped in Dane's arm and a vein bulged in his neck. He was really one-handedly keeping that boat from swamping...or showing off big time.

"Settle down there, champ," she said.

"Use your own phone," the girl groused.

"I left it at the cabin," the boy said

"Take a picture for your brother," the father said, mumbling under his breath about how the boy had at least the courtesy not to bring his phone on their fishing trip.

"Your sister will take a picture of you and me together, won't you little lady?" Dane said in his deep, slightly raspy *Hawk* voice that females seemed to swoon over. But not her. Definitely not.

Dane had a stilling hand on the boy's shoulder and was bathing the girl in his high wattage smile. She was blushing, her fingers flying over the phone's keyboard.

"I'll just finish this twee—" She glanced into Dane's blinding smile and her fingers went still.

"So," Kelly said, turning her attention back to the father, "Catch anything yet?" mentally, ticking off her script of Conservation Officers questions.

The father eyed his kids huddled in the bow of the boat getting their pictures taken with Dane St. John. "Just a movie star."

#

Kelly kind of knew how the father felt. A double major in conservation and criminal justice and trained alongside Michigan State Police candidates and she was still being handed fluff jobs like babysitting an actor researching his next movie role. Boat stowed and morning duties behind her, she led her charge along a ridge through the woods, stewing over the fact she still had to prove she was more than the token minority hire.

"Nice family back there," her charge said, dogging her heels...too close. "But since you scoped them out with your binoculars, why'd you still check on them?"

"The girl was giving her dad grief about her life-preserver. Didn't want to buckle it up. That's something we can't ignore."

"So you'd have given him a ticket because she refused to buckle up?"

"I could have if she hadn't buckled up by the time I got to their boat," she said.

"But you wouldn't have, right?"

There was something in the tone of his question—something almost pleading as if he would have found her lacking if she even admitted she would have written a ticket. And damn, but it made her want to tell him what he wanted to hear.

"A true law and order C.O.—" *Like my father.* "—would have written a ticket."

"But there's room to give a person a break, right?"

"Kids and life-preservers, that's black and white—life and death," she said, avoiding giving him a straight answer.

"But the dad was trying to do the right thing and teenagers can be contrary."

She glanced over her shoulder at Dane. "What do

you know about teenagers?"

He grinned. "I was one for seven years."

Before she could stop herself, she rolled her eyes. One corner of his mouth twitched. She stifled a groan and turned her attention back to the trail in front of them.

"You wouldn't have ticketed him," Dane said, sounding way too sure of his assumption.

"It's a moot point," she said. "By the time we caught up to them, the dad had gotten the daughter to buckle up."

"Yeah," he said, still sounding like he didn't believe she'd have ticketed the father.

Maybe she wouldn't have. Maybe the threat would have been enough to make an impression on the girl about how serious her lack of compliance was. She did see things more in shades of gray than black and white like her father. That was one of her issues—her failings as her father saw it.

Behind her, Dane's nerve ruffling voice lifted. "I heard you tell that dad where to take his kids for some fishing action this evening. That was nice of you."

"Just spreading a little good will," she returned. "Good for the tourist trade."

"Is that part of the job?"

"As a matter of fact, it is."

"So, I learn another aspect of the job," he said.

"And what else did you learn today?" she asked before she remembered she didn't really care what he learned, if anything.

"I learned there're no shades of gray when it comes to safety laws and binoculars are a C.O.'s best friend."

Surprised he even extracted that much from her

morning duties, she gave him a cursory glance. His grin stretched.

"Surveilling the boaters on the lake before we—"

"We?" she cast over her shoulder, intent on reminding him that she hadn't allowed him to help her in any aspect of *her* job.

"Correction," he said, giving her a conceding nod. "Surveilling the boaters on the lake before *you* even launched the boat saved a lot of unnecessary stops once we were on the water."

"That's why binoculars are a good tool of the job," she said.

"That's what I was saying."

She huffed and trudged off along the trail, sweet trickling down her flanks. Ordinarily, she'd have taken the afternoon off after a morning of marine surveillance then gone back out in the evening or night. July afternoons were generally too hot for field work unless there was something specific to deal with. But she was in no mood to make anything easy for *Joe Hollywood.* So, she'd taken him hiking through a dense, mosquito filled woods. The only problem was they were quickly sweating off their insect repellent. Good thing they carried a fresh supply in their backpacks. Oh yeah, she'd made him don a backpack under the guise of *you wanted the full experience.*

"So," he said way too close behind her. "Just what are we out here looking for?"

Your breaking point. "Any sign of poaching."

"And what would that look like?"

"Animal carcasses. Make-shift hunting blinds. Worn patches where someone might have been sticking up." *Mostly the sort of poaching evidence left over from the winter that we look for in spring rather than hot mid-summer. Not that she was about to inform of that fact.*

"Circling crows overhead mean there's a carcass on the ground, right?"

In her peripheral vision she caught the upward sweep of his arm and glanced up. Just her luck, *Jo Hollywood* was some sort of Boy Scout. She exhaled heavily.

"Looks like they're over the highway. Probably just road kill."

"So, is this all you do, wander around the woods looking for signs of something illegal?" he asked, all but tripping on her heels.

"Yup," she said without so much as a backward glance. "Nice and mundane."

"Is that another reference to how my portrayal of field work in my last movie missed the mark?"

"I may not have been on this job very long, but I'm the daughter of a C.O. and not once in his thirty year career did he come home sooty and singed from an explosion."

"That's because he never played a C.O. in an action movie."

She stopped short and wheeled around at him. "None of that over-the-top crap happens in real life."

He shoved his hands in his pockets and grinned down at her. "Reality doesn't make for interesting action films. Besides, I portray a Game Warden along the Texas/Mexican border. Things get a little more heated when the bad guys carry Oozies rather than fishing poles."

"So your Game Warden character stumbles across drug mules for a drug cartel and winds up in an all-out war. Does *that* really happen even in Texas?"

He shrugged, his grin oozing charm. "Wouldn't know. I didn't write the script."

"Yet you come all the way to the Upper Peninsula of Michigan to *research* the next installment of your gung-ho game warden movies?"

"Figured, if they were going to create a series around my character, I had an obligation to learn a little more about him and what he'd encounter in movie number two."

"And you think the Texas Department of Natural Resources would send one of their Game Wardens to the U.P.?"

"Actually," he said. "My character's supposed to be taking a vacation after all the mayhem he encountered in the first movie."

"And they thought nice, boring Upper Michigan was just the place for him to recuperate from...how many shots did you duck and explosions did you narrowly miss?"

His grin stretched and he hovered closer. "You really hate all that action crap, don't you?"

"Tell me they aren't going to blow up my woods for the sake of a movie."

His grin turned into a grimace. "Wouldn't be much of an action film if there weren't some fireworks. Besides, where the Hawk goes trouble follows."

She groaned at reference to one of the tag lines hyping his movie character, turned, and trudged off, calling back to him, "Just stay on the trail and watch your step. I'm responsible for your safety."

"Yes, ma'aaaam."

The humorous note in his voice turned into a wail and Kelly turned to see her charge somersaulting down the slope the ridge bordered.

About the Author

An obsessive writer who'd rather write than breathe, Barbara Raffin wrote her first novel at age twelve in retaliation to the lack of female leads in the adventure stories she loved reading. But it was a love of playing with words, exploring the human psyche, and telling stories that kept her writing.

This award-winning author lives on the Michigan-Wisconsin border with her Keeshond dogs Katie and Slippers and her avid outdoorsman husband who has always supported her love affair with reading and writing. Learn more about Barbara Raffin and her books, or contact her through her web site at www.BarbaraRaffin.com